MIDNIGHT BLUE

SIMONE VAN DER VLUGT

TRANSLATED BY JENNY WATSON

LARGE
PRINT

First published in Great Britain 2017
by
Harper
an imprint of HarperCollins*Publishers*

First Isis Edition
published 2017
by arrangement with
HarperCollins*Publishers*

A catalogue record for this book is available
from the British Library.

ISBN 978–1–78541–453–4 (hb)
ISBN 978–1–78541–459–6 (pb)

MIDNIGHT BLUE

1654: Following the death of her young husband, Catrin Barentsdochter takes a job as a housekeeper in Amsterdam. The city is flourishing; and as she assists her mistress with painting lessons, she dreams of developing her own skill as an artist. But when the past catches up with her, Catrin must leave behind the comfortable security of her new home for the smaller city of Delft. There she is introduced to Evert van Nulandt, owner of a pottery factory. Working together, they dream of replicating the prized blue-and-white porcelain arriving from the Far East. And Catrin dreams of a life in which her secret stays safely buried . . .

SPECIAL MESSAGE TO READERS

THE ULVERSCROFT FOUNDATION
(registered UK charity number 264873)
was established in 1972 to provide funds for
research, diagnosis and treatment of eye diseases.
Examples of major projects funded by
the Ulverscroft Foundation are:-

- The Children's Eye Unit at Moorfields Eye Hospital, London
- The Ulverscroft Children's Eye Unit at Great Ormond Street Hospital for Sick Children
- Funding research into eye diseases and treatment at the Department of Ophthalmology, University of Leicester
- The Ulverscroft Vision Research Group, Institute of Child Health
- Twin operating theatres at the Western Ophthalmic Hospital, London
- The Chair of Ophthalmology at the Royal Australian College of Ophthalmologists

You can help further the work of the Foundation
by making a donation or leaving a legacy.
Every contribution is gratefully received. If you
would like to help support the Foundation or
require further information, please contact:

THE ULVERSCROFT FOUNDATION
The Green, Bradgate Road, Anstey
Leicester LE7 7FU, England
Tel: (0116) 236 4325

website: www.foundation.ulverscroft.com

CHAPTER
ONE

De Rijp, March 1654

The funeral was a week ago and I still feel more relieved than anything else. I know that's indefensible, that I should be grieving, but it's impossible.

I stand with my arms folded, gazing out of the top half of the kitchen door at the fields and meadows surrounding the farm, but don't really see them.

It should never have come to this. Looking back, I can't understand what came over me that night. For years I'd thought of Govert as just another man from the village, not someone I paid any particular attention to. I never gave him much thought at all. Not that he wasn't an attractive man, in a certain way he was. The first time I noticed him was at the village fair, when he pulled me up to dance and held me to him. I'd been drinking, of course I had been drinking, but not so much that I couldn't hear his heavy breathing or feel his body pressing against mine, his muscular arms clasping me so tentatively.

With every turn our hips brushed and the grip with which he steered me through the other dancing couples tightened. It was an exciting feeling. I realised he was in love with me. The off-putting way he stared at me whenever we passed one another, with that furrowed brow of his, had been an expression of desire rather than disapproval.

Did I feel flattered by his attention? Had I turned down too many potential suitors in the hope of something better? Was I afraid of being a spinster all my days? Or was I in love at that moment?

When he took my hand in his and led me outside to a quiet corner of the orchard I didn't protest.

Govert was happy when I finally told him, four months later, that I was pregnant, all set to marry me and start a family. As a widower of around forty and not without means, he was a fair prospect, even if he wasn't what I'd pictured.

Not that there was much choice. One moment of madness at the fair, one moment of total lunacy, and my future was set. Gone was the chance to someday leave the village and begin a new life, gone were my dreams.

The worst thing was that I wondered what I'd even seen in him that night. Whatever it had been, the next morning it was gone too.

We were married a month later, and six weeks after that my pregnancy ended in a premature birth. The child, a boy, was stillborn. That was over a year ago too.

And now Govert himself is lying beneath the cold, dark earth. The only mirror in the house is turned to the wall and the shutters have been closed for weeks. Today I'm opening them again. I let the morning light stream in with a feeling of utter pleasure. The living room, which was packed with visitors for days, is eerily quiet. I've lived in De Rijp all my life, and the support of relatives, neighbours and friends is heart-warming. My in-laws were notably absent. They probably find it hard to accept that I'm about to inherit all of Govert's property after one year of marriage. It's understandable, but there's nothing I can do about it. And God knows I earned that inheritance.

I allow my gaze to wander around the room, from the round table next to the window to the fireplace and the furniture I painted myself. Sunlight falls on the flagstone floor and brings a little warmth. Not much, it's only the beginning of March. The smoke drifts along the beams hung with sausages and bacon and up into the loft, which is still half full of winter stores.

It's strange to have the house to myself, but I have no time to take it in. There's work to be done and now that Govert's gone there's even more than usual.

Although I have a maid and a farmhand, there's plenty left for me to do. Every day's the same. I milk the cows, feed the pigs and chickens, tend the vegetable patch, churn the butter and make the cheese. I use the remaining time to wash and mend clothes, spin and weave and, very occasionally, to paint.

Now and then, when I glance at the shiny surface of a copper kettle, I catch a glimpse of my mother, her braided hair under a white cap. She's always busy, always tired. I'm twenty-five but I feel much older.

Just keep going, I think as I head to the barn to check on the animals. The mourning period is only six weeks, not so long.

Jacob, the farmhand, has already started the milking. He greets me with a slight tilt of his chin. I nod by way of an answer.

"I might be able to go and work for Abraham Goen," he says as I sit down on my stool.

"That's good."

"Now it's only Jannet who has to find a job."

"It'll all work out. If there's nothing for her here, she'll find something in Graft."

"When are you leaving?" Jacob asks.

"As soon as everything's sold. The auction's next week."

Jacob nods. "Jannet would like to take the churn. Then she can make her own butter."

"I can't give it to her. I've promised it to my mother."

"Oh. That's a shame." Jacob pulls the full pail out from under the cow and stands up. The way he stands there makes me think he has something else to say, and I look at him expectantly.

"About the boss . . ."

"Yes?"

"His brother's been telling tales around the village."

I stop milking. "What kind of tales?"

He hesitates.

"What is it, Jacob?" I say, a little too sharply, sounding impatient.

"I think you know," he says, and walks away.

Yesterday I made buttermilk curds. Today, for lunch, I smear some of the sour leftovers onto a slice of rye bread. Jacob and Jannet are sitting at the table too. We don't say much, all three of us are deep in thought.

After the meal, I leave the work to them. I pull on a pair of clogs and set off along the dyke towards De Rijp. The farm backs onto the circular canal around the Beemster polder, which is surrounded by marshy lowlands. My parents' farm is on the far side of the village, and the quickest way there is to walk through it. I walk along Kralingergracht and onto the main street, where the shabby buildings give way to grand homes with green and red painted gables. Closer to the centre of the village there are even a few stone houses with stepped gables, which look like they've been left here by accident.

On the way, I say hello to people I know, who reply somewhat reluctantly. Are they avoiding me? Are people staring at me?

By the time I get to the Kleine Dam and the bustle around the weighing-house, I can no longer dismiss my concerns. People are throwing curious glances my way and whispering behind my back. Only one person comes up to ask how I am and whether it's true that I'm leaving.

The people here are proud of their village, their families have lived here for generations. Leaving is unheard of, practically a betrayal. But the villagers always thought I was a bit odd, so my plans should come as no surprise.

"Are you getting rid of that dresser as well? The one you painted so nicely?" says Sybrigh the wholesaler. "I'd be happy to take that off your hands."

"The auction's next week," I answer, and keep on walking with an apologetic smile.

I turn into narrow Church Street and leave the village. I can see my parents' farm in the distance. When I reach the muddy track that will take me there, I quicken my pace.

"Mart was just here." My mother is rinsing out milk churns under the pump. In the pale winter light her face looks thin and old, and when she straightens she presses a hand to her back. "He came to speak to you but he was yelling so much that I sent him away."

I grab a milk churn and shove it under the pump.

"He'd heard you were leaving. He was furious, Catrin."

"Why? Isn't that up to me?"

"Of course, but now? So soon after the funeral? Lots of people find it strange. You've got a farm, cattle, everything, and it's all yours now. Men are lining up for you. Take Gerrit, if you got together you'd both be rich."

"I'm moving to the city."

"To go and work as a housekeeper. Even though here you're completely free."

I sigh. "We've been over this so many times, Mother. I'm not planning to be a housekeeper forever. I want to save up, remarry and make a new life in town."

"Yes, I suppose that is what you've always wanted. As a little girl, you were always desperate to come along when we took the cheese to market. I never understood why; the others weren't like that. Four hours on a barge to get to town and another four back."

"Crying because I wanted to stay."

We look at each other and smile.

"Well, you should do what you want to do. You're not a little girl any more, I can't stop you," my mother says after a short pause. "It's just . . ."

In the silence that follows, I study her expression. "What is it?"

"People are talking."

"People in villages always talk, that's another reason I want to leave. I've had more than enough of all the gossiping and meddling."

A look of resignation appears on my mother's face. "I'll miss you," she says. "But maybe it *is* better that you go."

CHAPTER
TWO

A week later everything is sold. Govert and I had been renting the farmhouse and land but the animals and furniture belonged to us. During the auction, which takes place on the farm's threshing floor, I see my possessions pass into other people's hands. The proceeds — around a hundred guilders — are welcome. They're enough to keep me going for a while and maybe set up a business. Perhaps painting pottery. That has always been a dream of mine. As a little girl I decorated furniture with beetroot juice. Later on, when I was given commissions by rich farmers and important people from the village and started decorating dressers and foot warmers for them, I used real paint.

"It reminds me of those colourful pieces they make up in Hindeloopen," Cornelis Vinck, the notary said one day. "You've got talent, Cat. You should try selling a few things up in town."

"I can't, sir. I'm not a member of the guild," I said.

"At the annual fair in September out-of-towners are allowed to sell whatever they like. As long as they don't set up their own business."

In my scarce free time I started painting plates and footstools, which I did end up managing to sell quite easily at the fair.

From that day on I longed for the city.

I've only known a few villagers leave De Rijp and they were boys who signed on for VOC ships or went off to become whalers. In the neighbouring village of Graft, there was a girl who found a job as a housemaid in Alkmaar and that seemed like a good idea for me too. Of course, life as a housemaid is hard work, but at least I wouldn't be stuck here with nothing but reeds and mud as far as the eye can see. Town is where things happen, there are amusements and diversions, the people there really live and I long to be part of it. I heard from Emil and Bertha, friends who live in Alkmaar, that a rich resident of the city was in need of a housekeeper. A few weeks ago, when I had to go into town for the cheese market, I walked over to Oudegracht to offer my services. To my astonishment and delight, I was hired on the spot.

I look around the barn, at the early morning light that falls on the packed earth floor. The possessions which had been piled up here have been taken away by their new owners. The only things I still have are a few trinkets and some clothes.

Outside in the farmyard, my parents and brothers stand waiting in the morning mist. As the only surviving daughter, I could always rely on their care and protection and I see from the boys' faces that they're not happy I'm leaving. There's a big age gap between Dirk, my eldest brother, and Laurens, left by a number of miscarriages and brothers and sisters who died young. Maybe that's why Laurie is the one I'm most attached to; we're the ones who had to make up for those losses.

Our parting is brief. I hug everyone, my parents the longest. Laurie has to go to Alkmaar too and will be accompanying me. A good idea now that I'm carrying so much money.

"We'll see each other again soon," says my father. "I'm bringing a load up to Alkmaar next week."

"See you then, Pa. You know where I'll be."

Another kiss, a hug, and we set off. Laurie takes the bundle with my things under his arm and we walk along the East Dyke, which leads to the quay. I look back a couple of times and wave to my family. My heart is full but I have no regrets.

It's a long journey to Alkmaar. Squashed in between the cargo, huddled together for warmth, we watch the polder landscape of flat, neatly laid-out fields and ditches go by. The barge doesn't go particularly fast, but I'm used to that. I've made this journey many times. I know every bend in the canal, every hamlet we pass. On some stretches there's hardly any wind and we make so little progress that the bargee has to use his pole. He leans on the bargepole with his whole weight, works it into the mud at the bottom and levers the boat forward.

I sit next to my brother and point out things I notice in the landscape. I don't get much response.

"So you're not coming back then?" says Laurie, just as I'm about to give up my efforts to start a conversation.

"Of course I will. Now and again."

"If I were you, I wouldn't stay in Alkmaar. Mart is turning the whole village against you."

"Do they believe him?"

"I don't know." He's quiet for a moment, then says: "You could go to Haarlem or Amsterdam instead."

Now it's my turn to pause. "So far away?" I say quietly.

"It isn't that far really. What I mean to say, Cat, is that you mustn't let us hold you back. If another town is . . . better for you, that's where you have to go. We know what's being said about you is nonsense, but not everyone is convinced."

"I should have stayed in mourning for longer, cried more." I look up at my brother. "Is it a sin to be glad someone's dead?"

Laurie puts his arm around my shoulders and gives me a squeeze. "No," he says, "in this case I'd say it's only human."

We sail along the shore of Alkmaar Lake and pass the lock at Akersloot. Rays of sunlight pierce the mist, breaking up the grey haze and bringing a little warmth. A stiff breeze fills the sails and drives the boat through the waves. In the distance, the towers and city walls of Alkmaar are visible, and the gallows field.

A shudder goes through me when I see the sinister posts with their dangling corpses. I quickly turn my gaze to the hustle and bustle of the port further up by the Customs Tower, where incoming goods are weighed and taxed by the city authorities.

The broad expanse of the River Zeglis stretches out glistening in the sun ahead of us. On the banks on either side, swarms of people are walking towards the city, a man is driving a couple of pigs in front of him. Carts lurch and crash over the potholes, a beggar narrowly manages to jump out of the way of their wheels.

The barge moors up just outside the city walls. Laurie and I struggle to our feet and pay the skipper. A few minutes later, we cross the small wooden bridge leading to Tree Gate. We say goodbye at the Customs Tower. Laurie has an appointment in an inn on Brewer's Quay.

He hesitates, as if he wants to say something but can't find the right words. "Well, Sis, good luck. I'll come and look you up next time I'm in town." He hugs me. "Think about what I said."

I kiss Laurie on the cheek and take my bag of clothes from him. We look each other in the eye for a moment, then smile and part ways. When I glance back, I see my brother watching me. I wave and turn right.

Stiff from sitting so long, I walk up River Street, clutching my bag. The canal is full of little barges and flat-bottomed boats, goods are being loaded and unloaded everywhere.

I make a beeline through the familiar streets to the other side of the city, where the cathedral towers over the rooftops. I enter the church through the door on

Choir Street and wander through the gigantic apse with its pillars and stained-glass windows to the front, right up to the altar. I sit down on the front pew and close my eyes. For a while I sit like that, listening to my own breathing and the irregular beating of my heart.

It is only when everything inside me has quieted down that I open my eyes again. The silence hanging between the white walls and arches has a calming effect.

I clasp my hands together. The content of my prayers is no different than at the village church in De Rijp but here it feels different — as if here, among the massive stone vaults, I will be heard more clearly. I don't know whether my entreaties make any difference. I don't feel any relief yet. With my head still bowed, I leave the church. Outside, I blink at the sunlight and stand dazed for a moment before allowing myself to be swallowed up once more in the bustle of the city.

Near the cathedral is the inn and tavern, the Thirteen Beams, which is run by friends of mine. Bertha and her husband Emil do a roaring trade because their inn is the first one travellers come to when they enter the city from the west through Goblin Gate. It's a large building with a stepped gable and a wrought-iron sign that swings merrily in the wind.

My hands are so cold they're almost frozen; I open the door and let out a sigh of relief as the warm air washes over me. The small taproom is full to the rafters. I make my way through the mass of people standing and sitting between me and the bar. Emil is pouring beer. Bertha is just walking off with two foaming tankards in her hands.

"Emil!" I shout, leaning across the bar.

"Cat! Hello! Lovely to see you. It's a bit busy right now but I'll catch up with you in a minute!" he shouts.

I nod and whip around as someone puts their hand on my shoulder. It's Bertha. Her dark curls have worked their way out from under her cap to frame her face. "There you are! Do you want something to eat?"

"Yes, please."

Bertha disappears into the kitchen and comes back a moment later with a hearty-looking soup and a hunk of bread. I quickly find somewhere to sit. By the time I've finished eating, it's a bit quieter in the inn and Bertha comes to join me. She asks how the journey has been.

"Long and cold, but Laurie came with me," I say. "Can I sleep here tonight? I don't need to be at my boss's house until tomorrow."

Bertha's expression turns solemn.

"What is it? Are you full? It doesn't matter, I'm sure I can go to the Morien's Head," I say.

"You can stay here as long as you want, but I have bad news. The gentleman who wanted you to be his housekeeper, Willebrand Nordingen, died two days ago. He fell ill — something to do with his lungs. Of course he was quite old, but his death still took us by surprise."

For a moment I've no idea what to say. This is bad news. Not only for Nordingen, who seemed like a kind man, but for me too.

14

"What do I do now? I've sold all my things, given up my lease."

"Then buy or rent a house here and find another job."

"There's nothing else I *can* do. And I can't go back to De Rijp."

"We'll help you," says Bertha. "You can stay here until you get a place of your own and we'll ask around about a job for you. An inn is the perfect place to do that."

It's reassuring to know I'm not alone, but it takes a while for me to accept that everything isn't going to go as planned. It's a good job I've got enough money to pay my way for the time being.

Emil comes and puts his hand on my shoulder. "You'll find something," he says. "There's plenty of work in Alkmaar."

CHAPTER
THREE

I spend all week searching for work. I crisscross the whole city, from the grand houses along Mient Canal, the fanciest thoroughfare in town, to the salt works on Oudegracht and the brewery on Dove Lane. I try my luck at the city orphanage on Doelen Street and the adjoining silk-weaving workshop, then at Saint Catherine's Cloister and various inns and taverns. I don't care what I have to do — cleaning, fetching and carrying, nursing the sick — as long as I have a job.

The end of the week finds me sitting across from Bertha in the inn, utterly disillusioned.

"I didn't think it would be so hard to find work," I say. "There are jobs for men, but it's much harder for women."

"You could set up on your own. A small business of some kind."

"Selling what? Pots and pans? The city's full of those already."

"But you paint them so beautifully. And now that you're a resident of Alkmaar, you're allowed to set up a business."

I shake my head. "You know it's not that easy. I'd have to serve an apprenticeship, pay fees to learn and pass an exam to become a master. And that's assuming a guild would even take me on."

"A woman joined the Guild of Saint Lucas a while ago — Isabella Bardesius. Now she's a painter with her own studio."

"Then she's almost certainly from a rich family that paid for her education. They don't let you in without training, Bertha." I stare into space, thinking. "Perhaps I should take that job in the infirmary after all. That's the only offer I've had."

"In the pest house? Are you insane?!"

"There's no plague. The people in there have other diseases."

"Yes, and they're just as infectious and just as deadly. That would be my last resort."

"It *is* my last resort. If I don't find something soon, I'll have to go back to De Rijp."

Next to us, someone clears their throat. A man of around thirty with mid-length dirty blond hair is standing by the table. "Hello, Bertha. Sorry for interrupting, but I couldn't help overhear your conversation."

"Matthias, it's good to see you. How are you?" Bertha's face, breaks into a broad smile.

"Very well, thanks," says the man. "I'm passing through on my way to Den Helder and I've got a few bits of business to take care of in Alkmaar."

"Mister Van Nulandt is one of our regular guests," Bertha tells me.

The man takes off his hat and bows slightly. "A pleasure to meet you," he says with a winning smile.

I nod and tell him my name. Matthias sits down on the stool opposite us.

"It's not a complete coincidence I was listening to your conversation," he tells Bertha. "Emil mentioned the situation. He told me a few things about your friend here and asked whether I could help."

"And?" Bertha asks.

"As it happens, I can. My brother is in need of a housekeeper. Would that suit you?" Matthias asks, turning to me.

"I don't know. I mean, yes, I think so. But you don't know me," I say, astounded.

"Emil and Bertha know you, that's good enough for me. And Emil speaks very highly of you."

A wave of excitement bubbles up inside me. "A housekeeper . . . that would be wonderful. Who is your brother and where does he live?"

"His name is Adriaan van Nulandt," Matthias says, "and he lives in Amsterdam."

Amsterdam! The shock obviously shows on my face because Matthias asks, "Is that a problem?"

"It's so far away. I don't know anyone there . . ."

Matthias shrugs this off. "It's not that far, and once you're there you'll soon get to know people."

I exchange glances with Bertha, who looks a bit flabbergasted. "It *is* an opportunity for you, Cat," she says. "And since there's no job for you here, it's Amsterdam or De Rijp."

I don't have to think for long. Even though I'm not keen on the idea of leaving everyone I love behind, I have no choice. What's more, this is a better move for

18

me. I would never have gone to Amsterdam on my own initiative. Perhaps it's fate.

While I'm thinking, Matthias goes out to settle his business affairs. When he returns that evening, I go and talk to him.

"I've decided to do it. I'd be very grateful if you would recommend me to your brother."

"Of course, I'll write a glowing recommendation. But for that I reckon we need to get to know each other a little better. Will you join me for a drink?"

We draw up two chairs at a table in the corner and Matthias orders a jug of wine. "So tell me," he asks as he fills my cup, "why did you leave your village?"

I tell him everything. About my longing for the city and how that one night at the dance sent my life in a different direction. About my stillborn son and Govert's unexpected death. Matthias listens attentively.

"So you're a widow," he says when I've finished. "A very young widow. I'm sorry about that."

"Oh, it wasn't a happy marriage." I stare into the distance, thinking of the life I would have had if Govert hadn't died. "He hit me. From the moment we were married, and more and more as time went on. I don't know why. There was no reason for him to do it. We never argued, I didn't answer him back, I worked hard." I laugh wryly. "I purposely made sure we didn't argue and I never answered him back, but he hit me anyway." My voice betrays the bitterness I always feel when I think of all that violence.

"Some men are like that," Matthias says gently. "But not all of them."

"No . . ." I sigh. "The problem is, you can't tell by looking whether they are or not. You only know when it's too late, when you're already married."

"Next time, if it ever happens to you again, have the rascal up before the judge. It's illegal to beat your spouse, did you know that? It is not what God intended between man and wife."

"Are you married?"

"No, and I don't plan to be. I want to travel, see the world. I work for my brother's company. He's a trader and one of the directors of the East India Company. He has no desire to go off gallivanting so I do it for him."

"Where do you go?"

"Italy and Norway for the most part, no long voyages. I wish I could go further. To the East, to China and the Indies. Don't you ever wonder what's on the other side of the world? What it looks like and how people live there?"

"Finding out what the world outside De Rijp and Alkmaar is like is good enough for me," I say, and he laughs.

Maybe it's the familiar way he talks to me, the way the skin around his eyes crinkles when he laughs or the sound of his voice that make me edge closer to him. He's nice. Really nice. Apparently, he thinks the same of me because he keeps leaning towards me and touching me now and again as we talk. His face is alive with enthusiasm and I can't stop looking at him. A tingling feeling spreads through my body, like little bubbles of air under my skin.

As the evening draws on, the world shrinks until all that exists is the table we're sitting at, lit by a flickering candle. It's long after midnight when I make a move to go to bed. Matthias walks me upstairs. On the landing he gives me a long look. The wine has weakened my resolve and when his mouth finds mine, I let him kiss me. His lips are firm yet gentle. Desire wells up in me and I throw my arms around his neck. He caresses my back in response, before letting his hand descend to my bottom and then up along my side.

It's only when he tries to undo the laces of my bodice that I push him away, gently but firmly. He smiles regretfully.

"I like you, Catrin." His mouth is by my ear. "A lot. I'm glad I met you. Hopefully we'll meet again in Amsterdam."

"Yes, I hope so too."

"If my brother is so stupid as to decide not take you on, be sure to tell the maid where I can find you."

I nod and promise that I will. We kiss again, at first softly and then with more and more feeling. I feel my body respond again, so much so that I put an end to it by stepping smartly back and opening my door. I smile at Matthias and go inside. Before I shut the door he blows me a kiss.

"See you in Amsterdam," he says.

The next morning, I go down to the taproom, but to my disappointment, Matthias has already left;

"He had an early appointment in Den Helder. Asked me to give you this." Emil hands me a roll of paper.

21

The letter of recommendation. I turn it over in my hands a couple of times. "Did he say anything else?"

"That the house is on the first part of Keizersgracht and he hopes he'll see you soon."

I can read a bit, the pastor in De Rijp set up a class when I was little. He thought it was important to teach girls to read so they could give their children Bible lessons. I can remember enough of it that I'd be able to tell what is in the letter, but the roll is sealed.

"You two got on well last night." There's a note of enquiry in Emil's voice.

"Yes," I say with a smile. "Very well." I pretend not to notice Emil's curiosity and choose a table at the window.

After a light breakfast of bread and cheese, I take leave of my friends.

"My family will be shocked when they hear I'm not in Alkmaar any more," I say as I give Bertha a hug.

"We'll explain. Send word when you've found a job, won't you?"

I promise I will, say goodbye to Emil and set off. I walk along Lang Street to Mient Canal and past the fishmongers' stalls, where everything is busy and messy. Taking pains not to slip on the fish guts, I buy myself a couple of herrings. After that I head up River Street and it comes as a relief when at last I reach the River Zeglis. Much as I love the city's liveliness, it takes some getting used to.

After asking around, I find a boat I can travel on.

"I don't go any further than Haarlem, mistress," says the captain. "But getting to Amsterdam from Haarlem isn't difficult, you can just take the water coach."

I've heard of water coaches, though I've never been on one because they don't run as far as Alkmaar. According to the captain, they work perfectly. From Midway they've dug a long, straight ditch alongside the water for the horses pulling the barges. "All the way to Amsterdam," he says.

I pay him the required coins, allow my bag to be carried on board and climb aboard myself. I find a spot among the baskets and crates and settle down on the blanket laid out by the captain for passengers to sit on.

Wrapped in my cloak with the hood up over my head, I watch as the city gets smaller. I've never been further than Alkmaar before and have no idea what awaits me in Amsterdam. The only thing I do know is that I will have to face whatever it is entirely alone.

CHAPTER
FOUR

The journey to Haarlem takes all day. It's only once we pass Beverwyck and are on Wyck Lake that we start making decent headway. Once we get to Spaarndam we rely on locks and canals again, but by then Haarlem is in sight. It's almost dark and I'm exhausted. When the boat moors at Gravestone Bridge I get up stiffly and clamber onto the quay. I'm so tired I stagger into the first inn I see. Fortunately, there's still a bed free. I don't care that I have to share a room.

In the taproom, sitting beside the fire and with a hot meal in front of me, I come round a little. Out of the corner of my eye I see men staring at me. I make sure I avoid eye contact and appear as unapproachable as possible, which isn't difficult, given how tired I am. To my relief, they leave me in peace. As the evening wears on, the mood gets rowdy, but by then I'm already in bed. Despite the long day I've had, it takes a while to fall asleep. I lie with my eyes closed and listen to the snores and breathing of my roommates and the racket from the taproom. My thoughts turn to my family and suddenly I find myself thinking back to when I was little.

I nearly drowned once as a child. During a violent winter storm, the dykes protecting Waterland from the sea burst, followed by the ring of canals protecting the Beemster. Many people and animals died, and mud-built farms with thatched roofs were washed away. The somewhat higher centre of De Rijp was spared, even if the well-to-do people there didn't manage to keep their respectable feet entirely dry.

I was five when the flood came. I only know the details of the disaster from stories. But I still remember the feeling of powerlessness as the roof my family and I were sitting on collapsed and the water carried me away. I couldn't swim, but it wouldn't have made much difference anyway. As soon as the sea began to ebb, the flood carried everyone with it. Anyone who couldn't manage to hold onto something was lost. I was fished from the waves by one of our neighbours and pulled into a boat. My parents and brothers managed to save themselves. Allie and Johanna, my two older sisters, drowned.

In the grey light of dawn, I lie and think about my family. Meanwhile, the other guests start to emerge from their beds. People yawn and mumble good mornings. Some begin chatting quietly. I get up too but don't make the effort to talk to anyone.

I take my time getting dressed, putting on a linen blouse, skirt, apron, fichu, bodice, jerkin and cap. Now and then I glance out of the window. Outside, the quay is busy, despite the hour. Freight and passenger ships both set out at first light.

I pack my things. The letter from Matthias is among my clothes and I smile. If I get this job, I'll see him again. A little more certain now about my decision to go to Amsterdam, I square my shoulders. If I hurry, I can still make the first barge.

Compared to yesterday's voyage, the journey to Amsterdam is as nothing. The pleasingly short distance remaining is encouraging, and the comfort of the horse-drawn barge couldn't be more different from the open boat that brought me from Alkmaar. There's a deck house complete with benches where passengers can take shelter from the elements. Since we're not dependent on the wind, we travel at an even pace. There are inns along the route where passengers can get off for a meal and the barge can take on fresh horses. The Haarlem Ship Canal stretches in a straight line through the polders past windmills and farms to Amsterdam.

From time to time, I leave the deck house to feel the wind and sun on my face and admire the beauty of the wide, cloudy skies and green meadows. Milkmaids, pedlars and travellers on horses or in carts pass by on the dyke along the canal. Occasionally, someone waves. I smile and wave back.

My nervousness only resurfaces when we reach Amsterdam. I've heard a lot about the city, about its size, how busy it is, and with a touch of trepidation I ask myself whether a country mouse like me belongs in such a place.

My uncertainty gives way to excitement when I see the high walls looming ahead. I gaze in awe at the windmills atop the bastions, their sails spinning at top speed.

It's busy at the entryways and on the water, as if the whole world is on its way to Amsterdam. The mighty IJ bay, an arm of the sea reaching far inland, is clogged with cranes, flat-bottomed barges, market boats and fishing vessels. Just beyond the pales that fence off the harbour, merchant ships lie at anchor, sterns gleaming in the sunlight. The last leg of our journey follows the shore of the IJ and we moor at Herring Merchants' Gate.

I grab my things and allow someone to help me ashore. Much as I would like to go directly to Keizersgracht and search for Van Nulandt's house, I'm too tired and hungry. Having decided to go and have something to eat first, I order a simple meal at City Inn on a jetty in the IJ.

I wolf down the fish and bread, pay at the counter and carry on up the quay.

So this is Amsterdam, the centre of the world. What a crowd, what a commotion! Boat masts loom up into the sky as far as the eye can see; the quay is covered in bales, crates and baskets that have been unloaded and people calling and shouting out over each other.

Curious to explore the rest of the city, I turn right, walk over the quayside known as Damrak and reach a large square with a wooden town hall and a weighing-house. There are traders everywhere, I hear all kinds of languages. An outlandishly dressed man with a scarf around his head and a little monkey on his shoulder walks past me, magnificently dressed women greet each other and exchange pleasantries. I breathe it all in. Far from scaring me, the cacophony fills me with joy. This is where it is all happening, this is where different worlds meet.

I stand in the middle of the square, drinking in the bewildering new world around me, and know I will never go back to my hometown.

In contrast to Damrak, Keizersgracht appears brand new. The gaps between the paving stones have yet to be touched by dirt, the paint on the doors and window frames is gleaming and the cobblestones look like they've not long been cut. Young linden trees have been planted along the canal. One day I'm sure they will lend Keizersgracht even more grandeur, but for now the saplings droop a little sadly against their supports.

I've asked around to find out where the Van Nulandt family lives and now find myself gazing up at the gable of their enormous house. Somewhat nervous, I ascend the front steps and let the knocker fall against the door. A young girl opens it and regards me with undisguised curiosity.

"I'm Catrin Barentsdochter and I have a letter for Mister Van Nulandt from his brother."

The girl puts her hand out for the letter but I shake my head. "I would prefer to give it to him myself."

"I'll tell the master." She lets me in and disappears into the passage.

While I'm waiting, my eyes wander around the hall, taking in the carved wood winding staircase, the

28

paintings on the walls and the expensive vases on the side tables.

A door opens and a man of around forty dressed in sombre black approaches me. I curtsy and repeat my message.

"A letter from my brother? Why, has something happened?" asks Adriaan van Nulandt in alarm.

"No, don't worry," I say. "We met in Alkmaar, where he was staying overnight, and got to talking. I said I was looking for a job and your brother said he might know of something for me."

Adriaan van Nulandt takes the letter, breaks the seal and reads it. Halfway through he takes his eyes from the letter, sizes me up, and then carries on reading. "So you're hoping for a position as a housekeeper," he says once he's finished.

"Yes, sir."

I come under his scrutiny once more, for longer this time. "Follow me," he says.

He leads me into a beautifully decorated chamber. There's an oak table with six chairs, but he makes no move to sit down. Instead he perches on the edge of the table and leaves me to stand. With my head held high, I endure Van Nulandt's appraisal.

"Give me one good reason why I should employ you," he says finally.

"I'm no stranger to hard work, sir."

"My brother writes you're a farmgirl. You don't look like one."

By way of reply, I show him my raw, calloused hands. He spares them only a cursory glance before looking me directly in the eye for a long time. His penetrating gaze makes me nervous, even though I don't let it show. I return his gaze as calmly as possible, only to cast my eyes down when it becomes unbearable.

Finally, Mister Van Nulandt breaks the silence. "Tell me about yourself. What brings you to Amsterdam?"

"I'm a widow, sir. I could have remarried, but I always wanted to live in the city. Friends found me a situation in Alkmaar but it didn't go through. I had resigned myself to returning to De Rijp when I was fortunate enough to meet your brother. It was as if God steered me into his path."

This last addition is a nice touch; it emphasises my piety. The paintings around me are all of religious subjects so it should please Van Nulandt. I look up to meet his eyes and see a glimmer of respect. That gives me courage.

"You could try me out for a few days," I say.

His face betrays no emotion. "You're not shy, Catrin Barentsdochter."

"I know what I'm capable of, sir."

Van Nulandt skims the letter again, then sets it aside. "I need someone who can keep house and manage the maid. I can give you a monthly salary of twenty stivers with room and board. You'll have a day off every two weeks. When can you start?"

"At once, sir."

"Good, then I'll give you a chance, Catrin," Adriaan says. "I shall introduce you to my wife. Follow me."

CHAPTER
FIVE

Adriaan van Nulandt leads the way into the passage and walks into a room at the front of the house. Daylight streams in, along with the sounds of the street and the water.

Next to the window a woman is standing at an easel in an attitude of intense concentration. She glances up, annoyed.

"Brigitta, I've come to introduce the new housekeeper. This is Catrin Barentsdochter," Adriaan says.

I take a couple of steps into the room and curtsy. Mistress Van Nulandt is still young, around the same age as me, and glances at me without much interest.

"A pleasure to meet you, madam," I venture, when no one says anything.

"Is she starting today?" Brigitta asks her husband. Adriaan nods and she smiles contentedly. "Good, then Greta will stop coming to disturb me. If you two will excuse me, I have work to do." She peers intently at the painting she's working on and dips her brush in the paint.

Adriaan motions for me to follow him and shows me the house. It is huge. Upstairs are bedrooms and the attic where beds are made up for servants. Downstairs are the reception rooms, along with the entrance hall and parlour, and the private rooms, including the living, breakfast and dining rooms, and the kitchen. Adriaan tells me the parlour is only used to receive guests and that it's my job to clean it. The maid is not allowed to set foot in there.

"Be especially careful with these." He points to two blue-and-white vases on the floor either side of the hearth. "Don't move them, just work around them. And whatever you do, don't knock into them. These vases are extremely valuable."

I gaze at them in wonder. "I can understand that, sir. They are magnificent."

"They are imported from China and made of porcelain. That's a special kind of pottery."

"Can I have a closer look?"

"As long as you don't touch them."

I make sure I'm careful. Reverentially, I bob down next to one of the vases and look at the exotic scenes painted in different shades of blue on the brilliant white background. I have never seen pottery so white.

"China," I say. "That must be a long way away."

"On the other side of the world. Come with me."

I stand up and follow him. It's strange to be given instructions by the man of the house and not his wife. Brigitta van Nulandt obviously has no interest whatsoever in household matters.

As the master shows me around, I listen closely and stare in wonder at the house. So this is how the rich folk of Amsterdam live: in houses full of paintings, oriental porcelain and silver. The furniture is oak with fine carvings, the bedsteads are hung with velvet curtains, the floor is covered in black and white tiles and the walls are decorated with panelling or more tiles.

Even the kitchen comes as a surprise. It's much larger than anything I'm used to and has a scullery. There are cupboards for crockery and pans rather than shelves along the walls. The hearth takes up much of the wall and there's a long table down the middle of the room. A door with the top half propped open leads to a small courtyard.

Adriaan goes outside and I follow him. A girl is hanging out washing and turns to face us.

"Greta, this is Catrin, the new housekeeper. She's starting today. I trust you will show her the ropes."

The girl nods shyly.

Without saying another word, Adriaan walks off, leaving me and Greta to stand in silence.

"Right then, let's get to work," I say. "When you've finished hanging out the washing, Greta, come and help me in the kitchen. Then we can get to know each other."

I smile encouragingly at the girl, turn around and go inside.

Greta has not long turned fifteen. She had to make do without a housekeeper for a while and is thus used to a lot of freedom, but also had double the amount of work.

"Hester got sick and a couple of days later she was dead. She *was* getting on a bit, forty or so," Greta tells me as she accompanies me to the produce market on Prinsengracht that afternoon. "I'm happy you're here, though. It was much too much work for me on my own."

"If there's a problem, do you go to the master or the mistress?" I ask.

"To the master, even though he's not home much. The mistress gets angry if I disturb her while she's painting."

"She can't paint all day, surely?"

"No, but even when she's finished, she doesn't want to listen. She's not interested in housekeeping. It always seems as if she's only half there."

I think about the absent way Brigitta looked at me and understand what Greta means. "But the master has a brother too, doesn't he? Do you see much of him?"

"Yes. When he's not travelling, he stays with us. The bedroom at the back of the house is his. Master Matthias is ever so kind. He brought me a comb once. I don't know where from, but it was far away."

"How nice. When is Master Matthias coming back?"

"I think he should be back next week."

"Oh. And where are you from, Greta?"

"From Sloterdijk. It's a little village near here."

"Do you go home often?"

"When I can. But since Hester passed away, I've not been home at all."

I sneak a sidelong glance and see the girl's sad face. "You'll be able to go again soon. I'll arrange it with the master."

34

At once Greta cheers up. "That would be good! Look, there's the market on the bridge. I always get vegetables there. And fish on the Dam, but the herring is better at Herring Merchants' Gate. The dairy market is next to Droogbak. I get beer around the corner on Brewersgracht at Hasselar Brewery." There's no trace left of her shyness; she talks and talks, telling me all about the crooked and reliable traders she knows.

When we return home with our heavy baskets, I pour two small glasses of beer and put them on the table. "Sit down for a minute, Greta, let's have a drink."

Surprised, the girl sits down.

"You see," I say. "There's a time to work and a time to have a sit down. I reckon you've had a lot of work over the last few weeks."

"Hester gave me an earful if she caught me sitting down."

"I have no intention of giving you an earful," I say. "Not as long as the work gets done. And with the two of us that should be easy enough."

We don't sit for long. From the studio comes the sound of things being thrown, followed by hysterical crying. I look up in alarm.

"That's the mistress," says Greta. "She often has outbursts like that."

"I'll go to her." I shove my chair back.

"Take this." Greta stands up, grabs a tiny crockery jug and pours a goblet of wine from it. "Her medicine."

"What kind of medicine?"

"I can never remember what it's called. You put it in the wine."

I nod, take the cup and walk to the hall. Noises are coming from Brigitta's studio again. I quicken my pace and open the door without knocking.

Brigitta is standing at the window, her gown covered in paint and her hair a mess. She has torn off her cap and thrown it among the pots of paint and paintbrushes on the floor.

Her easel lies face down on the painting she was working on.

A couple of paint pots have been smashed against the wall, leaving a rather interesting still life on the wainscoting.

I take everything in at a glance. Deciding the mess isn't important, I help Brigitta into a chair and give her the wine. "Here, drink this, madam. It'll make you feel much better."

As if suddenly robbed of all her energy, Brigitta slumps into the chair. She accepts the cup without enthusiasm. "It was going so well. I haven't needed this for two days."

"Do you normally take it every day?"

"My husband thinks it's best. I would rather I didn't, but if I don't take it . . ." Brigitta looks around as if she has only now realised what she's done and bursts into tears.

Cautiously — I don't know whether the gesture will be appreciated — I put my hand on her shoulder. "Don't worry. I'll have this cleared up in a jiffy. And your painting doesn't seem to be damaged."

Brigitta snorts contemptuously. "What does it matter? It's rubbish. Everything I make is rubbish."

"Well, what I've seen was very pretty."

"You're a servant — you have no grasp of art. You can't come up with shoddy trash like this in the circles I move in."

I don't say anything more. I only caught a glimpse of the painting when I was introduced to Brigitta; I praised it because it seemed like the right thing to do. As Brigitta drinks her wine in tiny sips, I stand the easel back up. I put the painting on it and take a couple of steps back to have a proper look.

It's nothing special. The flowers of the still life lack depth and the colours are unnatural.

"See, you don't like it either. I can see it on your face." Brigitta slams her goblet down on the table. She stares into space for a moment and begins weeping softly. "I wouldn't know what to do with myself if I didn't paint. Sit inside all day, go to market now and again, play a bit of harpsichord and hope my husband won't come home too late . . . What kind of life is that? I would be bored to tears."

"You don't have to stop painting, madam. It's not about the result, it's about the enjoyment of doing it."

"Of course it's about the result. You can't think I'd want to spend days producing something worthless. It may be difficult for someone like you to understand, but I have ambition. It's normal for me to be critical. Did you know artists are highly sensitive, emotional people?"

"I have heard that, madam."

"Then you understand how hard life is if you're a perfectionist. Making art is a process with ups and downs."

I think carefully, weighing my words. "In the village I come from, there was a girl who really liked painting too. Everyone said she had talent. Lots of talent. But unfortunately it did her no good."

"Why not?"

"Because there was work to do on the farm. When she had time, she painted with beetroot juice on wooden panels she'd sanded smooth. She thought about painting all the time. She looked at the world in paint, as she once put it. The sun that shone on the meadows and ditches, the farm amid all that green, even the milk churns in the farmyard — she saw a still life in everything. But there was no time or material to paint it."

Brigitta dries her eyes on her sleeve. "What happened to her?"

"She got married and then she had even less time."

We look at each other.

"I know what you're trying to say, Catrin. I realise how lucky I am to come from a rich family and have a husband who doesn't mind me sitting in my studio all day. But painting is more than a hobby for me. The fact that I don't have to earn a living doing it doesn't mean I should lower my standards. Have you heard of Rembrandt van Rijn? We have a couple of his canvases in the house. Artworks admired by everyone, but he himself was critical when he saw them again. A true artist is never satisfied with his own work."

"That's true, madam. And we can't all be Rembrandt van Rijn. I think we should be satisfied with the talent we've been given and take pleasure in it."

Brigitta says nothing and stares out through the leaded windows.

"What I mean is that you should paint for yourself, madam. For the pleasure it gives you, even if it means setting your standards slightly lower."

Brigitta turns slowly to face me. For a moment I'm afraid I've gone too far. She holds my gaze for a few seconds then stands up.

"If you'll tidy up my studio, Catrin, I'll take a turn in the garden. I need to think."

I nod and stoop to gather the paint pots up off the floor. Brigitta leaves the room with rustling skirts and a pleasant silence falls. I open the top part of the window to let in some fresh air and get to work. Once everything is tidy, I clean the brushes. I stroke the soft hairs with my fingertips. What would it be like to dip such a beautiful paintbrush into some paint and put it to a canvas? No doubt very different from my homemade brushes made from pigs' bristles. I carefully pat them dry and lay them neatly next to each other on the table.

CHAPTER
SIX

During the day everything is fine. I get up at daybreak to start my chores and don't go to bed until late in the evening. The work distracts me from the thoughts I don't want to have and the silence I don't want to hear. But everything that allows itself to be pushed into the background during the day returns at night, and it's even stronger for having been repressed. Regardless how cold the nights get, I always leave the doors of my box bed open. When I close them I feel as though I've been buried alive. Often I jerk awake from a nightmare, thrashing around, struggling to breathe. When that happens, I leap out of bed and go to stand at the window to cool off and calm down. The deep blue of the night always has a calming effect on me. At home I used to sit at the window and gaze at the stars when I couldn't sleep, wondering what was up there. Heaven? What do you have to do to get in? And how easily do you go to hell?

Back then, I didn't concern myself with questions like that. Now, they keep me awake for hours.

"Have you settled in here a bit now?" Adriaan van Nulandt has summoned me to his office and is looking at me from behind his desk.

"Yes, sir. Greta has been a great help."

"Good. And your mistress?"

"Oh yes. She is most kind."

"Kind." Adriaan stares out the window onto Keizersgracht, absorbed in thought. "Yes, she is. But not always. Not to herself, at any rate."

"She's rather harsh on herself when it comes to her painting."

Adriaan sighs. "She shouldn't take it so seriously. I mean, it's a wonderful pastime and I would happily fill the house with her work, but that isn't enough for her. She wants praise in artistic circles and to sell her work. But if she keeps on destroying her paintings, that's not going to happen."

"May I ask what kind of medicine your wife takes?"

"Laudanum. It's a spiced wine containing opium. Opium eases the pain, soothes the nerves and stimulates creativity. Maybe too much; all she does is paint."

"In Alkmaar one woman was allowed to join the Guild of Saint Lucas. She was given training and now works as a master painter in her own studio."

Adriaan pulls at his goatee and leans back. "I know what you're driving at, but there is no way my wife can start an apprenticeship as a master painter."

"That's not what I meant, sir. I just meant to say that nowadays painting is becoming more than a hobby for women. I was wondering . . ." I hesitate.

"What were you wondering? Speak your mind, I have no objection."

"She could take lessons to improve her technique. There are many great painters in Amsterdam who could help her get better. I think then she wouldn't need those draughts any more."

A pause follows and I wonder whether I've been too free with my opinions. But Adriaan's expression is more thoughtful than annoyed and eventually he says, "I shall have to think about it."

The day passes with all manner of small chores. I'm scrubbing a kettle when Brigitta comes into the kitchen.

"I'm hungry, is there any cheese?" she asks.

"Of course, madam. Should I cut a piece for you?"

"No need, I'll do it myself." Brigitta picks up the pewter plate the cheese is kept on. She cuts a slice, pops it straight into her mouth and looks around. "It's clean in here. Much cleaner than before."

"Thank you."

"You're a good housekeeper, Catrin. We're very happy with you." She walks to the window that overlooks the garden and stands with her back to me, gazing out. "Where are you from originally?"

"De Rijp, madam."

"That's quite a distance away. Why did you come to Amsterdam?"

"My husband died two months ago, madam."

Brigitta turns around. "How dreadful. But surely that's no reason to leave your village?"

"I wanted to leave. I've always wanted to live in the city."

"I can imagine." She looks at me, consumed in thought. "Did you marry for love, Catrin?"

42

The question makes me uneasy. I don't answer straightaway and Brigitta sighs sympathetically. "You didn't, did you? People seldom marry for love. I'm jealous of everyone who does."

It doesn't seem fitting for me to respond.

"So your husband died? What of?"

"One day he was dead in his bed."

"Wasn't he sick?"

I shake my head and add, "But he drank a lot. Ever such a lot."

"Then you can count yourself lucky you're rid of him. It's no good having a drunk as a husband."

The ease with which she reaches this conclusion and skips over my feelings doesn't surprise me. Rich people have a habit of doing that, as if their employees aren't made of flesh and blood. I smile noncommittally and say nothing.

Brigitta is about to say something else when the knocker on the front door sounds. I wipe my hands on my apron and rush into the hall. Brigitta follows me and waits by the stairs to see who the visitor is.

As soon as I open the door I am hit by a jolt of happiness. It's Matthias. He's standing there talking to a passing acquaintance and turns to face me. For a split second I think the broad smile on his face is for me. Then I notice he's looking over my shoulder: Brigitta has appeared behind me. She throws her arms around Matthias's neck.

"And here we have the most beautiful woman in Amsterdam! Are you still her?" He holds her at arm's length and inspects her. "Yes, you're still her. Always a pleasure to see you, my beautiful sister-in-law."

Brigitta laughs and gives him a tap on the arm. "You've barely been gone a week."

"A lot can happen in a week." Matthias turns to me and takes off his hat. I expect him to make some kind of sweeping gesture with it and bow to me, but instead he presses it into my hands.

"This is Catrin, our new housekeeper," says Brigitta.

"I know, I recommended her to Adriaan myself. Welcome, Catrin."

Our eyes meet for a few seconds longer than necessary. I think I can see a somewhat warmer greeting in his gaze but as he walks into the hall with Brigitta that feeling disappears again.

"Bring cheese and wine to the living room, Catrin," says Brigitta over her shoulder. She links arms with her brother-in-law and leads him off.

I return to the kitchen, where the kettle is still waiting for me on the table. I scrub as hard as I can. I let Greta take in the cheese and wine.

I keep to the kitchen all afternoon. Brigitta and Matthias are sitting in the living room, their laughter ringing through the house. I work even harder than usual and give myself a good talking to. I'm the housekeeper. Unless I want to find myself unmarried and pregnant for the second time, I'd do well to remember that.

Late that evening, by the time I check the locks and cover the fire with a basket, I've got a grip on myself again.

But even so, I jump when Matthias comes strolling into the kitchen. By the light of the moon and the candle in my hand I can see little more than his silhouette.

"Catrin, I've been waiting to catch you on your own." His voice sounds soft and warm.

I consider politely asking whether I can be of any service but opt instead for a blunt, "Why?"

"Because I couldn't very well say hello the way I wanted when I arrived." He walks over to me slowly.

I hold the candlestick in front of me so he can't come too close. Without another word, Matthias takes the candlestick, sets it down on the table and pulls me to him. All my good intentions vanish. The sound of his voice alone is enough to make them dissolve. All my senses cry out for his touch and as soon as his lips brush mine, there is no more controlling them. One moment our kiss is cautious, the next it's forceful and urgent. Suddenly I come to my senses. I push Matthias away and we look at each other, out of breath.

"This isn't a good idea," I say.

"No, you're right. I'm sorry. I mean, I'm not *sorry*, but . . ." He runs his fingers through his hair so it looks even more dishevelled. "I've been thinking about you a lot, Catrin."

"So that's why you ignored me when you came to the door this afternoon."

"What was I supposed to do? Give you the kind of greeting I just gave you?"

Despite everything, I'm forced to laugh, which gives him the courage to take me in his arms again. "If I'd said hello to you properly before, Brigitta would have fired you. I couldn't pay too much attention to you. I was desperate to do this the moment you opened the door." He kisses me at length and I let him. After a while I break free and look at him earnestly.

"We can't go on like this, Matthias. This can't go any further. I'm a servant and I'd like to keep my job."

"But we can make it work."

"No, we can't. You're from a distinguished family, what would you want with someone like me?"

"My family isn't *that* distinguished. My parents had a pottery and had to work hard for their money. If my father hadn't bought shares in a VOC expedition, I would have probably ended up a potter and we wouldn't be having this discussion."

I like the way he looks at things but I can't dismiss the differences between us so easily. "This can't happen any more," I say, quietly but firmly. "You don't stand to lose anything here, but I could lose everything."

"You're right." The light-hearted tone in his voice makes way for seriousness. "I don't want to cause you any trouble. As long as you work here, I'll keep my distance. In a month I'm going away again to Antwerp, and when I come back we'll talk. Agreed?" He puts his hand on my cheek and looks deep into my eyes.

"We'll see," I say.

CHAPTER
SEVEN

Over the next few days we have only brief moments of
contact. Though we must restrict ourselves to the
occasional wink, a fleeting touch, or a couple of
whispered words, it's enough. No matter how attracted
I feel to Matthias, my job is more important. And
whatever he says, I'm not so naive as to believe a man
of such high standing could ever have a serious interest
in me. I'm too often confronted with the effects of his
charm on other women to believe that. Even Greta is
smitten with him. What is it about that man? Is it the
genuine interest on his face when he looks at you and
listens to you, his sunny disposition, his handsome face?
He knows he's attractive. I see it in the way he preens
in front of the mirror and the elegant grey and light
brown suits he favours over the old-fashioned black
ones most Amsterdam businessmen wear. Perhaps it's a
legacy of his travels in Italy. No ruff for him but rather
a fine lace collar that covers only the shoulders; no tall,
black hat but a smart little one, complete with a
feather.

"He doesn't need to take any more interest in his
appearance than he already does," says Brigitta from

behind her easel. "If Adriaan dressed like that, it would seem odd. But it suits Matthias."

I've prepared the midday meal and set the table in the studio. As I pour a cup of milk, there's a note in Brigitta's voice that makes me look up.

"Master Matthias is very modern. All the women look at him," I say.

"Yes. I'm curious to see who will finally manage to snag him."

"Doesn't the master plan to marry?"

Brigitta bursts out laughing. "Oh no, why should he? He enjoys his freedom. Can you picture Matthias living a regular life?"

"Not really, madam."

"Me neither. And that is precisely why I married his brother and not him."

I hold my breath, shocked. "Did Master Matthias want to marry you?"

"He never formally proposed, but it was clear enough. Have you seen the way he looks at me? He's never been able to accept the fact that I chose Adriaan."

I look down at her with the milk jug clutched to my chest. "What does your husband think of that?"

Brigitta shrugs, unconcerned. "No idea. It annoys him, I think. But I married *him*, so he has no need to worry. He's a good man and I care for him a great deal. Have you heard what he's arranged for me?"

I shake my head.

"I'm to have painting lessons! From Nicholas Maes, one of Rembrandt van Rijn's apprentices."

"How wonderful, madam!"

Brigitta glances up at me. "Yes," she says after a pause. "It seems Rembrandt has heard about my talent and made enquiries. He has no time to give me lessons himself, but he very much wants me to progress. That's why he has recommended one of his best apprentices. Adriaan and I are going along to visit him at his studio this afternoon."

"Are you having your lessons there?"

"Of course not, Catrin. We're going to buy a painting from him. Nicholas will come here twice a week, to my studio. It wouldn't be appropriate for the two of us to be alone, so you will have to sit in. Bring some of your mending, if you're afraid you'll be bored." Brigitta looks up at me and I hastily adopt the appropriate expression.

"I'll be fine, madam."

I'm going to meet an apprentice to Rembrandt van Rijn! Rembrandt, *the* greatest painter of the age, the name known by everyone with an interest in painting. Perhaps I'll even get to meet him. And whatever happens, I'm definitely going to meet Nicholas Maes. I've never heard of him, but if he's a student of the master, he must be good.

"You look happy," says Matthias.

I break off from hanging the washing and turn to him. "I'm going to meet one of Rembrandt van Rijn's apprentices!"

Matthias is smoking and takes his pipe out of his mouth. "Do you know him?"

"The apprentice? No. But I do know of Rembrandt. I've heard a lot about him."

"I thought he was only well known in Amsterdam. So you'll like being there while Brigitta has her lessons?"

"Oh, very much. Back home in De Rijp, I did a bit of painting myself."

"Really?"

"Yes. But not on canvas. I decorated furniture and plates."

Matthias laughs. "Well, that is rather different." He sticks his pipe back in his mouth and puffs on it. "Adriaan is going to buy a painting from Van Rijn this afternoon. Would you like to come along to the studio?"

I stare at him in surprise. "Am I allowed?"

"I'll tell them they can't possibly go visiting without taking a present, and you should go with them to carry it."

Adriaan has no objections to my accompanying him and Brigitta. According to him, everyone should have an opportunity to meet the greatest artist of the age, even servants. "But do try to remain inconspicuous," he says.

That afternoon we drive up Keizersgracht in a hired coach, turning onto Bree Street where Van Rijn lives and works. The studio is on the western side of the city, which I've never visited. I've not seen much of Amsterdam yet; my life plays out in the immediate vicinity of the house I work in. Perhaps because of this I enjoy the trip all the more: the chaos of horses, coaches and pedestrians. At the end of Keizersgracht we come to the place where they're digging a new canal ring. Diggers and carpenters are busy laying a foundation in the muddy bottom. Windmills are used to pump out the water and workmen are busily cutting the wood and stone to build up the banks in places where the foundation has been laid. The work is arousing no end of curiosity.

"It would have been quicker to walk," says Brigitta when we eventually turn away from the building works and are able to carry on.

"I don't think so, it's a bit too far for that. Too far for you in your dainty silk slippers, in any case. And you'd have had to throw them away afterwards," says her husband.

It's true that the streets are filthy now that we've left the chic new canal district. The fish market on the Dam has just closed for the day, and heads and scales stick to the wheels of the cart. The horse pushes its way on to Dam Street, where you can barely make your way through the stalls full of goods. At the end of Old Doelen Street we turn right and not long after that the coach rattles its way onto Bree Street.

"We're here." Adriaan climbs out and offers his wife a hand down.

I get out too, the jug of wine we've brought as a gift clutched to my chest. I gaze up in wonder. The building we've come to is magnificent, with a gable covered in red and green tiles.

The servant opens the door and shows us into a black-and-white-tiled hall with several doors. She leads the way up the stairs to the second floor. The workshop windows open out onto the street. It is a large, light room where five apprentices are at work. The artist himself is standing at his easel and doesn't look up for a second. It's only when his servant coughs that he puts down his paintbrush.

"Mister Van Rijn, Mistress Van Nulandt." Rembrandt van Rijn turns, wipes his paint-covered hand on his shirt and makes a half bow.

"It's so nice to meet you," says Brigitta, blushing.

Van Rijn smiles faintly and a silence falls. Just as it's getting awkward, Adriaan points to the canvas on the easel. "I see you are busy."

"I'm always busy, Mister Van Nulandt. Always. This is a commission. It has to be ready in four weeks' time." Van Rijn glances at the canvas with a look that suggests he'd rather carry on painting.

"We shan't keep you long." Adriaan waves me over from where I'm standing by the door. I give Adriaan the jug of wine and he presents it to Van Rijn with a bow.

An exchange of pleasantries follows, but I pay no attention to what's being said. I only have eyes for the painting Rembrandt is working on. A young woman looks up out of the canvas with such lifelike eyes it seems she can really see me. How is it possible for someone to paint something so realistic? It's unbelievable.

Van Rijn obviously notices my fascination because he turns to me and asks, "Do you like it?"

I'm struck dumb for a second by this direct question but I recover quickly. "The woman is looking straight

52

into my soul, as if she knows me. It's almost unnerving," I say, full of awe. "And the way the light falls, and the colours! It is the most beautiful thing I've ever seen."

A smile spreads over Rembrandt's face. "Do you like art?"

I nod fervently before noticing my employers' faces.

I hastily shuffle backwards. As Adriaan and Brigitta take over the conversation, I wander around the messy studio, watching as the apprentices grind pigment, wash brushes, or sit and paint. Then I stand for a long time in front of the paintings by the master himself, which are dotted about the studio.

Much too soon, Adriaan and Brigitta are making their farewells. I'm the last to leave the studio and turn back for a final look. Van Rijn is smiling at me and I smile back.

"Really!" says Brigitta once we're back in the coach, "I expected more than that. What a surly man. He didn't even offer us a drink."

"I got the impression we were disturbing him. He was busy," says Adriaan.

"So what? We've commissioned a painting, he should have made more time for us."

Brigitta turns to me. "What did you think of him? He was rude, wasn't he?"

"He should have offered you something to drink, madam. On the other hand, when you're busy painting you don't like being disturbed either."

Brigitta looks thoughtful. "There is that. True artists can't bring themselves to waste time with chitchat. But he had no cause to be so surly. I don't know whether I like Mister Van Rijn."

As I stare out at the hustle and bustle on the street, I can still feel the warmth of Rembrandt's smile.

CHAPTER
EIGHT

A few days later Matthias leaves for Antwerp. Despite my resolution to keep my distance, I miss him. The house is quiet. There's no laughter or whistling, and days go by where I only speak to Greta and Brigitta, and Brigitta only says the bare minimum. Since her lessons started, she's working even harder. Nicholas Maes comes twice a week to instruct her. He's a nice boy, still very young. One day when I let him in and Brigitta keeps him waiting, we get to talking. He says he's twenty and comes from Dordrecht. However much he likes Amsterdam, he still plans to go back to his hometown later this year, once he's finished his master work.

"I'll always be a Dordrechter at heart," he says with an apologetic smile. "I'm homesick."

"That I understand all too well." I smile back and let him into the studio.

From my corner, where I sit with a pile of mending that never seems to get any smaller, I have a good view of the painting Brigitta and Nicholas are working on. Because I'm sitting behind them, they have no idea I'm watching the lessons with such interest.

★   ★   ★

Sometimes, when I have time to stop and take stock, I think back on my reluctance to come to Amsterdam and smile. I couldn't have made a better decision. From the first moment I set foot on the quayside, I felt the heart of the city beating and sensed her lust for life.

It's infectious. The fact that I have to work hard for long hours doesn't bother me. Whether I'm walking along Keizersgracht as the spring sun's glittering on the water, diving into the hustle and bustle of the market, or looking around the harbour at the VOC ships, I savour every moment, revelling in the bustle around me. The weeks pass and it's May before I know it.

On my day off, I walk out of the city to the countryside with its polder meadows and vegetable gardens. Whenever I see farmers sailing towards Amsterdam with barges full of milk cans and cheese, it brings a stab of homesickness.

I wrote a letter home and received a couple of words back, just the once. I will have to be satisfied with that.

On Sundays we go to church. The master and mistress sit in special pews reserved for patricians. The lower orders have to stand. Not that I mind. However painful my feet and knees, I stand motionless, my eyes fixed on the pulpit, and sing and pray.

Adriaan praises my piety. "You have to stand through the entire service, yet you're always the last to leave the church. Many people would do well to follow your example."

He and Matthias are originally from Delft, where their elder brother Evert still lives. Their parents had a pottery in Delft and did a fair trade. It was a smart move on the part of Conrad van Nulandt to invest in the first voyage to the East. The expedition hadn't done that well but a second voyage brought enormous profits. The pottery was expanded to a second site, which also did brilliantly. After the death of their parents, Evert took over the largest pottery and the younger brothers sold the second one. Adriaan left for Amsterdam with his share of the inheritance and worked his way up to become one of the masters of the East India Company. Matthias, not yet twenty when his parents died, rapidly ran through a large portion of his fortune and went to work for his brother.

One windy day in June, Adriaan announces he's going to Delft to pay a visit to his oldest brother.

"I'll be gone for a week. Take good care of my wife, will you?" he says.

"Of course, sir. There's no need to worry."

"How are her painting lessons going?"

"Young Master Maes gives useful advice."

"So it's going well. Is he satisfied with her progress?"

"Her work is getting better and better."

"Good. You may go, Catrin. Thank you."

I rush up to the living room, which is in need of a good clean. Greta can wash the furniture and scrub the floor, but she has to steer clear of the porcelain.

I take dusting cloths and move all the objects arranged on the dresser onto the table. Then I wipe away the dust, polish the silver and clean the pair of porcelain decorative vases. They aren't as big as the vases in the parlour but they are just as beautiful. Relieved not to have damaged anything, I take a step back. As always, I allow myself a minute or two to admire the cobalt-blue motifs.

Looking at the vases is like looking into another world. Every time I find myself hypnotised by the tiny figures with their long, pointed beards and baggy robes, the landscapes with mountains and birds I don't recognise and the strange buildings.

All the patterns are painted with such hair-fine lines I almost can't believe they were made by a human hand. You'd need a steady brush to work with such precision. The lines, curves and loops are exactly the same all over. Nowhere has the line been broken or applied too thickly; these are masterpieces. It's strange to think that someone on the other side of the world sat hunched over these vases and that they spent months after that in the hold of a ship before winding up here on the dresser.

"Catrin?"

I jump and turn around. Brigitta is standing at the door, her hair sticking up around her head. She has a weary expression on her face. "Will you help me mix some paint? I'm up to my ears."

"Shouldn't I finish my work first, madam?"

Brigitta flaps her hand impatiently. "This room isn't important, I need you."

"I'll just give Greta her instructions and then I'll be right there, madam."

Grinding pigment. As if I have time for that. With a sigh I go to the kitchen and tell Greta what she needs to do, then walk to the studio.

Brigitta stands waiting at a table of little bowls.

"I'll show you how to do it." She holds up a pestle and a piece of ivory.

"I know how to make paint, madam. I've done it before."

"Very good. I only need blue and black. Go steady with the lapis lazuli, it's expensive. Don't knock over the bowl."

"No, madam."

We get to work, grinding chunks of black ivory and lapis lazuli to powder by crushing them with the pestle. Eventually a splash of linseed oil is added and mixed with the powder to make a smooth paste.

When Adriaan comes to say goodbye, he finds his wife with a blue-and-black-powdered apron and hands. He laughs. "Are you sure you won't come to Delft? Will you manage for the whole week on your own?"

"Of course I'll manage," says Brigitta sweetly. "Have you got the painting I did for Evert?"

"It's with my things. You're not working too hard, are you, my dear? You look very pale."

"I feel fine. I'll see you next week, darling." Brigitta stops grinding to give her husband a kiss, but not for long. As he goes out the door, Adriaan turns back. When Brigitta doesn't look up, he leaves.

CHAPTER
NINE

For most of the morning we work side by side in comfortable silence. After a while, Brigitta puts a canvas on the easel and wanders around the studio in search of objects to paint.

"I don't want flowers," she says. "Nicholas wants me to paint a single object with as little colour as possible."

"You could take one of those beautiful vases from the dresser."

Brigitta considers this and nods. "Yes, that's a good idea. Fetch one, will you?"

I wipe my hands on my apron. In the kitchen I wash them thoroughly with soap and go to the living room. I pick up the vase with care and walk with it to the studio.

"Put it down there." Brigitta nods towards a side table across from her easel. "Don't drop it."

Delicately, I place the vase on the little table. "Hard to believe it's come all the way from China. I don't even know where that is."

"There's a map of the world on the wall in the living room, have a look at it some time. It really is ludicrously far away. It would take a ship at least six months to get there."

The vase is stable and I take a step back. "How much is something like that worth, madam?"

"That? I think about a hundred guilders. The two big ones next to the hearth in the parlour, easily double that." Brigitta laughs. "If my husband saw you walking around with *them* he'd have a fit."

I return to my post behind the work bench and carry on grinding blue pigment. It's not a difficult task, but I'm worried about the shopping that still needs to be done today. Greta will struggle to carry everything on her own.

My gaze wanders to Brigitta, who is holding on to the edge of the table. "Anything the matter, madam?"

"I don't know. I don't feel very well."

"What's wrong?" I stare at her in concern.

Brigitta never has much colour in her cheeks but now she's deathly white and there are dark circles under her eyes. Suddenly she wobbles and I rush around the table to her side.

"Are you all right, madam?"

"Everything's fine, I'm a little dizzy, that's all."

"Perhaps you were bent over for too long."

"Yes, perhaps." Brigitta sinks onto a chair and groans.

I squat down beside her, take in her pale face and feel her forehead. "You've got a fever! Madam, you're ill."

"No, no, I'm fine. It's nothing . . ." Brigitta groans again and looks to me for help. "You're right, I don't feel well at all."

"You have to go to bed. I'll help you."

"No, that's impossible. That painting needs finishing. Nicholas is coming today and he'll want to see whether I've made use of chiaroscuro, and . . ."

"You can't have your lesson if you're sick. I'll tell Mister Maes it's cancelled." Fully resolved, I lead a weakly protesting Brigitta to the living room, to the box bed. Once there she gives up all resistance. She trembles as she lets me help her out of her clothes and into bed.

"I'm cold," she whispers.

"I'll light the fire and fill the warming pans. Do you want an extra blanket?" I leave the room and hurry to the kitchen. "Greta, the mistress is ill. Fill the warming pans with hot coals and fetch a blanket."

As Greta walks away I pour a flagon of watered beer, walk with it to the living room and set it on the table next to the bed. I touch Brigitta's forehead again and am shocked to feel how warm she is. Even so, her teeth are chattering and she's pulled the blanket right up.

"I've put something to drink next to your bed. If you need me, just say so, I'll stay close by. Try to sleep a little." I grab a chair, set it beside the box bed and sit down.

After a while Brigitta's breathing becomes more regular and when I'm certain that she's asleep I get up. I beckon to Greta, who is peeping around the door frame into the room, and tell her in a low voice, "I wanted to go to the market with you today but someone needs to stay with the mistress. Go on your own and get them to deliver anything you can't carry. Come on, let's see what we need."

62

"I have to clean upstairs."

"That can wait. No one but us will see that it's dirty anyway. I'd like you to call at the doctor's and ask whether he can come to see the mistress. That fever worries me."

"She'll not have anything serious, though, will she? Or anything catching?"

"I don't think so. She hasn't taken very good care of herself, that's all. We're going to make sure that changes from now on."

"And that draught, what's it called again?"

"Laudanum. I'm glad you brought it up, we've nearly run out. Go to the apothecary's on Rokin and pick up a jug. And I know it's a long way, but you need to go to Mister Maes as well and tell him the mistress's painting lesson is cancelled."

Greta casts a happy glance at the glorious weather outside, puts on her shawl and grabs a basket. The front door closes behind her and I look around. What should I do now? Greta has taken a lot of work off my hands by doing the shopping on her own and now that I don't need to mix any paint I have some spare time. That makes me think of the layer of paint covering the table and floor of the studio.

A few minutes later I'm marching through the hall with a bucket of suds. In the studio I pause to inspect the painting Brigitta just started. She has outlined the contours of the vase and its decoration in pencil and part of the sketch is already filled in with paint.

As I scrub the floor around the table, my eye keeps being drawn to the canvas on the easel. Something is wrong with the placement of the light. I can't say for certain what it is, but it's not right. I study the painting closely. The blue is too dark, Brigitta should have used a lighter shade on the side. And she should have left the lightest bits white. Nicholas explained that the other day.

I take a couple of steps towards the easel and examine the brushstrokes close up. Maybe if Brigitta scratches off some of the blue and paints over the top she can still save the picture, even though it would be easier to start again and use the white of the canvas. I would have gone about the whole thing completely differently.

Sunlight falls in through the leaded windows and warms my fidgeting fingers. I *could* have a go. Not a complete picture, I don't have time for that. Just a section. Just to know how it feels to paint with a real brush and a real canvas. I could use that little one Brigitta never chooses because she prefers to work on something bigger. I'd have to buy a new canvas later to replace it, but now that Brigitta is sick she's not so likely to notice anything is missing.

Even as my head is screaming that I shouldn't be so stupid, my hands are already busy. They grab Brigitta's painting and set it against the wall, pick out a smaller canvas and place it on the easel. I'm trembling a little but I can't bring myself to reverse my decision. Everything in me is longing to let a paintbrush glide across the linen. First I make a sketch. I make hair-fine lines with a piece of charcoal. The vase is soon on the canvas, but the figures on it are a little more complicated. In the end, I only draw the most important bits and miss some of the details.

I choose a paintbrush with care. My first brushstrokes are somewhat tentative but I soon gain confidence. What a difference, to be painting on canvas. Earthenware is porous and sucks up the paint, linen is much finer. And the brush! It caresses the canvas, as if it has a mind of its own. By changing the firmness of the brush stroke and the amount of water added to the paint, I make different shades of blue, creating the same light, whimsical effect as on the vase. The people and animals come to life with every stroke.

Absorbed, I keep on working and forget the time. It's only when there's a knock at the door that I finally look up. It can't be Greta; the household staff use the servants' entrance. I hurriedly put down the brush, make sure there's no paint on my hands and walk into the hall. I open the door and find myself face to face with an older gentleman dressed in a black suit. He's wearing a hat and a ruff.

"I'm Doctor Geelvinck," he says. "I understand Mistress Van Nulandt is unwell."

"It's good of you to come so quickly. I'll show you to her." I close the door behind us and lead the way to the living room.

Brigitta wakes up when she hears our footsteps. "Catrin?" she says hoarsely.

"I'm here. And the doctor is with me."

"Good day, Mistress Van Nulandt, what seems to be the trouble?" Geelvinck goes over to the bed and peers down at Brigitta.

She tries to sit up but falls back onto her pillows. "I'm dizzy and I have a headache."

As the doctor examines Brigitta, I stand by with my arms folded. It would be unthinkable for me to leave the mistress alone with a man, even the doctor.

After Geelvinck has felt her forehead, looked at her tongue and asked her some questions, he leaves the room so Brigitta can use the chamber pot. When he comes back, he pours the urine into a glass beaker, holds it up to the light, scrutinises the liquid and sniffs it briefly.

"Nothing serious," he says after a while. "The colour and smell is normal. I suspect you have exhausted yourself again, Mistress Van Nulandt. You work too hard and don't spend enough time outdoors. It isn't healthy to be amidst paint and turpentine fumes all day." He turns to me. "Make sure she rests and have her walk in the garden as soon as the fever has subsided." He bids farewell to Brigitta and allows me to lead him back into the hall.

"Should I give her that draught, the laudanum?" I ask.

"Yes, of course. It relieves tension and settles the nerves. There are healing substances in it, as in opium. It even helps against the plague. I take it during every epidemic." Geelvinck glances into the studio through the wide open door. At first he only looks in absently, as if by chance, but then his eyes fill with interest. "Was she working on that canvas? That is a beautiful piece of work. A truly beautiful piece of work."

CHAPTER
TEN

To my horror, Doctor Geelvinck goes into the studio, making a beeline for the painting. He examines the half-finished picture in minute detail.

"What a fascinating subject," he says. "Mistress Van Nulandt usually paints flowers. I didn't know she was an admirer of Chinese porcelain. It's remarkably well done. See how beautifully the sunlight falls onto the vase. And how precisely all those little Chinese fellows have been painted. You need a really steady, skilled hand for that."

I stand behind him and say nothing. The doctor doesn't seem to be expecting me to because he doesn't look round once.

"That would be wonderful above my mantelpiece," he says. "Oriental porcelain is too expensive for me, but a painting like that would be just as nice."

There's a commotion in the kitchen. I glance over my shoulder, afraid Greta will appear. The doctor has heard the noise too and goes back out into the hall. After repeating his instructions about Brigitta's care, he finally leaves. Relieved, I shut the door behind him and turn to Greta, who's just approaching.

"I got everything," she says. "It was a lot, but I managed nearly everything on my own. A few more things are being delivered. Was that the doctor?"

"Yes." I close the door to the studio. "He says the mistress hasn't got anything serious. She's tired, that's all."

"No surprises there, shutting herself up in that pigsty all day and working all the hours God sends. I fetched that draught from the apothecary's. Does the mistress need to take it?"

"I'll give it to her in a minute. Go and unpack the shopping." I watch Greta go down the hall and disappear into the kitchen. Then I nip into the studio and swap the canvasses. I run upstairs with my painting and hide it in the drawer under my bed. Back downstairs I heave a sigh of relief. I'll get another canvas first thing tomorrow.

The next day the fever has broken, but Brigitta still feels weak and tired.

"You should stay in bed. Shall I fetch you something to read? *The Journal of Willem Bontekoe*, perhaps? You said the other day you hadn't got round to it."

"I'd really rather be painting."

"I don't think that's such a good idea, madam. The doctor said I had to make sure you were fully rested. If the fever hasn't returned by this afternoon, you can sit in the garden. The weather is glorious."

To my surprise, Brigitta listens. "Maybe you're right. Bring me the shipping almanac, will you?"

I fetch the book from the cupboard and hand it to her. If only Brigitta had just gone back to sleep, I would have been able to dash out and buy a fresh canvas and a piece of lapis lazuli.

"Greta, I need to pop out to the market. There's no treacle left to bottle the poultry."

Greta, who is busy scrubbing the floor in the hall, glances up. "Yes there is! There's another jar in the cellar."

"That one's gone off, it smells strange. I'll buy another." I throw on my shawl.

"Should I go?"

"No, thank you. I'll just nip out myself." I hurry to the front door but Brigitta's voice stops me in my tracks.

"I fancy a trip out. Let's have a stroll and look at the progress they're making on the new development, Catrin. Adriaan wants to buy a house there if everything keeps going well. The gardens are much bigger than around here."

I turn to face her. "That's quite a step, madam. Are you sure you feel well enough?"

"I think a walk is exactly what I could do with. Were you on your way out?"

"Yes, we need treacle."

"Then we'll pick some up while we're out. Step aside, Greta, you can see I'm trying to get past. And don't make such a mess on the floor — I might slip." Brigitta walks into the hall holding onto the wall for support and picks up her cloak. "I feel a lot better than yesterday," she tells me. "Tomorrow I'm going to get right back to work."

By the time we return in the afternoon there's little left of Brigitta's energetic mood. I help her into bed and gently close the door behind me as I leave the room.

"Keep the noise down," I tell Greta when she comes into the kitchen with clattering buckets. "I don't want the mistress to wake up. I'm going to slip out and get the treacle."

"Weren't you supposed to have picked that up while you were out?"

"The mistress got so tired on the way back, we took a shortcut home. I'll be back before you know it." I leave the house again without waiting for a response. Normally I take my time when I go out shopping; I don't often get out of the house. Now I march along at a swift pace.

Luckily, it isn't too busy at the apothecary's. I've brought a few coins from my stash and use them to buy the lapis lazuli. I wince at the price, but there's no other option. After that I go to the frame-maker and pick out a canvas the same size as the one I used. With the stone in my hand and the frame under my arm, I head back to Keizersgracht.

Once I arrive at the house, I go in through the servants' entrance, slip into the studio and set the canvas against the wall. I place the lapis lazuli on the work bench and decide to go back and grind it into powder as soon as possible. In the hall I run into Brigitta.

"Mistress!" I say in surprise. "You're up again already?"

"I wanted something to drink. Why didn't you come when I called?" says Brigitta sharply.

"I didn't hear you, I was busy in the cellar."

Brigitta eyes me suspiciously. "Then why have you come from my studio? What were you doing there?"

I rack my brains for an excuse. "I put away a piece of lapis lazuli, madam. I've just been to buy it."

"Why?"

"I knocked over a pot of paint. I used my own money to buy a new piece."

"Really? That must have cost you an arm and a leg."

"I'm afraid so, madam. But it's my own fault, I should have been watching what I was doing."

"Next time you will. Make sure you get it ground today. I'm going to sleep a while longer, but tomorrow I want to get back to work."

"I'll do it at once. You go back to bed and I'll bring you something to drink." There's a knock at the door and I look round.

"That could be Adriaan," says Brigitta. "He's supposed to be back today or tomorrow."

It isn't Adriaan on the doorstep but Doctor Geelvinck. Brigitta steps forward to greet the doctor. "How good of you to drop by. I'm much better now. The fever is definitely gone, anyway."

"And are you still dizzy?"

"No. Just a little tired. I'm going to rest up today and get back to painting tomorrow."

Geelvinck glances at the closed door of the studio. "I saw the painting you're working on. You've got a great deal of talent."

Brigitta looks at him with a glow of satisfaction. "You saw my vase? Did you think it was pretty?"

"Really pretty. Do you ever sell any of your work?"

"Of course, if there's an interest in it. I can hardly keep everything I make, I paint so much."

I clear my throat so she turns round. "Mistress, do you want me to take care of upstairs or . . ."

"Not now, Catrin. You can see I'm trying to have a conversation." Brigitta turns back to the doctor abruptly.

Doctor Geelvinck bows. "Then I think you have a customer. I would be glad to buy that painting from you when it's finished."

His eyes stray back to the studio and for a second I fear he'll ask to go inside.

"Mistress, could you tell me what you'd like me to do?" I say.

"Yes, yes, we'll discuss it in a minute. Doctor, if you will excuse me . . ." With a few more pleasantries she shows Geelvinck to the door. Once he's gone she looks at me in delight. "Did you hear that? He loved my painting!"

"I heard, madam."

"I always suspected Doctor Geelvinck was a man of taste. He has that air about him. And he's quite well off; he only takes on the city's more well-to-do patients. If he buys my painting, perhaps I'll get more orders. I could start painting on commission!"

"That would be wonderful, madam."

"Indeed, that *would* be wonderful. Have you ground the lapis lazuli yet? I want to get to work, I feel well enough."

"Are you sure —"

72

"Go and make the paint, Catrin. I have no intention of going back to bed and wasting my time. Come on, hurry now."

I should be starting the evening meal, but there's no point in saying so. I push open the door of the studio and study the painting on the easel. On closer inspection, it isn't that bad. What possessed me to mess around in the mistress's studio? If it comes out, I'll lose my job for sure.

My mind full of woes, I grab the pestle and get to work.

CHAPTER
ELEVEN

A couple of days later, Matthias returns from Antwerp. I'm putting a pile of freshly ironed linen in the cupboard when I hear his voice and a jolt goes through me. I'd have liked to run to the hall, but I stay where I am and listen as he and Brigitta greet each other. I straighten the pile of clothes and walk back to the kitchen. As I do, I cast a quick glance into the hall, just in time to see Matthias pulling his sister-in-law into an embrace.

The two disappear into the living room and before long they are strolling around the garden arm in arm, their heads almost touching. It costs me no little effort to concentrate on my work, my attention keeps wandering outside.

"Master Matthias is back!" Greta appears next to me, full of excitement.

"Yes, he's walking in the garden with the mistress." I take my eyes off Matthias and grab a piece of cheese from the side. "He'll be hungry. Bring some bread and a jug of red wine, Greta. It seems they're staying out there." I look outside again to where Matthias and Brigitta are settling down on a bench in the sun. Brigitta gestures with some object or other and laughs. She seems so young and happy, sitting there like that.

"Do I have to do it? I look awful, my hair's sticking up and my face is all red. I can't let the master see me like this," says Greta in a panic.

"Don't worry, he'll not be paying any attention to you." It's only when I see how crestfallen Greta is that I realise the effect my words have had, but by then the girl is already on her way out into the garden with the plate of cheese and bread. She pushes a couple of stray hairs under her cap and does a curtsy before putting the plate down on the arm of the bench. Matthias looks up, smiles and has a little conversation with her.

It says a lot about him that he treats a maid so kindly. On the other hand, it could lead to misunderstandings and give Greta the wrong impression. It takes a minute for me to realise the same applies just as much to me.

When we meet face to face it somehow still comes out of the blue. Brigitta is painting, Greta is cleaning furniture and I'm hanging a pot over the fire to make some parsnip puree when Matthias walks into the kitchen.

"Hello, Catrin."

I straighten up and wipe my hands on my apron. There he is, tall, handsome and brimming with self-assurance.

"Are you busy?" he asks.

"I'm always busy."

"But you've got a bit of time for me, I bet. I've brought you something." He offers me a pretty little package and even though I'd rather keep my distance, I can't help walking over to take it. "I saw this in Antwerp and thought: this is for Catrin."

I carefully unwrap a long, thin object and look at it.

"It's an Italian fan." Matthias takes the thing off me and opens it. It unfolds into a beautiful painted canvas. "In Italy, the fancy ladies wave these to cool themselves off. It's boiling hot there in summer."

"I'm no fancy lady."

"But you get too hot sometimes, I'm sure. Have a wave of it."

I use the fan and look up at Matthias. "It's magnificent. How kind of you to bring me a present. Thank you."

He pulls me to him and kisses me tenderly on the mouth. "I've missed you." His eyes are so close to mine. I want to say something but he kisses me again, for longer this time. He only lets me go when we hear footsteps approaching. "Put the fan away, otherwise Brigitta will see that yours is much prettier than the one I brought her." He winks and saunters off.

For a couple of beats I stand motionless, holding the fan to my heart. Then I slide it into my apron pocket and get back to work.

The next day Adriaan returns too and the house is once more filled with voices, footsteps and slamming doors. It is impossible to steal another moment alone with Matthias, but I'm happy that way. His attention confuses me. How seriously can I take him? Not very, I fear. I've heard stories about maids who allowed the

76

master of the house to turn their heads and they seldom ended well for the girl in question.

Of course, there are exceptions. Brigitta told me that after the death of his wife Saskia, Rembrandt van Rijn started a relationship with his maid, Geertie Dircx. It seems they live openly as man and wife. That kind of story gives me hope, even though I don't know many of them.

Brigitta's painting is complete. This time she's as satisfied as she is critical the rest of the time. In high spirits she leads her husband to the studio with great ceremony and tells him how wonderful Doctor Geelvinck thought it was.

I happen to be passing in the hall and see them standing together before the canvas. For a moment I'm torn between carrying on and stopping to listen. I choose the latter.

"It's . . . different," says Adriaan hesitantly.

"It needed to be. An artist can't keep making the same thing. What do you think?" Brigitta looks eagerly at her husband.

My heart sinks a little.

Adriaan tugs at his beard thoughtfully. He takes a step back to take in the whole thing again.

"You don't think it's pretty," says Brigitta disappointedly. "I can see it on your face."

"Darling, what I think doesn't come into it. What do I know about art? Geelvinck understands it, he's an enthusiast. If he says your painting is good, then it is."

"I want you to think that it's good. Don't you understand how important this is to me?" Brigitta's voice quavers.

"Of course I understand. I think it's wonderful. It only took a minute to get used to it because I was expecting a still life with flowers. You're right, you can't always paint the same thing. It's admirable that you've tried something else."

"Really? You like it?"

"You're a great talent." Adriaan kisses his wife and takes another look at the painting. "What did Nicholas think of it?"

"He hasn't seen it yet. I missed a lesson when I was ill. But what does that matter? Nicholas isn't the only one who understands art."

"Well, I would like to hear his opinion. When are you going to show him?"

"Do you think he won't like it? Is that what you're trying to say?" Brigitta's voice goes up a couple of octaves.

I put on my jacket, and with Adriaan's murmured denials echoing in my ears I rush down the stairs into the cellar and out of the house.

A while later I'm walking along Keizersgracht. It's a sunny day with a stiff breeze. Clouds are scudding across the blue sky, the water in the canal is rippling and the sails of the windmills on the city bulwark are whizzing round. The wind refreshes me but fails to take my worries with it.

What should I do? Tell the doctor the painting he saw wasn't made by Brigitta? Impossible. I may as well quit now.

In a sombre mood, I turn right on to Brewersgracht, cross Singel and find myself by the harbour. The wind is blowing even harder here, the smell of fish, tar and salt hits me with every gust. I breathe it all in and go to stand as close to the water as I dare. The IJ stretches out before me, grey and restless and full of ships. It seems so long ago that I arrived here on the water coach, on the way to another life. I'm overcome by an intense feeling of homesickness. My mother would know what to do. I hear her voice in my head and know what she would say: Confess, Catrin, there's nothing else for it.

With a sigh, I join the queue in front of the stalls outside Herring Merchants' Gate and wait for my turn. I don't mind that it's busy, I'm glad to be outside.

A good while later, I'm placing a supply of fresh herring in my basket. As I walk back along the quay, a figure emerges from the shade of the inn wall. The man walks up to me and I quicken my pace without meeting his eye. Then he grabs my arm and I look up at him in shock.

"Hello, Catrin, don't you know me any more?" he says.

CHAPTER
TWELVE

For a moment I don't recognise him without his farmer's smock, but then I see it's my former farmhand.

"Jacob? What are you doing here?" A stab of anxiety goes through me. "Nothing's happened to my family, has it?"

"Do you think I'd come to Amsterdam to tell you something had happened to your family?" Jacob raises his eyebrows.

"Probably not, no. But what *are* you doing here?" Something tells me it's no coincidence that we've run into each other. He had walked up to me with too much intention for that, as if he had been there waiting.

"I need to talk to you." He shoves his hands in his pockets and fixes me with his gaze.

Anxiety rushes through me again. The look on his face tells me Jacob is not here for a cosy chat and I have a fearful suspicion that I know what this conversation is going to be about.

"I can't take you to the house where I work," I say.

"There's no need for that anyway. We can talk in the tavern here." He gestures to the building he has been leaning against.

I agree with a relieved nod. We go inside and sit at a table in the corner of the taproom.

"How are my parents and my brothers?" I ask, before Jacob has time to start talking. "Good."

"Is that all you have to say?"

"What do you expect me to say? Everything's fine with them. The usual." He waves to the innkeeper, points to the two empty beer mugs on our table and the man nods. A while later he comes over with two full mugs.

"The question you should be asking is: how is everything with me?" says Jacob after taking a hefty swig.

"That would have been my next question."

Jacob eyes me narrowly. "So you do care."

"Yes, of course. What's going on? If you need to tell me something then spit it out."

"The point is . . ." Jacob says, "that it's not going so well. I have debts and no job."

"How awful for you."

"Yes, awful. It's strange, isn't it? The way your life can change from one moment to the next. Then there's nothing to be found in your village, then you have to leave. But you know all about that, of course."

"Have you left De Rijp for good?"

"That's what I'm saying. I tried my luck in other villages but no one needed a farmhand. So in the end I came to Amsterdam."

"And? Can you find a job here?"

"Maybe, but I'd prefer to go into business for myself."

I don't like the way he says this, eyeing me over the rim of his mug. "Good idea," I say, and leave it at that.

"It is, isn't it? That's what I thought too. The only problem is, I've got no money."

We look at each other in silence.

"That *is* a problem."

"It doesn't have to be. You and I both know whose fault it is that I lost my job, and that you were left with a big pile of money, while I had to fend for myself."

"I assumed you'd find something else."

Jacob laughs a rough, humourless laugh. "You should never assume anything, Catrin. It's not smart. Never assume that everything is going to work out."

I take a sip of beer in an attempt to wash away my unpleasant sense of foreboding.

"You thought you were alone, didn't you?" Jacob leans closer to me. His voice is soft but his eyes are like flints. "You should have checked that no one was by the door or outside the window. Because I saw you."

In the silence that falls, the only thing I hear is the frantic beating of my own heart. The chatter of the other customers has become a distant murmur. It becomes so quiet that I am even aware of Jacob's breathing, but then he is very close. His arms are on the table and he leans so far forward that I pull back slightly. His eyes stay glued to my face. I realise he's studying my reaction and that my first words are of crucial importance.

"What are you talking about? I thought you had something to tell me. If you're going to sit there speaking in riddles, then I'm leaving, I've got enough to do as it is." I set my mug down on the table, slightly too hard. The foam slops over the rim.

He laughs again. "Don't be afraid, I'm not going to tell on you. We'll find a way out of this together."

"Jacob, for the last time, what are you talking about?"

"It all happened so fast." He leans back and stares into the distance as if he's reliving the moment. "I wondered why he didn't fight back. Maybe he was too far gone. He did react, though; his arms and legs were moving, and his head. But you put a stop to that pretty fast."

I sit frozen and stare at the face across the table, at the mouth speaking words that turn my future to rubble.

"I don't know what you think you saw, but I found my husband dead in bed. I panicked and shook him as hard as I could."

"With a pillow in your hands? No, Catrin, that's not what happened. I don't blame you, you know. Govert was a bastard. To women, at any rate. I had no problem with him, but I wasn't the one he was kicking the stuffing out of. So I do understand and I'll do my best to keep my mouth shut. But then I *have* lost my job. Everyone is better off, apart from me. How is that fair?"

"What do you want?"

"Fifty guilders."

"That's half of what I own!"

"I know. And it's enough for me to make a new start. I could have asked for the lot, but I'm not like that. And when you think about it, isn't fifty guilders a small price to pay? What good would money do you when you're dangling from the gallows?"

Our eyes meet: his challenging, mine cold. Or so I hope. Perhaps he can see the fear I'm trying to hide.

"I'm not saying you saw what you think you saw, Jacob. As I said, I was shaking Govert, nothing more. But I don't want you spreading this nonsense about me around the village. You can have twenty guilders."

"Fifty," says Jacob. "I know what I saw, you know it too. I don't like having to ask you this, but I have to think about my own future. You probably had no other choice when you did what you did, and now I have no other choice."

I close my eyes and consider his proposition, even though I've known all along that I'll have to accept it. "So if you get fifty guilders you'll keep your mouth shut?"

"I swear it."

"And you won't come back for more?"

"No, that's enough for me. I know that you think I'm a scoundrel, but I'm not that bad. I'm leaving you something."

"How noble of you."

He grins at me. "I'm glad you see it that way. Now, shall we go to the house where you work? Then you can give me the money and I'll be off."

I could spend more time thinking about it, but in the end I have little choice. "Fine," I say.

CHAPTER
THIRTEEN

The short walk to Keizersgracht seems to take twice as long as usual. With each step I'm aware of Jacob's presence and my mind keeps on searching for a way out. As the loss of half my fortune draws nearer, Jacob talks animatedly about the latest news from the village. I don't hear a single word of it and when we reach the house, I cut him dead.

"I'll go and get the money, you wait here. If I come back and we're not alone, pretend you're collecting payment for a bill." I turn my back on him and go inside.

I hear the voices of Matthias and Brigitta coming from the back of the house. I rush upstairs to my room in the attic. With shaking hands, I fetch my purse from the drawer under my bed and count out fifty coins. Fifty! I could cry. But I really am getting off lightly. As he said, Jacob could have asked for the lot.

With the coins in a piece of cloth with the corners knotted, I rush back outside. Jacob is standing with his back to me further up the canal, watching the barges go by. At that moment he turns around, as if he can feel my presence. "Have you got it?" I hold out the little bundle to him without saying anything. He opens it and counts the contents. "Great, then I'll be off."

"I never want to see you again."

"Don't worry about that. Goodbye, Catrin, all the best." He doffs his cap and walks away whistling.

I watch him go. There's something about the greedy way he counted the coins that makes me uneasy. Jacob has never been any good with money. He always ran through his wages as soon as he got them, he thought saving was a waste of time. He'll be back for more.

Over the preceding weeks, I had often wondered whether I would make the same decision as I did back then, when I stood over Govert with a split lip, a couple of fresh bruises and a pillow in my hands. I don't know. Despair takes over, switches off your mind and clouds the consequences of your actions. The life I would have led if I'd had second thoughts doesn't appeal to me, but at least I would have had a life. Now I might be free from the blows and kicks, but the internal turmoil that has come in their stead, the spectre of the gallows, make for a poor exchange. As long as I'd still believed no one else knew about my crime, it had been different. Now everything has changed.

I can't rely on Jacob keeping his mouth shut, I have to leave. God wasn't looking the other way when I gave in to my baser instincts and smothered my husband. Now he's punishing me.

Later that same afternoon, I make a decision. I wait for Adriaan to come back from a meeting in the VOC building and ask to speak to him. He nods, leads me into his office and closes the door behind us.

"Sit down." He gestures to a chair and sits down without waiting for me. "What do you need to talk to me about? I hope you like it here because I'm very pleased with your work."

I sit down and straighten my back. "Thank you. I do like it here, and I'd really like to stay but unfortunately I need to give notice."

"You want to give notice? Why?"

"Something has happened."

"It can't be so bad that you need to leave. Although . . ." He studies me with knitted brows. "It doesn't have anything to do with my brother, does it?"

"With Mister Matthias? No, not at all."

"Oh good. I was afraid . . ." He makes a gesture. "But that isn't it. Tell me, perhaps I can help."

I know that I owe him an explanation. One that will convince him it's better for me to leave. I take a deep breath and tell him the truth about the painting. That I painted it in Brigitta's studio, that I used her canvas and paints and replaced them later, that I got myself into an impossible position now that Doctor Geelvinck wants to buy the painting.

Adriaan listens to me with an expression of growing astonishment. "I wouldn't have expected that of you," he says finally. "You hear of servants who wear their mistress's clothes, put on her jewellery or try out her bed. All highly objectionable. I never thought you'd take the liberty of painting in my wife's studio while she lay sick in bed."

"I'm so sorry. I should have bought my own materials and sat in the kitchen. It's only that then I'd have to use the table where we prepare food and there are poisonous substances in paint so —"

"Enough." Adriaan holds up his hand. "I don't like it, but I don't see any reason to dismiss you. Certainly not now that you've confessed of your own volition. I'll make sure everything is resolved with Brigitta's painting. I'll have someone buy it and tell Geelvinck that there was a higher bidder. It's not an issue."

"There's something else."

Adriaan's eyes narrow to slits.

"I'm being threatened by someone from my village. He's tracked me here and I ran into him this morning."

"Why is he threatening you?"

A silence falls in which I cast down my eyes. "I'd rather not say, sir."

"Is it someone who you promised to marry or something? Has he come to fetch you home?"

I nod.

"So you left your village to escape a marriage. But hadn't you recently been widowed?"

"It's a complicated story, sir."

Adriaan heaves a sigh. "Say no more then. It's a pity you want to leave. Brigitta is happy with you and she doesn't warm to people easily. I understand you've been helping her make paint. She said you were very quick and deft, and now I see why." He pauses before adding: "I'd like to take a look at that painting of yours."

"It's in the drawer under my bed."

"Go and fetch it."

I hesitate. "Is it a good idea to walk through the house with it, sir?"

"You're right, that isn't a good idea. I'll come with you."

We leave the office and go upstairs to my room. The little window doesn't let in much light. I pull out the painting and take it onto the landing where Adriaan is waiting. I hold up the canvas without saying anything.

For a long time, Adriaan studies the half-finished vase while I wait, nervously. Maybe he'll get angry after all and throw me out without my final wages.

"Do you know what you're going to do?" he asks finally.

"No, sir. The one thing I'm certain of is that I'm not going home, whatever happens."

"Do you want to leave Amsterdam?"

"Yes, I think that would be best."

"The further the better, I assume."

I nod.

"What do you think of going to Delft?"

I gawp at him, dumbfounded. "Delft?"

"Is that far enough away?"

"Yes, I think it would be. But if that man comes here and asks where I am —"

"Then I'll tell him I have no idea," Adriaan says.

CHAPTER
FOURTEEN

That night I'm troubled by a dream that's been haunting me for weeks. I'm standing over Govert with a pillow in my hands. He's sleeping it off, mouth open, stinking of booze. I count to three and press the pillow down hard on his face. He wakes up, moves, but he's too drunk to realise what's happening. By the time he realises, suffocation has robbed him of his strength.

I press the pillow to his face until he's still. Only when I'm sure he's dead do I remove it. I look down at him, not daring to breathe. When my eyes meet his vacant gaze, I scream.

I thought Amsterdam was far away, now I'm headed even further south. If someone had told me four months ago I'd be doing this, I would have stared at them in disbelief. Back then my life had still been simple and predictable, now everything has been turned upside down.

Adriaan tells me his other brother Evert, a widower, is in desperate need of help and asks whether I would like to go into his service. "Just think about it," he says.

Later that day he comes to find me. "You can travel with Matthias. He has a cargo that needs to be taken to

Delfshaven. You could leave next week — if you want the job, that is."

At first I can only nod, then I say, "Yes, I would like that very much. Thank you."

Feeling a little lightheaded, I walk to the kitchen and pull out a chair. I flop down onto it and stare out of the window. In other circumstances I would have looked forward to travelling with Matthias. But now I'm preoccupied with other things. All I want is to leave here as soon as possible.

Saying farewell a week later isn't difficult, I've not been in the house on Keizersgracht long enough for that. It's a windless, sunny day. We aren't taking the water coach, which only carries passengers, but instead are travelling on a cargo ship full of freight going to Delfshaven. The boat has a closed deck house where passengers can make themselves comfortable. We aren't the only ones using it, several merchants are travelling with us, but after Haarlem it gets much quieter. I kill time darning while Matthias spends most of the morning talking to the captain and keeping an eye on the cargo.

It's not until we are crossing Haarlem Lake, where the wind picks up and it gets colder, that he comes to keep me company.

"Goods have disappeared a couple of times," he says. "Sometimes they get unloaded at the wrong port by accident, but people do steal things too. So whenever we put in anywhere, I stay with the load."

"Sensible," I reply. "How do you do that when we stop overnight in Leiden?"

"The boat's kept under guard then."

I nod and a silence stretches out between us. I have often fantasised about what it would be like to spend time alone with Matthias, but now that it's happening, I don't quite know what to say. Matthias does. The two merchants we're sharing the boat with are up on deck so straightaway he brings up the very subject I'd been hoping to avoid.

"Now you must tell me why you quit. Adriaan refused to give me any details. I thought you liked it with us." He adopts a tortured expression and I realise I'm not going to get away without offering an explanation. Luckily the story of the painting is a plausible reason for me to leave, so I tell him that. To my surprise, Matthias ends up laughing.

"So Geelvinck wanted to buy the painting! Hearing that must have given you a fright."

"It isn't funny. I thought it was a shame for Brigitta."

"Why? Everything she makes is hideous. It's high time she realised that. My brother always protects her, pays others to buy her work, but is he making her happy by doing that? This way she keeps on believing she can paint."

"What's so bad about that? She enjoys it."

"And that's all well and good, as long as you don't lose sight of reality. Brigitta lives in a fantasy world, which Adriaan maintains. I'm forever telling him that he has to stop. But he's afraid she'll become despondent again. She nearly took her own life once."

"Really? How awful. Why did she do that?"

"She thought her life was meaningless. She can't have children and she didn't know what to do with herself. It was only when she started painting that she rediscovered her lust for life. That was wonderful, of course, but she loses herself in it. As if there was nothing more to life than painting. I don't understand. There's so much to discover and enjoy."

"For a man, yes."

"And not for a woman?" He looks askance at me. "You're not one to rest on your laurels — I liked that about you from the start."

Something flutters in my belly. I push the happy feeling away.

"When a woman casts her life into chaos, it tends to be out of necessity, Matthias. It's men who leave everything behind because they want to have fun. Men like you."

He mulls over my words for a moment and then nods. "You're right. But there aren't many men who dare to break free, either."

"Because they have families they need to take care of. Because what you think of as fun costs money, and not everyone has it."

"I mean men of my social class, who *can* afford it. My brothers would love to see the East, but they daren't make the long voyage. They don't dare leave their businesses behind, not even in the hands of their family. If you live in fear, you only live half a life."

"But it's often a much longer one. I wouldn't want to spend six months on a boat either. I've heard too many stories about what can go wrong."

"You wouldn't dare? That doesn't seem like you, Catrin."

I smile at him. "You don't know me."

"That's true, but we're going to do something about that. By the way, is that the painting you were talking about?" Matthias points his toe at the canvas, which is leaning up against the bench wrapped in old rags.

"Yes, do you want to see it?" I pick it up and unwind the rags.

Matthias takes the painting and studies it in admiration. "That's quite something! Now I understand Geelvinck's reaction."

"You think it's pretty?" I say, blushing.

"More than pretty. I want you to finish it and sell it to me."

"It will be a gift."

We look at each other and Matthias leans towards me. His lips brush mine, warm and loving.

"I'm glad you needed to bring the cargo," I say quietly.

He grins. "That cargo could easily have waited another week, but I did my best to convince Adriaan that it needed to go now. You don't think I'd have allowed you to go alone, do you?"

As the day draws to a close we sail into Leiden. We make our way to an expensive-looking inn called the Leiden Market Boat where Matthias books only one room. I don't protest. Something between us has changed, something I can't put my finger on but which can be seen in every word and gesture. A feeling of familiarity combined with desire and the knowledge that you have to grab hold of happiness where you find it.

I don't know whether this love has a chance or if Matthias is serious about it. I do know that I could get pregnant and that he might abandon me. I should be holding him resolutely at arm's length. But I don't.

As soon as we're in our room, we turn to each other and start taking off our clothes. We kiss, touch and caress without saying a word. The last pieces of clothing fall to the floor and we topple onto the bed. His naked body covers mine, our mouths meld together, so urgently that our teeth clash and I feel his tongue everywhere. After that he works his way down. He doesn't neglect a single inch of my body, until my skin glows and a wave of pleasure crashes over me which drowns out any qualms.

CHAPTER
FIFTEEN

The voyage from Leiden to Delft can't go slowly enough. My instincts say it's all too good to be true, sobering reality is going to come bursting in any second. Until that happens I want to believe in a life of love and happiness, and I savour every moment of it. Even the spring is doing its part to make this a pleasant journey. The polder landscape between Leiden and Delft is a succession of dykes with willow trees, lush green meadows and sprawling farms and windmills. I stand on deck watching the clouds that flit across the sun, the blue that re-emerges in their wake. I feel the wind on my skin, the weight of Matthias's arm around my shoulders and I sigh.

"What's that sigh for?" Matthias asks with a smile.

"Nothing in particular, it's just for the moment. It's a sigh of contentment."

He pulls me even closer.

"We do need to discuss something, though," I say.

"And what's that?"

"Well, how we're going to do this. I mean, you live in Amsterdam and I'm moving to Delft. That's going to be inconvenient."

He doesn't reply and stares off into the distance. I feel a vague sense of unease rising inside me.

"What are your plans?" I ask tentatively.

It takes a long time for him to answer, too long. And when he does answer it sounds like he's doing it against his will. "I don't have any plans. I take each day as it comes."

I regard him silently for a moment. "Ye-es," I say eventually, "but everyone has to make a decision or two now and again, surely?"

"Is that so? I'd rather not if I can avoid it. I prefer to drift along and see what happens."

I have to let this information sink in. "And you mean you want to do things that way with us as well."

"Do you think that's a bad thing? Just waiting and seeing how it goes?"

If I start raising objections now, I'll scare him off. And after all, there's still the chance that one day . . .

"Catrin?"

I manage a reassuring smile. "No, I don't think that's a bad thing. I've been married once and I wasn't all that taken with it."

The relief is all over his face. He kisses me briskly. "I knew we were cut from the same cloth. We like adventure and change, new experiences."

I say nothing. I love him *and* I love a regular life. But if that's the way he wants it, I'll happily play the game.

We head up the Vliet towards Delft. The sun is beginning to set and the trees and windmills cast long shadows into the canal. Matthias has to go even further, to Delfshaven, and we agree that he'll come to find me tomorrow.

"By the time you reach Delft, it'll be too late to go to my brother's," he says. "And you're probably tired as well. Go to the Mechelen Inn on the market square — they know me there. Ask for Johannes or Digna and give them this note. It says they can put all the expenses on my slate."

"Thank you. When will you get there?"

"At nightfall tomorrow, if I've taken care of all my business. Will you manage without me until then?" He taps me teasingly on the nose.

"Of course," I say. "I've spent my whole life until now managing just fine without you."

Even though it's only for a day and a night, I don't like saying goodbye. After a long embrace and an even longer kiss, I climb onto the dock at Noordeinde. With my bundle at my feet, I stand and wave to Matthias as the cargo ship continues on its way up the Vliet. It disappears from view as it rounds a bend and a feeling of intense loneliness washes over me. I sounded so tough when I said I could manage just fine without Matthias, and of course it was true, but I do feel a sudden absence at my side.

I take a deep breath, pick up my things and ask a passer-by how to get to the marketplace.

"Walk," says the man with a grin, but he does point me in the right direction. "Go down Old Delft Street and take a left at New Street. Then you're there."

After a swift thank you, I head off. The working day is over and it's busy on the streets. Maids and workers are heading home, farmers are leaving the city before the gates shut and shopkeepers are fastening the drop-down hatches they've been displaying their goods on. Delft isn't all that much bigger than Alkmaar, and there are similarities, with all their little canals and houses with stepped gables. It gives me a pleasant sense of homecoming.

Most of the streets are in the shade by this time; the sun only shines on the buildings in a small corner of the market square.

My gaze sweeps over the stepped gables and stops at a building next to the church. The sign above the door depicts a beer barrel and a bed. To be certain, I ask a woman selling brooms whether it is the Mechelen Inn, and it is.

It's busy inside, all the tables are taken. A young man is standing at the bar and I approach him. "I'm looking for Johannes."

"That's me," he says, giving me a quizzical look.

"I'm Catrin Barentsdochter. Matthias van Nulandt recommended this inn to me." I produce the rolled-up note.

Johannes reads it and when he looks up, he greets me with a smile this time. "Any friend of the Van Nulandt family is a friend of mine. Welcome, Catrin. You've had a long journey, you must be tired and hungry." He turns to a woman with dark hair and a curious expression who is on her way over to us. "This is Catrin, a friend of Matthias van Nulandt. Catrin, this is my mother, Digna. Have we got anything tasty left for her, Ma?"

"Of course." Digna nods politely. "The only thing is, you'll have to share a table with some of the other guests. Johannes, see if there's a seat free."

Her son leads me to a long table where a number of ladies and gentlemen are having a meal. I notice the clientele seem wealthy. The inn is fancy, too; rather than bare boards it has a green tiled floor covered in sand to absorb spilled drinks. The taproom is large and long, it has several fireplaces and the walls are adorned with paintings of tavern scenes. This is no cheap place to doss down for the night. I feel out of place in my simple, rumpled clothes and sit quietly at the end of the table without venturing to speak to any of the other guests.

The food, white beans in plum syrup, is delicious. After a flagon of beer to wash it down, a wave of tiredness engulfs me. A maid takes me to my room — which I don't have to share — and I fall asleep as soon as I lie down.

CHAPTER
SIXTEEN

"Did you have a painting with you yesterday?" Johannes enquires, setting a dish of baked kidneys and a piece of bread down on the table.

I'm sitting in the sunshine near the window in the taproom. I've been asleep for so long I'm in a daze and all the other guests have already left.

"Yes," I say.

"Do you like art?"

"I love art. I painted it myself."

"Really? How wonderful. Yes, I noticed because I'm not just an innkeeper, I'm a painter and art dealer as well."

"So that's why there are so many paintings in here." I look around.

"I painted a couple myself. I was still in training back then."

"You're not any more?"

"No, the guild examined and approved my official masterpiece last year; now I can legally call myself a master painter."

"Which ones are yours?"

Johannes stands up and points to a couple of inn scenes, signed J. Vermeer.

I study them with deep admiration. "They're magnificent."

"Thank you. They're not bad, otherwise I wouldn't have hung them up, but I'd do a lot of things differently now."

"That's always the way," I say, still examining the paintings. "Where did you do your apprenticeship? Here in Delft?"

He nods. "Under various masters. One year with one, two years with another, one year with another one. Totally chaotic, but the advantage was that I learned a lot of different techniques. It made it easier to develop my own style."

"Because you weren't stuck with one specific style of painting."

"Exactly. And what brings you to this city, Catrin Barentsdochter?" Johannes moves to sit down and I follow his example.

"I'm looking for work. Matthias says his brother has something for me, so I'm going over to see him in a minute."

Johannes says nothing, merely stares at me intently. I start feeling a bit uncomfortable, try to break his gaze a couple of times by glancing away and finally look him right in the eye. "What?"

Startled by my directness, he leans back. "No, nothing. Sorry for staring at you like that. It's because you remind me of someone."

"Is that right?"

"Yes, but the likeness isn't all that strong up close. You're much prettier."

I eye him suspiciously but Johannes doesn't seem to be flirting. His expression is earnest, even a little concerned. He looks up when a door opens and a young woman comes in. She's blonde, with strikingly pale skin, and a resolute expression.

"This is my wife, Catherina," Johannes says. "Catherina, this is Catrin. She's a friend of Matthias."

Catherina's greeting is as reserved as her husband's and mother-in-law's were warm. She looks me up and down and nods coolly before giving Johannes a meaningful glance.

He stands up, suddenly uncomfortable. "Well, Catrin, I hope you find a job. I'm sure I'll hear whether you have later. I assume you'll leave your things in your room?"

I nod. "I'll probably stay here another night. Matthias is arriving today as well. He'll pay the bill."

"I've no worries on that score. I've known the Van Nulandt family for a long time. Do you know where you're going? It's not far. You cross the market square, walk along the Corn Market and then you're on The Gheer. Good luck!" He nods to me and bustles away.

Catherina watches him go, gives me another swift appraising glance and walks off without saying a word.

I shrug it off and leave the inn. As soon as I get outside the racket from the various markets being held in the square smacks me in the face. I slowly make my way through the stalls and up Corn Market along the canal.

I ask a passer-by for the Van Nulandt house. The man takes a pipe out of his mouth and points along the quay with it. "Down there, where they're loading up that barge."

I carry on, somewhat confused. I'd expected a fancy house, but Adriaan's brother has a shop. A drop-down hatch in front of the window that serves as a counter is covered in pottery. Two boys are carrying a crate out onto a boat. I let them pass and open the door. A jingling bell announces my arrival. As soon as I'm inside, I'm surrounded by walls piled high with bowls, jugs and mugs. Simple brown earthenware but also colourful majolica dishes and bright flatware cover every inch of the shelves. A ladder leans against one of the walls; a man is standing on it, reaching for a plate just out of his reach. As he reaches out even further, the ladder wobbles. I rush over to grab hold of it.

"Thank you." The man looks down and his mouth falls open in shock. He slowly descends the ladder with the brightly coloured dish under his arm.

"Are you Evert van Nulandt?" By the time I've asked the question I have little doubt that he is. The man is somewhat older and heavier than Matthias, but his eyes are the same vivid blue and aside from the beginnings of a double chin, his profile is identical.

"Yes, whom do I have the pleasure of addressing?" He's standing right in front of me now, half a head taller, and staring at me.

"I'm Catrin Barentsdochter. Your brother Adriaan sent me." Without further ado, I hand him the letter from Adriaan.

Evert van Nulandt unrolls the letter and skims it. "You're looking for a job."

"Yes." He seems to be a man of few words, so I don't say any more than is necessary.

"I was saying a while ago that I could use another pair of hands. But not a woman."

I raise my eyebrows. "Why not?"

"Good question. It's not that a woman couldn't do the work, that isn't the problem. Have you been trained?"

"Not really. But I have lots of practical experience."

"I thought so. Well, we shall see. The letter says you were responsible for the housekeeping and that you paint."

"Yes, that's right. When I have time."

"Did you teach yourself? Without any training?"

"Yes, I come from a farming family. My parents placed more value on milking cows and making cheese than on painting."

He laughs. "Do you paint on canvas?"

"Mainly on wood or earthenware, actually. At home, I decorated cupboards and tables for my own pleasure; plates and jugs as well sometimes. I didn't have much time for it because of the work on the farm."

Evert has been listening intently. When I finish my tale, I venture to ask what my artistic abilities have to do with the job I've come for. Evert seems surprised.

"Everything, of course," he says. "It's not a bad thing that you haven't been trained, because you obviously have talent. I think that's much more important, really. Talent and love of the craft. I'm curious to see what you can do with a pot."

For a moment I don't understand, but then it begins to dawn on me. "You're looking for a man to paint pottery."

"Or a woman. It depends how skilled you are. Painting on canvas is one thing, but painting on porous ceramics is something completely different. We'll have to do a test piece first, of course."

"Yes," I say. "Yes, of course."

The painting workshop is right behind the shop. The kiln shed is behind that. The doors are open and I feel the heat of the ovens hit me as I follow Evert. Three people are at work in the area where the pottery is painted: two men and a boy. They look up as we enter and stare at me.

"You can sit here. Frans, grab a misfire. And paint and a brush," says Evert.

As I awkwardly take my seat, the requested items appear. Frans, a tall, bald man of around thirty, fetches a pot from the shelf and sets it down in front of me. I smile but receive a disparaging look in return.

"Turn it into something pretty," says Evert, and walks off. He disappears into an adjoining room and from then on keeps wandering in and out. He probably wants to keep an eye on his painters' reactions. They are clearly startled to find a woman in their midst and keep glaring at me.

I ignore their sharp looks, show them my back and focus on my work. I saw in the shop that most of the pottery is decorated with flower vines. As luck would have it. I happen to be very good at those.

106

Deep in concentration, I set to work and it doesn't take long before I'm oblivious to everything around me. As usual, I become one with my brush. I don't even notice that somebody has come to stand next to me, and I am startled when an arm covered in scars appears in my peripheral vision.

"That's *good*," says the man, in a tone betraying a touch of surprise. "You'll definitely get taken on with that, missy. What's your name? Mine's Quentin. I'm the assistant potter."

This is the first encouragement I've been given and it's most welcome. I smile at the man. "Thank you," I say. "I'm Catrin."

CHAPTER
SEVENTEEN

Evert takes his time examining my work, then nods. "Good enough. You'll receive four guilders a week. I'll have a contract drawn up right away. You can start tomorrow."

A few minutes later I'm back outside, a little dazed by how smoothly it all went. With a spring in my step, I walk back to the market square, enjoying the pleasant weather and the future laid out before me. I'm going to be a pottery painter! Who would have thought I would ever earn a living painting?

Buoyed up, I push open the door to the Mechelen Inn. The common room is busy again, though a couple of tables are still free. Digna and Catherina are walking up and down with dishes of food, Johannes is pouring beer.

"How did it go?" he asks as I come in.

"Very well indeed — I start tomorrow. As an artist painter."

They gawp at me, thunderstruck.

"I thought you were after a job as a housekeeper," says Digna.

I laugh, saying that's what I'd thought as well, and tell her all about my love of painting.

"Well, that's wonderful. Congratulations," says Digna. "You don't hear of that too often, a female pottery painter. But I can understand Evert. You're young, beautiful and you obviously have talent."

"I hope it was the last one that swung it for me."

"Of course it will have been. Evert is too good a businessman to be swayed by his feelings." Digna exchanges a glance with her son, who nods to her. "But there's something I think you should know. Let's sit down." She leads me to a quiet corner and points to a wooden bench. Once we're both seated, she says, "Evert is a good friend of ours. He's been through a bad time so we try to help and protect him a little." She fixes me with her earnest gaze.

"I understand, but what does that have to do with me?"

"Four years ago, something terrible happened. Back then, Evert owned a pottery on Corn Market. He lived with his family above the shop. No one knows how it happened, because Evert was always so careful and particular, but one day a fire broke out. The whole family was in bed when Evert smelled the smoke. He went downstairs to see what was going on and the fire came rushing up to meet him. Before he knew it, the whole place was in flames: the hall, the stairs, the shop. He only just managed to escape. In a few moments, everything he had was lost. His wife and children died."

"How awful," I murmur.

"He's never got over it. He has no desire to remarry and doesn't want any more children."

"I can well understand that, after such a loss."

"Me too, even if I don't think it's sensible. We all worry about Evert. So when a lovely young woman turns up who bears a striking resemblance to his deceased wife, it gives us a fright. Even more so when he employs her just like that. Do you follow?"

"Do I look like his wife?"

"At first I thought it was Gesina walking in. I can imagine Evert jumped too."

I think back to when he was on the ladder and looked at me dumbstruck. "I wondered why he was staring at me like that."

"Now you know why. It would be best if you didn't take the job. But I don't think I can ask you to turn it down."

"I assume Evert knows what he's doing. And his brothers too. Adriaan would never have sent me here if he thought it wasn't good for Evert."

"Oh, I don't know. You know what men can be like when it comes to that kind of thing. They never stop and think. But fine, I've told you what's what. Do what you want." Digna stands up. "You seem like a nice lass. Perhaps it's meant to be."

My mind is occupied with other concerns. I need somewhere to live. Johannes helps me out, he has an acquaintance who rents out houses.

"Go to Isaac van Palland on Choir Street. Say I sent you and you'll be all sorted before you know it."

And before I know it, I am all sorted. Isaac van Palland organises everything straightaway. He walks with me to a little house with a stepped gable on

Achterom. It's only a single room with a loft, but the rent isn't much.

"Where are you from?" Isaac asks as he gives me the key. "Not from here, I don't think."

"No, I'm from Alkmaar."

"Oh? I used to live there — I was the bailiff. When I met my wife, we moved to Delft; she's from here."

"You were the bailiff in Alkmaar?" I feel the hairs on the back of my neck stand up.

"A long time ago."

"Do you ever go back there?"

"Now and then. I don't have much to go back for, since my parents died. Although I do still have family there: two brothers and a sister."

"It's quite a way away."

"Yes, as bailiff I'm too busy to leave Delft for long."

"You're the bailiff here as well?"

He nods. "And I've got my hands full with it."

"Yes . . . I can imagine," I say, feeling uneasy.

We talk for a while longer about the conditions of the lease, and afterwards I walk back to Isaac's house with him to sign it. I can read and write a little. Not enough to decipher all the terms and conditions, but Isaac reads them out and I make my mark. As I say goodbye in the hall, I glance at the portraits of Isaac and his wife. I resolve to give him a wide berth.

Outside I stand and look down Choir Street, which is full of stalls and shops with hatches on the front. A good place to acquire some essential household items. I've still got a fair sum set aside, but I can't permit myself any luxuries. Thankfully, my room comes with a bed, a table with two chairs and a built-in cupboard. As far as furniture goes, that's enough for now.

By the end of the day I've bought everything I need, fetched my belongings from the inn and brought everything to my new lodgings. I look around with satisfaction. With flowers from the garden and some decorations on the unpainted furniture, it could be quite something. But the most important thing is that I have a house, a job, and still a decent amount set aside. I couldn't ask for more. That's not entirely true. Something, or rather someone, is missing. From the moment I said goodbye to Matthias, he hasn't been far from my thoughts and, now that I've sorted things out, I can't wait to see him. I don't know for certain what time he's arriving in Delft so I go back to the inn to wait for him. For the sake of convenience, I order a meal and sit down to eat, my eyes trained on the door.

"Hey, I forgot to ask about that painting of yours." Johannes comes to stand next to me. "I'm curious to see it. Will you show me?"

I turn to give him my full attention. "It isn't finished yet. And it's not all that good. I haven't had any training."

"So?" He shrugs. "Talent is the most important thing. You can learn technique, but you won't get far without talent."

"That's true. That's what Rembrandt says as well. According to one of his apprentices, anyway."

Johannes stares at me in astonishment. "Do you know Rembrandt van Rijn?"

"I met him once at his studio."

"Really? How wonderful. The things that man can do! The way he brings light into a painting is ingenious. On jewellery, in eyes, on water, everywhere. Carel Fabritius, my last master and one of my closest friends, was apprenticed to him. He said Rembrandt painted with light rather than paint."

"With highlights," I say. "According to his apprentice, that's the last thing he adds, with little dabs of white paint."

Johannes smiles and I see respect in his eyes. "You paid attention. I'm curious to see what you can do yourself. I'd like to see your painting."

"When it's finished."

"Deal."

Catherina enters the taproom. "Johannes, come give me a hand," she says brusquely before immediately disappearing back into the kitchen.

Johannes rolls his eyes.

"Who does this inn belong to? Is it yours or your mother's?" I ask, to break the awkward silence.

"My mother's. My father died two years ago. That's why I stayed here and Catherina moved in. Running an inn is a lot of work. On busy days, my sister Gertrude comes to lend a hand too."

"A real family business then." I smile, but I feel a stab of pain inside.

He nods and his eyes focus on something over my shoulder. "I think there's someone here to see you."

My eyes dart to the door but never make it all the way. Matthias is standing in the middle of the taproom.

CHAPTER
EIGHTEEN

Something's wrong. He's standing there, not smiling and looking at me solemnly. I find myself rooted to the spot too.

Eventually Matthias snaps out of it and I slowly stand up. I don't move to meet him but rather seek protection behind the table, as if it can somehow stop the imminent bad news from reaching me.

"Hi," says Matthias, once we're standing face to face.

He throws his arms around me and rests his forehead on mine, revealing my sense of foreboding to have been a false alarm. Or so it seems. I can't shake the feeling that he's different. Less enthusiastic. His heart beats in the same tempo as mine, I feel it against my chest, but his kiss is cautious, without the passion of the previous day.

"What's wrong?" I ask quietly.

"Do you know me so well already?" He chuckles unconvincingly but keeps hold of my hand. "Let's sit down."

I sink into a chair. Matthias takes one right next to mine. "Firstly, I want to say that I hesitated. It was all settled but I started doubting everything because of you. But I know I have to do it. Everything's been arranged."

"What's been arranged?"

"I'm going to the East."

"What?"

"To Batavia, in the Indies. I'm going on the *Delft*. We sail in two days."

No shock could have been greater. I gawp at Matthias, dumbfounded. I search his face in the vague hope that I've misunderstood.

"But a voyage like that could take a year," I splutter.

"Eighteen months, because I'm not coming straight back."

"Eighteen months! Why didn't you tell me about this?"

He sighs, grabs my hand and strokes it. "Because I started having doubts. It isn't hard to go away if there's nothing keeping you at home. When I met you, everything suddenly changed. But I have to go. Not only because I want to see the other side of the world but because it's important for business. There's a civil war in China and it's hindering the supply of porcelain. I don't need to explain to you how disastrous that is for us. Adriaan has insisted I go and see if there's a way to get the supply started again, either via another route or finding an alternative supplier for porcelain somewhere else, Japan for example. There are other merchants who want to do the same thing, so we agreed to organise a joint expedition. Do you understand?"

"Yes, but what I don't understand is why you kept this a secret from me. No, actually, I understand it perfectly well. You wanted one more little adventure before you went to sea. And of course I fell for it."

"No!" The grip on my hand tightens. "That isn't how things are. I've told you nothing but the truth. I meant everything I said."

We look at each other and I see my own pain mirrored in Matthias's eyes. "I believe you," I mutter. "But meaning something is not enough. The point is what you *do* about it."

"I'll be back in a year and a half. That's a long time, I know, but I am coming back. And then we still have the rest of our lives." His face is close to mine, his voice sounds rough. "I'd rather stay here, but I can't. I'm going on this voyage for you as well, so I'll have something to offer you. Wait for me. Will you do that?"

"You don't deal only in porcelain. It will be a blow, but more things come from the East than just that. Be honest and admit you're going away because you want to. I won't take it personally, I can imagine it myself. Why would you tie yourself down when the whole world is calling to you? Perhaps I would have done the same if I'd been born a man. But I'm not a man, and the world is very different for women." I stand up and look down at him. "So I can't promise I'll wait for you, Matthias. Who says another adventure won't entice you once you're back. It's better for both of us to put a stop to it now."

With these words I throw on my shawl and leave the inn before I can change my mind.

Some decisions are made with your heart, others with your head. Until now I've always balanced the two, giving in to my emotions in one instance and in the next, trusting to my intuition. Right from the start, an internal voice had been telling me he would break my heart; I have only myself to blame for the fact that I'm sitting here now with broken shards. Life isn't a fairy tale, it's a fight where dreamers get a tough comeuppance. Next thing I know I'll find I'm pregnant again. How am I supposed to raise a child and work at the same time? I'm going to lose my job, my wonderful job which suits me so well, before I've even started it.

I say a silent prayer and beg God to give me another chance.

I'll never dream again. From now on I'll let my head rule my heart. I've learned my lesson.

Once I'm home, I stare out of the window for a long time at the busy canal running along Achterom. It's a beautiful evening and there are still lots of people on the streets. Children are playing, women are standing chatting in the late sun. People cast curious glances at my window. I should go outside to say hello, but I can't bring myself to do it. Not today.

Glad that I've already eaten and that the house is in order, I crawl into my box bed and close the doors.

CHAPTER
NINETEEN

On my first day it's Frans rather than Evert who shows me the ropes. He is the master pottery painter, which means he has completed a five-year apprenticeship and is in charge of the studio.

The pottery itself consists of various buildings, stretching from The Gheer to Achterom. Frans shows me the clay house, where the treaders work the clay with bare feet for the potters making plates and vases. From there, the pieces are dipped into a glaze bath, fired and painted.

In all, there are ten people employed here, which I think is a lot, but Frans doesn't.

"There used to be many more," he says. "The boss had to lay off a fair number of employees. Things aren't going so well in the ceramics business."

"So why did he take me on?" I ask.

"In the end we were a painter short. There's always demand for simple earthenware. And he only needs to pay you half of what he'd have to pay a man."

If I'd been feeling smug about being hired, this remark puts an end to that. I trail after Frans in silence. Everyone looks at me curiously but no one says anything. Only Quentin waves. After a quick tour of the buildings, Frans takes me to the paint workshop and we get to work.

The work isn't difficult. Yesterday I showed them what I am capable of, but I am only required to cover the red earthenware in simple, white decorations. From behind my table, I have a view into the courtyard and am able to see Matthias suddenly appear there. My paintbrush falls still. Frans notices and follows my gaze outside.

"That's the boss's brother," he says.

"I know. I was in service to their other brother in Amsterdam."

Frans raises his eyebrows and turns away. His dismissive attitude doesn't bother me much. I have other things on my mind. It's all I can do to concentrate on my work. My hand trembles and I decide to go and grind pigment to avoid painting badly. Frans glances up, surprised, because there's still enough white lead paint on the table, but he says nothing.

I keep on grinding until he says, "We've plenty to be going on with now." As I sit down he adds, "You can ask Klaas to do that sort of thing. It wastes time otherwise."

"Fine." I take up my brush again.

At that moment the door opens and Evert appears in the doorway. "Catrin, could you step out for a second?"

I stand up and take a deep breath before following Evert. He leads me to a little office behind the shop and, as I expected, Matthias is there. Perched on the edge of the table, he watches as I approach.

"You've come to say goodbye," I say.

"Yes, the way we left things yesterday wasn't nice."

"I didn't think it was nice either, but there was no way it could be any different. There's nothing more to say."

"Except that I'll be back in a year and a half. I hope you'll still be here."

"A lot can happen in a year and a half."

"Yes . . ." He comes to stand before me and strokes my cheek. "You might meet somebody else."

"That could very well happen."

"You might be married by the time I see you next."

"Yes, that's possible."

"I'd rather you weren't."

I sigh. "If you don't want me to marry someone else, you'll have to marry me yourself. And if you don't want to do that, you'd better stop complaining."

He grins. "I love it when you're catty. I've got something for you."

For a second I feel a glimmer of hope, but the little package he gives me isn't the right shape. I open the ribbon and unwrap a bracelet of cornflower blue stones.

"Lapis lazuli," Matthias says.

"It's magnificent." Totally bowled over, I push away the feeling of disappointment and slide the bracelet onto my wrist.

Matthias pulls me to him. His lips find mine and kiss them lightly. "I'll be back," he murmurs. Then he turns and walks away. I just stand there.

His smell lingers in the air around me for a long time and I can still feel the warmth of his mouth. One brief conversation, one kiss and my defences are blown away. I lean on the table for support and suppress the urge to go after Matthias. Fighting back tears, I stare at the floor and take a couple of deep breaths. When I look up, Evert is in the doorway. He doesn't say anything.

Just as the silence becomes unbearable, he says, "I wouldn't take him too seriously."

"No," I say, my voice hoarse. "I won't."

In the days that follow, I try to think about Matthias as little as possible. Once I hear that the VOC ship *Delft* has left Delfshaven, I throw myself into my work. Firing pottery is a time-consuming process. It takes forty hours of stoking before the kiln is hot enough to fire clay and then another three days before it's cool enough to take out again.

Evert tells me that it was his father who started producing majolica, rough earthenware with an ornamental glaze that originated in Italy, and that he himself made the shift to faience when he inherited the pottery.

"Faience is a finer type of earthenware. It has something of porcelain about it, but it isn't so delicate. It's made a lot nowadays, we call it Dutch Porcelain," he says.

"It's magnificent." I carefully turn a blue-and-white-painted dish over in my hands.

"And extremely expensive," says Quentin, coming to stand beside us. "It costs three times as much as majolica. And there's less and less demand for it."

I look up at him. "And that's why you mainly make red earthenware?"

"Yes, it always sells well, even though it doesn't pay much. I've had to let some good painters go over the last few years because they were stuck painting little white flowers. Any apprentice can do that," says Evert.

"And me."

"You can do much more, and you cost less."

"Are things really going that badly for the potteries? There are a good number of people working here."

"Yes, but there aren't enough orders coming in for everyone to make a living. Chinese porcelain is in vogue and there's almost no way to compete with it."

"Matthias told me the supply of porcelain has been interrupted by a civil war in China," I say.

"That's true, but that doesn't mean people are going to go back to buying majolica or faience. The demand for oriental porcelain is still high." Evert sounds troubled. "If only we knew how to make it for ourselves. True porcelain is paper-thin but still strong, and it's white through and through. Dutchware has a white layer on top of a red background and is much heavier. We don't know how the Chinese manage to make it so fine."

"But if they can no longer obtain porcelain, people will have to buy something else. Something that looks similar," I say.

"Faience comes the closest to it, but it will never work. Rich people want the real thing, not an imitation."

"What exactly is it about Chinese porcelain that they find so beautiful?"

"Have you ever seen it?"

I picture the vases in his brother's parlour. "Yes."

"Did you think it was beautiful?"

"Yes, magnificent."

"Can you say why?"

"The colours. That deep blue on that gleaming white. And the designs. They were so . . . different."

"Exotic," says Evert.

"Yes. When I looked at them I felt like I'd stepped into another world. A world so far away from here you'd have to travel six months to get there. A world I'll never see."

"Apart from when you look at a dish or vase like that."

"I think that's what fascinates people so much: dragons, waterfalls, exotic flowers and the appearance of people on the other side of the globe. They're familiar with pictures of windmills and cows."

"You might be right there."

"That's how it is with me, anyway." I turn to Evert. "We could paint a couple of those decorative plates with Chinese subjects and see what happens."

Thus far Quentin has been standing and listening in silence; now he enters the discussion. "Waste of time. It would still be faience; an imitation."

"But maybe people don't care that much about the type of pottery. Maybe they want something to look at. Let me paint something like that," I insist.

For a long moment Evert stands looking at me, weighing it up in his mind. "Fine," he says eventually. "Give it a try."

CHAPTER
TWENTY

At the end of the day when all the other workers go home, I stay on in the paint studio. It's July, so it's light long enough in the evening to keep on working. I lay down the painting I did in Brigitta's studio and practise on a misfire before risking a good piece of earthenware.

To my surprise, Evert comes to keep me company. He's brought bread and roast chicken with him and sets this on the table as he eyes the painting.

"So that's what gave you the idea," he says. "You've painted something like that before. That's very good, Catrin."

"Thank you. The only thing is, this is totally different from working on canvas."

"Yes, I said as much. Earthenware is porous and doesn't take the paint so well." He glances at the little pot of paint standing before me. "I understand why you chose blue paint, but you should use black. Black paint with cobalt oxide dries to a beautiful light blue in the kiln." He laughs when he sees my face. "That blue paint gets too dark during firing. People prefer a lighter shade." He sits down next to me, takes his own plate and dips a brush into the paint. "Painting is not my strong suit, but

I can manage those little roses along the edge. Then if you take care of the more difficult motifs . . ."

In a comfortable silence, we set to work. The complicated figures demand my full attention. After a couple of hours, when the sun has stopped streaming in and the daylight has faded, we have decorated two plates.

We tidy up together and leave our work on the table. You can only fire pots if someone is there to watch the kilns overnight; the city watch comes round hourly to check. Since the kiln is no longer lit and the stoker has gone home, the firing will have to wait.

Even though I live nearby, Evert insists on walking me home. As I open the front door he says, "I won't regret taking you on, Catrin. I'm already sure of it."

I laugh. "Just wait until I ruin my first pot."

"Even then. Sleep well." He raises his hand and walks away.

I watch him go. It's not until he disappears around the corner that I go inside and shut the door.

"What's this?" Frans asks in consternation the next day. He's staring at the black-painted plates with oriental motifs waiting next to the kiln. Quentin is standing at the table too, also eyeing the new pottery.

"An experiment," I say. "All the potters are making the same thing, so I thought why not try something else."

"Did you stay yesterday evening to do this? Does the boss approve?"

"Evert helped me with it."

"Oh, so you're already on first-name terms. You don't waste time! It must have been a late night." He examines the plates without looking at me.

I glare at his back in annoyance. I have no intention of responding to the veiled insult. "I don't care for your insinuations, Frans. If you've something to say to me, then say it."

Frans puts down the plate and turns to me. "You can paint well, but not so well that I can understand why you were taken on so easily. It took years of training before I was allowed to do this work and you just swanned in here, easy as you like."

"Now, now," Quentin fusses.

"Maybe because I make half what a man would, as you so immediately informed me," I retort.

"Perhaps. But if you hadn't had a tooth in your head and were twice as fat or old, you wouldn't have managed it."

"Then lucky for me that isn't the case," I say in a frosty tone. "If you don't mind, I'll be getting to work now. I don't have time for this sort of nonsense."

Frans shrugs and walks off. It takes a while for me to recover my self-control.

"Don't pay any attention to him," says Quentin. "He can't stand having to work with a woman, let alone a woman who can produce work as good as his. If you have any problems with him, let me know."

"Thank you, I can take care of myself. I've known worse men."

"Yes, I think you are someone who can take care of herself. You remind me of my wife, Angelika. She looks

126

like she's made of porcelain but you'd better watch out. When she's angry, I run away."

I burst out laughing. "I'd like to meet this wife of yours."

"No doubt you will," he says, opening the door of the second kiln, which we seldom use. "It's a good job we've got another one. You have to maintain a different temperature for cobalt oxide." Quentin gives orders to stoke up the kiln and turns to me. "It'll be a while before it's hot enough."

I nod and get to work. At the end of the day I watch as the setters place my plates on the slatted shelves. I can't wait to see how they'll turn out. Unfortunately, the firing process takes a long time. Hard though it is, I need to be patient.

Three days later I'm craning to see in as the door is opened. The kiln is a large construction with thick walls and a furnace at the bottom. The furnace is separated from the upper oven, which consists of three layers, by a cover.

Normally, Evert lets Klaas, one of the apprentices, empty the kiln, but this time he does it himself. As soon as the door is open we huddle in closer. I peer inside, filled with curiosity. The man-sized kiln may be cool enough to be opened, but a wave of heat rushes over me even so.

It doesn't seem to bother Evert. He reaches inside again and again to remove the pottery. I look on in excitement. With tender care he sets the plates on the workbench and we crowd around them. It's quiet for the first few seconds but then everyone starts talking enthusiastically. We gaze at the results in amazement.

"Magnificent!" says Quentin, almost in awe.

And they are magnificent: the light blue on the perfect white background, the mysterious dragons and Chinese figures, the flowers and angels. Seen through the sheen of the extra layer of glaze they seem to come to life. I almost can't believe that I painted them. My face glows with pride and happiness.

With a big smile, I look over at Evert, who is bent almost deferentially over the pottery. He straightens and smiles at me.

A smile has even appeared on Frans's face. When our eyes meet, I see a glimmer of respect in them for the first time.

The plates go straight into the shop, on an expensive table of carved wood right in the window. Displayed like that, gleaming in the sun, they look their absolute best. They attract attention straightaway. That same morning Evert receives an order from a German merchant, Herman Fischer, whom he regularly does business with.

"Thirty decorative plates and twenty vases," he tells me and Frans. "With exactly the same motifs. They have to be shipped next week."

We get to work at once and when another order is placed the following day, Evert tells us to leave our old work. "Lambert can do those simple decorations. You concentrate on the new style," he says. "Frans, I have a load of clay coming from the Westerwald. Fischer says you can make thinner pottery with it and it dries to a lovely white. We're going to test it out."

From that moment on I do nothing except paint oriental motifs. Evert has some Chinese porcelain that serves as an example.

He increases my wages, which is very welcome, but the most important thing is that I like it at the pottery. Frans seems to have come around. At any rate, he hasn't made any more disparaging remarks.

One afternoon I leave the workshop to get something to drink from the kitchen. I hear voices in the shop and look round the corner. Evert is standing talking to a man and a woman with two children of around ten. When he sees me, he waves me over.

I wipe my hands on a rag and go into the shop.

"This is my newest business acquisition, a true artist. Give her a brush and she will work wonders with it." Evert sounds proud. "These are friends of mine, Catrin. You already know Isaac, you're renting your house from him. This is his wife Adelaide and their children, Janneke and Michael."

We nod to each other. With her dark hair and old-fashioned cap, Adelaide appears older than she could possibly be, since her face shows only a few wrinkles. Her husband towers over her, over all three of us. The children say good day politely. They are exactly the same size and are so alike that I suspect they must be twins.

Adelaide van Palland turns to me. "Evert tells me you're from Alkmaar, like my husband. What a coincidence."

"Yes, that's right," I say, instantly on my guard. I don't know for a fact that lawmen from different towns keep in touch with each other, and the chances that the bailiff of Alkmaar could track me down that way seem slim, but I feel uneasy all the same.

"It can't be easy for you, living alone in a strange town."

"So far I've not had much time to miss my family, but you're right, it isn't ideal. It's such a long way away."

"But your family will come to visit you, surely?"

"They're busy. The journey takes days and work needs to be done at home."

"Your surname is Barents, right, Catrin?" Isaac asks. "Did you keep your husband's name or is that your maiden name?"

"It's my maiden name. I don't think you'll know my husband's. We lived in De Rijp, not in Alkmaar." I break out in a cold sweat at the thought that he might well know Govert's name, that he might have heard from relatives in Alkmaar about his death under suspicious circumstances. Rumours spread so quickly.

"I'm in Alkmaar fairly often, but you're right, never in De Rijp." Isaac gives me a searching look, as if he has noticed my reserve.

"Drop in, if you have time. I'd love to get to know you better," says Adelaide warmly.

"That would be nice." I thank her with a weak smile. "I need to get back to work, if you'll excuse me . . ." I curtsy and bustle back to the studio.

"We'll see you in church on Sunday," Adelaide calls after me.

CHAPTER
TWENTY-ONE

I'd much rather stay out of Isaac and Adelaide's way but of course I can hardly avoid going to church. It also wouldn't be sensible to stay home, not when I've got so much to make up for with God. On the other hand, I see my breaking the bond with my family and giving up Matthias as a kind of penance. A new start in Delft, where I can spend my days painting, is more than I ever thought I'd have.

Meanwhile, the orders are flooding in. Evert has hired extra labour but the workload stays high. Inspiration and creativity no longer come into it. We need to deliver, and quickly.

Frans and I make drawings on paper, perforate the outlines of the design and lay them on top of the earthenware like a blueprint. We then fill in the perforations with charcoal, so the drawings become visible. After that, we only need to colour in the figures. The newcomers to the workshop use our stencils, driving up productivity.

The pottery grows exponentially. Over the course of the summer, sales double and then triple.

"The *Delft* has reached the Cape," says Evert one day, after work is over. "The Cape of Good Hope, the most southerly point of Africa," he adds when I look at him blankly. He beckons me to follow and leads me to his office, where a world map has been hanging ever since Matthias's departure. "This is the Republic, this is France and Spain. Below that is Africa. Matthias is here now."

I stand next to him and look at the dot he's pointing at. It's strange to think that Matthias is so far away. We never speak about him; Evert most likely because he wants to spare my feelings and me for the self-same reason.

What is he doing at this moment? Does he ever think of me? To my annoyance, I think about him all too often, even if the feeling of missing him has grown less raw.

"Where is he going?" I ask.

Evert's finger glides to a dot on the other half of the map. "You see how far away it is. Almost unimaginable. I wouldn't even think of going, but it's all he's ever wanted."

"Yes, he told me that."

Evert gives me a sidelong glance. "Catrin, there's something you need to know about Matthias."

"And what's that?"

"I told you a while ago not to count on him too much. Matthias has always had a problem with commitment. He loves variety. He has no interest in a settled life. I know he's very charming, but I hate to think how many women's hearts he's broken."

"He hasn't broken my heart."

"He nearly did. I saw the way you looked after he came in to say goodbye."

"He asked me whether I'd wait for him."

"Yes, I heard. And are you waiting for him?"

I stare at the map, at the dot where Matthias is now. "No. I don't think there's much point." But saying those words fills me with fresh misery.

To my surprise, Evert says, "I think he meant what he said."

"Really?"

"Matthias isn't a liar. If he says something like that, then he's being genuine. The problem is, he can't keep his promises. Not because he doesn't want to, but because he's not made the same way as other people. He needs the freedom to do or not do whatever he wants. He'll come back to you, but then he'll leave you again."

I listen to him in total silence. The tentative hope I've held onto despite everything is crushed. I know intuitively that Evert is right and his intentions in warning me are good. But there is something else at play too. I realise I would only have to take one step in his direction to relieve both our loneliness.

"Do you want to come to the fair?" asks Angelika, coming into the shop. She's got her two little daughters, Katherine and Gertrude, on each hand and her swollen stomach is clearly visible under her jacket.

I've spoken to her a few times before and instantly felt a strong, mutual connection. That feeling comes from Quentin too, who is always full of chatter about his wife and children and about the new baby on the way.

"I hope it's a boy this time," he confides in me one day. "Angelika gets furious when I say that. Any child is welcome as far as she's concerned, as long as it survives. And she's right, of course. But I still hope we'll have a boy."

"I can understand that," I say. "It's something special for a man to have a son, just as it is for a woman to have a daughter."

Now that Angelika is standing before me, I'm forced to think back to that conversation.

"Isn't the fair a bit busy for you?" I ask.

Angelika shakes her head, exasperated. "You're as bad as Quentin! He'd like me to stay at home all day. As if pregnancy is some kind of illness. A woman's body is made to carry a child. My previous births went fine, so it will be all right this time too."

I can't help but agree. "I'd love to go to the fair. I'm curious to see whether they celebrate it the same way here as in my village."

"Probably. In the end it all comes down to the same thing." Angelika mimes knocking back a beer, and I have to laugh.

"And you two? Are you going to the fair too?" I turn to the little girls, who seem a bit embarrassed at the attention. Katherine is five, Gertrude only three, and they nod without saying anything. Standing there in their little jerkins and skirts, their caps sitting jauntily on their curls, they're so adorable I feel a stab of longing. If he had lived, my little son would have been a year old now.

My eyes meet Angelika's. She is watching me with a tender expression. "The time will come for you too, Catrin, I'm certain of it."

"Are you?"

"Yes. Haven't you seen the way Evert looks at you? And he talks about you the whole time."

"We work closely together."

"He even introduces you to his friends. Believe me, he never did that with Frans or Quentin."

I burst out laughing. "No, I can't imagine he did. But to be honest, I don't know what to think of the situation."

"What situation?"

"Evert's wife who died. Everyone says I bear a resemblance to her. Is it any wonder that Evert looks at me? He's seeing her."

Angelika thinks for a moment. "I don't think so," she says finally. "Gesina has been gone for four years."

"That isn't long for such a terrible loss."

"No . . ." Angelika hesitates before continuing. "The loss of his children was the hardest thing for Evert." She gives me a searching look. "He said you were with his brother, Matthias. Is that true?"

"It wasn't anything serious. If it had been, Matthias wouldn't have gone away for a year and a half."

"Some men find that all too easy to do. They think women will wait for them for centuries. Listen, I don't want to be nosy, and you don't have to tell me anything. I only wanted to make it clear that Evert is a completely different kind of man. And he'd be a good husband for you. Love is wonderful, but in the end you're better off with a man who's there for you."

CHAPTER
TWENTY-TWO

At the end of July, the whole of Delft turns out for the fair. Even the rich lower themselves to mix with the ordinary people. Dressed in their finest clothes, they parade among the pedlars, tooth-pullers and clowns.

Delft's fair isn't all that different from the one in De Rijp, I realise as I make my way through the crowd with Evert, Quentin, Angelika and their children. It is, however, much bigger. There's more to see and do.

But even here the more hard-line parishioners, led by the pastor, warn of the sinful influence of the fair, which began as the yearly market on the day the Catholic church here in town was first dedicated. It is therefore an abomination to the Protestants. Most of the inhabitants of Delft are Protestant, but no one else seems to have any problem getting into the festive spirit.

On the market square, they've built a podium where one play after another is performed, and on the corner of the street there's a puppet show for the children. There are gypsy women in little tents who tell fortunes, astrologers, tightrope walkers and fire breathers. Not only the square but the streets around it are full of carts where you can stuff yourself silly, on lardy cakes, spiced buns and other sweet treats.

We bump into Isaac and Adelaide with their twins. We say hello, make polite conversation and keep walking.

There's enormous interest in the exhibition of physical curiosities. Giants and dwarves, hunchbacks and deformed people, all are thoroughly examined and discussed.

A little further on the Republic's Strongest Woman shows off how high she can lift a tree trunk into the air. A murmur of amazement ripples through the audience.

"Well, it looks like a man." I eye the woman's muscles with suspicion.

"It is," says Evert. "He probably borrowed his wife's clothes."

"Evert doesn't believe anything." Quentin nudges his friend, grinning. "Have your fortune told, Evert. I did that last year and was promised a son."

"I could make a prediction like that. You've got a fifty per cent chance of being right." Evert looks over at the fortune-teller's tent with a disparaging expression.

"Shall we go in?" Angelika asks.

"Yes, you two go in. And ask exactly when the baby's coming." Quentin grabs his purse and produces a coin.

"I can tell you that myself: not long now," Angelika says as she takes the offered coin. "Come on, Catrin, we're going in." She hands her daughters off to her husband and grabs my arm.

I look to Evert for help but he just laughs. "Why not?" he says. "As long as you don't take all that twaddle too seriously."

The tent is open, showing that the fortune-teller isn't with a customer, and we go in, feeling a bit giggly. Swags of dark cloth create an air of mystery. It smells strange, I can't put my finger on the scent.

A young gypsy woman dressed in a light-green robe with a transparent veil over her face smiles at us. "Take a seat, honoured ladies," she says in a soft, well-spoken voice.

We sit down and her eyes go immediately to Angelika. Without saying anything she puts out her hand and, after a slight hesitation, Angelika places hers in it. The fortune-teller closes her eyes and sits silently for a long time. Then her lashes flutter open. "I see a long, blessed life. Great wealth is on its way."

"You mean my child. Will it be a boy?" asks Angelika eagerly.

"Yes, it will be a boy. The birth will go well. And after him you'll bring many more healthy children into the world. But I was referring to your wealth in business too." She looks deep into Angelika's eyes, as if reading her future there. "You and your husband are going to start a business that will continue from generation to generation. It will become a big, successful company."

"My husband is an assistant potter."

"Then it's time he goes into business for himself." The gypsy's gaze turns to me. She lets go of Angelika's hand and takes mine. This time her eyes don't close but widen. She stares at me for several seconds. A feeling of dread comes over me.

"What?" I ask, fearful now.

"You must beware," she whispers. "Danger is lurking around the corner."

A shiver runs down my spine. "What sort of danger?"

"Several dangers. You must be strong and pray a lot to ward it off."

"Be strong? But what am I supposed to do?"

"Leave," says the woman firmly. "Go far away. That is the only solution."

A heavy silence falls in the tent. I swallow with an effort and see that Angelika is staring at me in shock. The fortune-teller has now closed her eyes but she keeps hold of my hand. When she starts trembling, I break free.

"I think you're talking rubbish," I say decisively, but even I can hear the fear in my voice.

"Yes, I think so too. Come on, Catrin, we're going." Angelika slaps the coin down on the table and stands up.

I get unsteadily to my feet, still watching the gypsy woman.

"Run," she urges, "while you still can."

It only takes one glance at my face for Evert to see something is wrong. He puts his hand on my shoulder. "You don't believe all that nonsense, I hope?" he says, sounding concerned.

"I don't know . . . It's not all rubbish. There are people who have real gifts of prophecy. It says so in the Bible."

"True, but there are many more who are charlatans. What did she have to say?"

Quentin comes to stand next to us and studies me with knitted eyebrows. "Angelika told me what that fortune-teller said. That you're in danger."

"She said it would be better if I went far away."

Evert's face contorts in fury and he marches into the tent with long strides. We all look at each other uncomfortably. He isn't in there for long. When he comes out his face is grim and he's pushing the fortune-teller ahead of him. "This woman has something to say to you, Catrin."

The young woman falls to her knees and grips my hand. "Forgive me, milady, I was only saying whatever came to mind. If I predict a glittering future for everyone, people don't believe me any more. I didn't see anything particular, so I made something up."

People crowd around and stare at me, wondering what's going on. Mortified, I try to pull my hand away, but the gypsy woman won't let go. "I'll try again and give you your money's worth." She turns over my hand and examines it frantically. "You have a long lifeline, that's good. And I see —"

The bystanders start to jeer and I wrench my hand away. "It's fine, I believe you." I turn to Evert. "Please, can we go?"

He nods, puts an arm around me and steers me through the growing crowd. Quentin and Angelika follow with the children. Behind them, people are yelling at the fortune-teller and pelting her with horse droppings. By the time we're standing in a quieter part of the square, I can see the fortune-teller's tent being broken down and torn to pieces.

Quentin sees my face. "Fortune-tellers know they're running a risk. According to the Church, they're not even allowed to be here. A hundred years ago they would have been flogged, so they're getting off lightly.

Shall we have a drink?" He nudges Evert, who looks as if he doesn't think flogging is such a bad idea, and laughs. "Come on, it's the fair!"

Evert relaxes and turns to me for confirmation.

"That seems like a good idea," I say.

We go into the Mechelen Inn, which is already pretty full. Digna and her daughter Gertrude wave to us but are too busy to stop and chat. Johannes is behind the bar. He makes time to come and stand with us for a minute.

"Catrin, I want to introduce you to someone," he says, putting his hand on a man's shoulder. "This is Carel Fabritius, my former master and one of my best friends."

A skinny man of about thirty with dark hair around his shoulders bows slightly. "I've heard about you, madam. You are the talk of Delft."

I laugh. "Is that so? All good, I hope."

"Very good. And now that I see you, I understand why. You're from De Rijp, I hear. And where else could you be from? Such a fresh, blonde beauty could only come from thereabouts."

"Carel was born in Middenbeemster," Johannes says meaningfully.

"That's near De Rijp," I say, surprised. "Has everyone from those parts moved to Delft?"

"It is indeed a coincidence. What's your surname?"

"Barentsdochter," Johannes supplies helpfully. "But you have been away from there for a while, Carel, so I don't think you'll have met before — or have you?"

"If we had, I am certain I would have remembered." Carel gives another small, courtly bow. "Indeed, I have

142

been away for a while. I lived in Amsterdam and I've been in Delft for four years now."

"Johannes told me. You were apprenticed to Rembrandt van Rijn, weren't you? I met him once, in my previous job. And one of his apprentices, Nicholas Maes. The woman I worked for had painting lessons from him," I say.

"I hear you paint yourself, too." Carel regards me with interest.

"A little. Not all that well."

"Don't sell yourself short. Johannes and I have something to confess. We looked at your painting. Evert showed it to us. He thinks you have talent and you should do something with it."

My eyes dart to Evert, who is watching from a short way off and beaming.

"Did he say that?"

"Yes, and he asked whether one of us wanted to give you lessons," says Carel.

"Which I would very much like to do, but I'm so busy at the inn that I hardly have time to paint myself," says Johannes.

"So I'm the one you're left with. I can't take on an apprentice for full training, but I do have time to teach you a few things. If you're interested, of course. I understand from Evert that you can be spared on Mondays, so I propose we begin this coming Monday." Carel looks to me for a reaction.

I'm dazed. Me? Painting lessons? My eye strays to Evert again, who has remained at a distance though he continues to watch me, a tender expression on his face. Bewildered, I turn to Carel.

"I'm content with the work I'm doing, but I would very much like to learn to paint better."

"Then it's agreed. I'll see you Monday morning at eight at my studio on Doelen Street." Carel nods and walks away.

Johannes winks at me and gets back to work.

Evert cuts a path through the crush in my direction and we stand looking at each other.

"Thank you," I say softly.

"Are you going to do it?"

"Yes, my first lesson's on Monday."

"That's splendid," Evert says with satisfaction. "I was able to agree a very reasonable price with Carel."

"I'm paying for it myself."

"Let me do this for you."

"I have money, I insist on paying for my lessons myself."

"And I insist on doing it for you. You've done me a great service by suggesting that we copy the Chinese porcelain. And what's more, I'll see what you learn with Carel in your work."

I can't do much in the face of this many arguments. All kinds of emotions are fighting inside me: surprise, gratitude, and something else that leaves me confused and in a dither. But the only thing I say is, "Thank you."

CHAPTER
TWENTY-THREE

Long past midnight, I'm sitting next to Evert on the edge of a set of steps, gazing out at the empty market square. A lone reveller is still staggering about, drunk and shouting, but otherwise the square is deserted. Flaming torches give off some light in the darkness, the pale moon is likewise doing its best. I fiddle with the bracelet I got from Matthias, but stop when I see Evert is looking.

"You have beautiful hands," he says. "So small and delicate. You should see mine." He holds up his hands, which are covered in scars, and we both laugh. "And a lovely bracelet. That's lapis lazuli, isn't it?"

I nod. "I got it from Matthias before he went away."

"I thought as much."

We both stare out at the square for a while in silence.

"Do you still love him?" Evert asks after a time.

His question hangs in the air like a bubble until I sigh. "I don't know. I was completely in love with him, but that feeling is fading. It would have been more difficult if he'd been here."

"It will pass."

I nod. "And Gesina?"

Now it's his turn to be silent. "Gesina and I were young and in love when we got married," he says eventually. "She was very beautiful, and I couldn't believe my luck when she said yes. Mostly because she came from a rich family and I wasn't such a good prospect for her. But the future looked promising. I inherited the pottery from my parents — along with my brothers, of course. I bought them out. I was determined to make something of the business. It didn't go as well as I'd thought. The competition in everyday earthenware was fierce and the rich preferred the exclusive porcelain from China. I did my best, but I couldn't give Gesina the life of luxury she'd been expecting. She hated having to help out in the shop, which she saw as a terrible insult to her dignity. Though she did it, I could feel her silent resentment. Even our children helped out in the business, as little as they were. I was training our son, Cornelis, as a potter; both the girls did chores."

He falls silent and it's only after a few minutes that I ask quietly how many children he had.

"Three," says Evert. "Cornelis was the oldest, then came Magteld and Johanna. They were twelve, eight and five when they died. Between them came two others, but they died as babies."

I don't say anything, I just squeeze his hand.

"For a long time I thought I could have rescued them. That I should have run upstairs, even though it was already an inferno, or at least tried to get up there. I know it would have been pointless. By the time I made it up there I would have been burned to a crisp,

I'd have died with my family. And that's how it should have been. Instead, I shrank from the flames, I stood hesitating for seconds, while upstairs I could hear my children screaming. I'll never forgive myself for that. And neither will God: he punishes me for it every night in my dreams."

A heavy silence stretches out between us.

"Sometimes I wonder," I say, "whether we don't punish ourselves much more harshly than God does."

"That might be true." He looks at me, but the darkness hides the expression on his face. I only have his voice to go on, and it sounds endlessly sad. Then he seems to rouse himself. He sits up a bit straighter and asks, "And what about you? What's your story?"

I shrug. "I'll tell you some other time."

As the summer wears on, each Monday finds me standing outside Carel's door on Doelen Street at eight o'clock. I'm not his only pupil but I am the only woman. On the other days of the week they paint nude models, but for the most part I paint city scenes and flowers.

"It isn't enough," I say one morning at the end of September. "If I'm to be able to paint the Chinese figures well, I can't carry on doing flowers and dragons. How can I paint people if I have no knowledge of anatomy?"

"But the Chinese wear baggy clothes." Carel is standing before a recently finished painting that is about to be picked up by a client. "You can hardly take part in the lessons with live models. I understand it's frustrating, but it simply isn't possible."

"How can women ever become master painters if they can't study the human form? Men get every opportunity to do so!"

"There are women enrolled in the Guild of Saint Luke. Judith Leyster from Haarlem, for example. A highly talented artist."

"I know, there's one in Alkmaar too: Isabella Bardesius. So how were they trained?"

"Same as you, by specialising in still lifes. Though they have also done portraits." Suddenly Carel turns the canvas he's been staring at so that it's facing me, easel and all. "Be honest, what's wrong with this kind of painting?"

I go and stand next to him. I hadn't seen his latest work yet, it's only just finished. The paint is wet and gleams in the morning light. On the canvas there's a little bird with yellow feathers and a red beak. Despite its fierce gaze, it's clear that this is a pet because the tiny creature is chained by its foot to a special perch fastened to a wall. It's a small, intimate painting. I look at it, struck dumb by its simplicity and beauty.

"Magnificent," I say eventually.

"I'm calling it *The Goldfinch*. I don't really want to part with it."

"I understand. Wouldn't you rather keep it yourself?"

"Yes, but that way I'd die of hunger."

We examine the painting in a companionable silence.

"You're right," I say. "There's nothing wrong with still lifes at all." I go back to my place behind my easel. "How did you end up in Delft?"

For a moment it seems as if Carel hasn't heard me, because he keeps his back to me and doesn't react. It's only when I resume painting that he starts to talk.

"Alice was my great love," he says, his eyes focused resolutely on the painting. "She was pretty, funny and my best friend. We grew up together, she was my neighbour. When we were little we agreed to marry each other when we were older." He turns and adds, "And that's what we did."

I can hear from his voice that this isn't the end of the story.

"Alice wanted to move to Amsterdam. She had wealthy relatives there, who helped me to pay my apprentice fees. That's how I was apprenticed to Rembrandt, and I soon received my own commissions once I was a master painter myself. It was a wonderful time, Alice and I enjoyed life. But things never stay as they are. Everything that's good and beautiful always falls apart." He comes and sits down next to me, staring with unseeing eyes at the canvas I'm working on. "Alice was desperate to have children. When she was still a child herself, she already knew what their names would be. We had three children, and not one of them made it to their first birthday. Alice died in childbirth during her third labour."

"How awful . . ."

"My career was going from strength to strength, but I'd had enough of Amsterdam. I went back to Middenbeemster and there I stayed until I met Agatha a couple of years ago. She was a widow, we understood each other's grief. After we got married we came to live in Delft, where she's from."

"What a sad story," I say softly.

"It's a normal story, there are so many of them. Sooner or later we all get our fair share of sorrow. The only thing you can hope is that it comes later rather than sooner, so you can at least know some happiness first. But I don't need to tell you that, do I?"

I look at him, confused.

"I know you, Catrin. I know who you are."

"You know who I am?"

"How many years separate us? Ten or so? De Rijp, Graft and Middenbeemster are right next to each other. I've got friends and relatives living in all three villages. I knew Govert, your husband, very well. And I go home sometimes, so I've heard the rumours."

This news comes like a kick to the gut. To hide my feelings, I carry on painting even though my hand is shaking. "What rumours?"

"I think you know exactly what I mean. Is that why you left, Catrin?" His face is friendly, his voice contains no accusation. "I know what Govert was like. He had two faces. On the outside he could be quite charming, but he had another side. I'm sure you found that out for yourself."

Unable to speak, I sit still as stone, like an animal in a trap. "Yes," I say eventually.

"So you'll have been relieved when he died."

"He was stone drunk. He was lying in bed, sleeping it off. When I left the room he was snoring loudly, when I came back half an hour later, he was dead."

He frowns. "Why did you leave De Rijp?"

"Why not? I always wanted to leave, even as a girl. After Govert died, there was nothing to keep me there."

"There are those who saw it as running away."

"It was. I was running away from the confinement of that village. I wanted a new life, to be free, to meet new people."

"And do you like it?"

I stare at him in confusion. "What do you mean?"

"What I said. Do you like your new, free life?"

I have to think about that for a minute. "Yes," I say finally. "I miss my family, but I don't want to go back. I can't go back."

"No," says Carel under his breath. "If I were you, that would be the last thing I'd do."

CHAPTER
TWENTY-FOUR

The week after that I attempt a portrait for the first time. Carel has received a commission from Simon Simonszoon, the verger of the cathedral, to paint his portrait, and Carel has his apprentices do the same.

Before we've even got started, Carel realises there's no more oil to mix paint with. Annoyed, he sets the empty jar on the table. "If one of you uses the last of it, it's helpful if that person tells me."

"It's my fault, I'm sorry," I say, ashamed.

"Go and get some more then. And be quick about it."

I get up at once, pull on my jerkin and glance apologetically over at the verger, who's sitting ready in his best linen suit. He nods reassuringly. "It looks as though there's enough for now."

I flash him a grateful smile, grab the empty jar and hurry out of the door. I run as fast as I can to Old Delft Street. At the oil merchant's, I get them to fill the jar to the brim, after that I head straight back again.

It's a glorious October day and the streets are busy. The hatches on all the shops are open, wares are on display and maids and housewives are doing their shopping from the street. I protect the jar with my arm as I move through the crowd. Just as I turn onto Fish Street there's a deafening crack, like an explosion. The noise is so overwhelmingly loud that I duck and lose my balance. The jar shatters and I smash into the wall. All around me people are running for cover or throwing themselves to the ground.

Before I've even understood what's going on, a second boom resounds. Panic breaks out in the narrow street, people fight to get away, pushing and shoving. The stench of smoke and powder burns my nostrils. I get to my feet, push a woman out of my way and run.

At the end of the street I come to a stop. Ink-black clouds of smoke are rolling towards me. I turn back in panic. Throngs of people block my path. I turn right, along the water of Verwersdijk.

Meanwhile it's getting darker and darker around me. Coughing, I look up at the cloud of smoke spreading ever wider above me and hanging like a black blanket over the city. A couple of streets further, flames roar; people are screaming, "Fire, fire!"

A third explosion thunders through the city. A roar so loud it seems to come straight from hell itself makes the houses and pavement shake and windows crack and fall to pieces. I feel glass pierce my skin but the pain I anticipate doesn't come. The only thing I feel is all-consuming terror.

In the distance, some kind of storm is raging towards us. It's as if the hand of God is tearing through the streets, sweeping off roof tiles left and right, smashing in gables, ripping off doors and shutters and casting them down. The water in the canal is boiling, slopping

153

over the edge of the quay. Boats are being turned to matchwood, debris flying everywhere, people are snatched up and thrown down again yards away. The storm howls down on me with terrifying speed.

I turn and run for my life. The wave of destruction is pursuing me, it will be here in a few seconds. I scream as I'm picked up and carried along with it. The next thing I know, I'm crashing to the ground.

I look around, dazed. To my surprise, I've been blasted into a house. The walls of the hall bulge back and forth, the wooden beams creak as if they could give way any second. When I try to move, my vision goes black. The pain goes through me in waves. I pass out. When I come round, I hear fire crackling. I open my eyes in alarm and look through the hole in the demolished roof, straight into hell. There's smoke everywhere, flames are roaring through the upper parts of the house and inching their way down.

With my teeth clenched I ease myself upright until I'm in a sitting position. The air around me is thick with smoke, making it harder to breathe. A shower of sparks falls on me, eating holes into my clothes. At the same time, I feel a burning pain in my scalp and smell something foul. I slap wildly at my head with both hands. My cap is gone and my hair is fertile ground for the sparks. I ignore the pain in my hands and beat out the flames. After that, I crawl to the hole where the door had been. Every movement is agony but I don't seem to have broken anything. The remains of the roof creak above me and before I can make it to the door, the whole thing comes down on me with a huge crash.

I scream, trying to protect my head with my arms. All kinds of things fall on me, planks, roof tiles, stones. I lie motionless in a cloud of dust, my eyes squeezed tight and my face pressed into the floor. Stabbing pains bite into my legs.

I wait, coughing, until the dust settles and I can breathe again.

I try with all my might to crawl out from under the rubble. Something on my legs stops me. No matter how much I struggle and twist, I can't find the strength to free myself. Meanwhile, sounds begin to float in from outside, shouts and cries, interspersed with piercing screams. The abrupt silence that follows makes me panic. You don't need much imagination to understand what's happening further on in the city. The fire has reached the far side of the canal and is destroying everyone and everything in its path. People like me, who aren't in any fit state to get away. The one faint hope I can cling to is that I have more time. The flames have yet to reach the buildings on this side. It won't be long, because most of the houses are made of wood and embers are raining down onto the street.

Once more I attempt to free myself from the weight on my legs. The wreckage is too heavy for me to kick it off, so I try to slide out from underneath. I grit my teeth and draw my legs towards me. Something sharp tears open my flesh and I scream. I lie panting. I've only managed to move an inch or so and the pain is so intense I don't know whether I can do it a second time. But I don't have much choice.

I take some time to overcome the waves of pain and muster the courage for another attempt. Almost in tears, I pull my legs up again. Blood streams over my skin and I give a raw cry to spur myself on. I gain another little bit of ground. Too little. One leg now has a bit of space to move, I can't move the other at all.

Lying on my side, I look at the street opposite, where the glow of the fire keeps getting redder. The ships on the canal are ablaze now, flames jump from them to the trees onto the freight on the quayside. I heave at my legs, again and again, with short, jerking movements. With every wrench, I grow shorter of breath and my vision keeps going dark more and more often. Whatever it is that's on top of me, it's not budging an inch. I feel the heat of the approaching fire and scream. My parents' and brothers' faces shimmer before my eyes, then those of Evert and Matthias. Before merciful unconsciousness overtakes me, I feel a brief but deep sorrow that I won't see them again.

CHAPTER
TWENTY-FIVE

Something's pulling at me. Muffled voices bring me back.

"Easy," someone says. "That leg's broken. I'll count to three and then we'll lift."

I open my eyes. There are figures bending over me. They count and I feel the weight being lifted off my leg. A chunk of stone is thrown aside with an enormous crash. Strong arms carry me outside. My leg dangles loosely as we move. The pain is terrible and I slip away.

When I come round for the second time, I'm on a wooden stretcher surrounded by an enormous crush of bodies. People are shouting to each other, jumping over the stretcher and knocking my wounded leg. I scream and a furious voice sends the bystanders away. I faint again, and the next time I wake I am in a bed. Not at home, judging by the foul smell coming from the sheets and the racket all around me.

I open my eyes and look to one side, into a room. The walls are lined with bunks from which a loud groaning emanates. More casualties are lying on the ground, on stretchers or on the flagstones. People force their way in between the bodies; people searching for family members, nurses. I surmise that I'm lying in the inn on Corn Market. And that I'm alive. I was saved from burning to death just in time.

I close my eyes and thank God. The relief is so great I can stand the pain a little better. I don't know exactly what's wrong with me, but I've got bandages almost everywhere. The worst injury is to my right leg. I can't make a single move without it sending a shock through me.

Gingerly, I lift the blanket and peer underneath. My leg is bound to a small plank. The strips of cloth binding it aren't particularly clean. They look grey and blood is seeping through them. My own blood or that of the previous patient?

My slight movement has already created dark spots before my eyes. I close them and try to ignore the chaos around me.

"Catrin . . ."

A familiar voice. Urgent and a little hoarse. I open my eyes, turn my head to the side and see Evert's face close to mine. His eyes are red and he's deathly pale. I raise my hand, which is also bandaged, and smile reassuringly at him.

"You're alive. Thank God you're alive. I thought . . ." He shakes his head speechlessly.

"I'd just left. Fetching oil for the paint."

"It saved your life. The whole neighbourhood exploded."

"Carel?"

"He's in here too, he's badly injured. His chances of recovery are slim. His apprentices are dead and so is Simon, the verger."

I close my eyes and let this information sink in. "What happened?"

"The artillery depot exploded. They still don't know what caused it. There must have been an enormous amount of powder in there, because the whole neighbourhood went up."

"How terrible . . ."

For a while we watch the stream of casualties still being brought in. The floor of the makeshift infirmary is full and the innkeeper gives instructions for them to take over the nave of the church next door. The wailing, screaming and shouting is deafening. There's blood everywhere and a heavy smell of iron in the air. An amputation is being carried out somewhere in the room and the patient is resisting, screeching mindlessly. The stench of burning oil, used to cauterise the blood vessels, mixes with the smell of burnt flesh.

Evert's face contorts with revulsion. "I can't leave you here. You're coming with me."

"I can't, my leg's broken."

"We're going to get you home. On a wagon or a stretcher."

The mere thought of having to bump and jolt my way through the city makes me shudder. "No, please. How am I going to cope alone at home?"

"I'll take you to my house."

His suggestion is touching, but I shake my head. "That would only give Delft another thing to gossip about. And incidentally, you have no time to be nursing me."

"Anna, my housekeeper, can do that."

I shake my head once more. "I can't bear the thought of being taken anywhere else. If I move even a tiny bit, the pain almost kills me. Really, this is the best place for me."

Evert looks around, unconvinced. "I think leaving you here is a terrible idea. It will be weeks before a break like that heals."

"I'll be feeling better in a week or two."

"Then I'm coming to fetch you in two weeks, whether you want me to or not."

Carel dies the same afternoon. Johannes and Digna tell me the news.

"Maybe it's for the best," Digna says. "The poor man was burnt to a crisp. He would have been terribly maimed for the rest of his life."

Johannes says nothing, he stares fixedly into the distance, as if he can't believe he's lost one of his best friends.

"We're so happy you survived." Digna places her hand on mine. "You must have had an angel on your shoulder."

"Yes . . . I don't know what I've done to earn it."

"It's all arbitrary," Johannes says hoarsely. "Luck, misfortune, death, survival. God acts at random."

His mother looks up at him, shocked. "Johannes!"

"But that's how it is, isn't it? I know no better man than Carel. Always concerned with the weak and needy, always ready to give alms, went to church every Sunday. What did he do to deserve a death like that? And don't say it's all part of God's great plan, Mother, because I can't hear that any more. I don't understand those plans at all."

Digna frowns and opens her mouth to silence Johannes, but I get in there first. "Johannes is right. I don't understand it either."

"That's not for us to do. Be grateful that He saved you."

"Of course I'm grateful." I look into the room and allow my gaze to fall on a young woman who sits crying beside her little boy, whose arms have been amputated. "But I don't understand it all the same."

In the days that follow, I hear the details of the disaster. Cornelis Soetens, the master of the powder store in the former Poor Clares Cloister, had gone inside with a burning torch. No one knows exactly what went wrong, because he didn't survive the accident. There were nearly 90,000 pounds of gunpowder stored in the depot, left over from the fight against the Spanish in the last century. The explosion destroyed the whole north-eastern side of Delft. A deep crater is all that's left of the place where the depot once stood. In the surrounding streets, there's not a single house left standing and body parts are still being uncovered in the rubble.

The damage is severe in the rest of the city too. All the church windows, including expensive stained-glass ones, have been smashed to tiny pieces and the roofs have been torn off many of the houses.

More than five hundred people have died and a huge number of people have been wounded, many seriously.

The number of blind and lame people in Delft has doubled in a single stroke. Luckily, Evert's pottery is far enough from the site of the disaster and not as much as a finger bowl has been damaged.

CHAPTER
TWENTY-SIX

Time passes slowly. I can't do much more than lie on my back. The only distraction is the hustle and bustle in the infirmary. The physician comes twice a day, accompanied by a surgeon, who does operations. The innkeeper and his wife have taken on tending to the wounded themselves with the help of a couple of maids and grooms.

The wailing from other parts of the ward makes me glad I've only got a broken leg. That, along with my burns and cuts, will heal on its own, unlike the wounds of many others here in the sick room. All day long, the physicians cauterise arteries, trepan skulls, cut away abscesses and amputate limbs. Even though they keep all the doors open during the day, the stench of the alcohol used to knock out the patients and that of rotting flesh persist.

Stinking poultices have been applied to my arms and legs to ward off infection. They don't seem to be helping. Several of my wounds now have fiery red edges and are starting to throb. In the beginning, only my broken leg had been giving me trouble, but now I'm burning up as if I have a fever.

Coming round from a brief doze, I'm surprised to find someone standing next to my bed. I slowly turn my head towards the visitor, half expecting it to be Evert. Instead it's Jacob. I blink, hoping my eyes are blurry from the fever, but when I open them he's still standing there.

"Hello, Catrin."

I can only stare at him.

Jacob sits down gingerly on the edge of the bed. He lifts the blankets slightly and frowns. "A broken leg, that's no good."

"What are you doing here?" I get out the words with difficulty.

"Seeing how you are. You were lucky."

"Depends on where you're standing."

"True. You live on the other side of town so you needn't have been anywhere near where it happened. But if you look around, I think you'll agree that I'm right to say you were lucky."

"How do you know where I live? Why are you here?"

He smiles. "You disappeared so suddenly. No one knew where you'd gone." Jacob picks something disgusting out from under his nail. "Those posh types you worked for looked straight through me when I spoke to them."

"So how did you find me?"

"I had a little dalliance with that housemaid of theirs, Greta. Everything soon became clear then."

I close my eyes, exhausted. I can't deal with this. Not now. "What do you want from me, Jacob? You've got half my money, have you come for the rest?"

"No, you can keep your money. I've only come to visit."

I look at him warily.

"Truly. I've known for a while that you were in Delft. When I heard what happened, I came at once to see how you were."

"Of course you did."

"I'm here, aren't I? And haven't I left you alone this whole time? I'm really not as bad as you think. And I wish you the very best."

"Well, as you can see, I'm fine."

He looks me over. "On the contrary, I don't think you look good at all. You've got a fever."

In a single movement he whips off the covers and peers with a furrowed brow at the dirty, fraying bandages that cover my wounds. "What have they put on them?"

"I don't know."

Without asking my permission, he unwraps one of the bandages and examines the substance underneath. "It reeks. I think you'd do better taking it off."

"The physician knows what he's doing."

"Do you remember what we used to smear on the cows when they got a cut? A salve made from marigold and bramble leaves." He uses the bandage to wipe off the dried poultice and moves on to the next dressing.

"What are you doing? Stop that! It'll start bleeding again and then —"

"It's not been bleeding for ages. Make sure they don't put any more of those dirty rags on you. I'll bring something else."

"I think that's a good idea." Evert appears by the bed, nodding with approval. "You seem to be getting worse rather than better, Catrin. It's time to try something else." He introduces himself to Jacob, who returns the courtesy.

"I'm an old friend of Catrin's," he says. "We're from the same village."

"Any friend of Catrin's is a friend of mine." Evert claps him on the shoulder. "Have you come here because of the disaster?"

"Yes, I was worried. I had been planning to drop in, and I set off as soon as I heard."

Apparently, Evert notices I'm not saying anything. He keeps looking back and forth between me and Jacob. "Thank you for coming," he says amiably. "I'd like to have a few minutes alone with Catrin now, if I may."

"Fine. I'll go and see about getting a different salve for her." Jacob stands up, bids us farewell and walks off.

Evert watches him go. "Who's that?"

"He used to work for Govert and me on the farm."

"Why has he come here?"

"I'm wondering that myself."

"He is right about the treatment you're getting here, though. Compresses that stink are no good."

Isaac and Adelaide come to visit me, but fortunately they don't stay for long. The fever is making me weak, I'd rather be alone. The next day, Adelaide returns. She lays a hand on my forehead, her face serious beneath her linen cap. "Would you like a drink?"

"Yes," I rasp. My mouth is dry; my lips are splitting.

She goes off and comes back with a pewter mug. She gently helps me into a more upright position and sets the mug to my lips. "I've been praying for you," she says.

Evert told me once that Adelaide secretly follows the old faith. She's very pious and trusts in God's plan. I myself don't always have so much faith in His intentions, and certainly haven't over the last few days. The ongoing chorus of groans around me makes me feel we're at His mercy rather than under His protection. But I don't say this to Adelaide, who's sitting next to me with her rosary hidden in the folds of her dress.

"You're being tested fiercely, Catrin. I find myself wondering how long I could bear it in here. But at least you're still alive. You were spared in a miraculous way."

"But why?" I try to bring her face into focus. It seems to be hanging in a mist, now close by, now further away. "Why is one person spared and another not?"

"Why indeed . . ."

"I don't understand. I've done such bad things, I'm a sinner."

"As are we all."

"Things that get you sent to hell. Things you have to burn for forever. When I was stuck under the rubble and the fire was coming down on me, I thought this is it. Hell. Do you know what you have to do to be given absolution? It's not so hard for Catholics, they buy an indulgence or say Hail Marys all day. Or they make a pilgrimage. I'd love to make a pilgrimage. Do you think God would forgive me then? I don't know. You have to feel remorse and I don't. I'd do the same again." A cool hand on my forehead quiets my words to a mumble. Adelaide's soothing voice comes to me from far away.

"Don't talk too much, Catrin. Sleep now. I'll stay with you. Get some sleep."

People come and go. When I'm awake, I hear muffled voices and see figures go past. It's as if I never fully wake up, as if I'm lying under water looking up at the surface, where faces ripple and dissolve.

One morning I finally return to the surface. The world is in focus again, sounds reach me clearly, the way they used to. Evert is sitting next to me, his face pale and drawn.

"At last," he says softly. "How do you feel?"

"Tired."

"I can imagine. You had a dangerous fever. We were afraid that . . ." He stops and runs a hand through his hair. "The physician didn't want you moved, so we've been watching over you in shifts. Jacob gave me a salve to put on your wounds."

"Really?"

"Yes, something with marigold, bramble leaf and fleawort. I'm glad I listened to him, because it helped straightaway."

Marigold prevents infections and fleawort is good for wounds, just like bramble leaf. Jacob knows a lot of herb lore. On the farm he always tended the sick and wounded animals. Even though I understand his ulterior motives in healing me, I'm grateful.

"I've talked it over with Angelika and Quentin, and you can stay with them. You're leaving here today," says Evert.

I wonder whether it's a good idea to saddle a heavily pregnant Angelika with receiving me, but I feel too weak to protest.

Later that same afternoon I am taken to my friends' house on a stretcher. There, I'm welcomed with a warmth and interest that touch me deeply. Angelika has a somewhat older housemaid who works hard and takes a practical view of things.

"It makes no odds to me whether I'm taking care of four people or five," says Truda as she throws back the doors of the box bed in the kitchen.

Evert and Quentin lower me gently inside. They've been treating me like I'm made of glass the whole way, but being moved has still worn me out. I lean back on the pillows woozily.

"Have a little nap," says Angelika. "I'm going to as well."

"Where are you sleeping? Surely not in the attic?"

"No, Truda's going up there. You're having her bed in the kitchen."

"All this fuss, just for me, and you in your condition . . ."

Angelika comes up to the edge of the bed and puts her hand on my arm. "Catrin, I'm just glad you're still with us, and that I can do this for you. It's no trouble really, it's Truda who does all the work. You'd be better thanking her."

Behind her, Truda shakes her head darkly. "We'll have come to a pretty pass the day I'm not willing to give someone with a broken leg a bite to eat."

But of course she does much more. That afternoon she changes all my bandages for clean, new dressings and combs and plaits my hair. "Otherwise we'll be having to cut it off, what with all these tangles."

I hear from Truda that Jacob was at the door, asking how I am, and had nodded with satisfaction and gone away again once she told him the fever had subsided.

"Didn't he want to come in?" I ask.

"Should I have asked him to? Do you want to see him?"

"No, I was just wondering."

"I did find it strange that he went straight off again," says Truda. "He must be a good friend if he's come all the way from the North to see how you are. He told me you're a widow, you haven't had it easy and that's why he's keeping an eye on you. He's found a job here in Delft, so he can stick around. I reckon he likes you."

She winks at me, but I don't respond. I pretend to be falling asleep and Truda goes away. As soon as I'm alone, I open my eyes and stare at the panels of the box bed.

CHAPTER
TWENTY-SEVEN

At the end of October, Angelika goes into labour. Her cries wake me a little after midnight and increase in volume and intensity with the passing of the hours. There's a buzz of excitement in the house. Quentin is up, Truda isn't leaving Angelika's side, Katherine and Gertrude wake up and come down in their nightdresses and sleeping caps to find me. I let them clamber into my bed and distract them with stories.

"Why haven't you got a baby, Catrin?" asks Gertrude.

"I nearly had a baby, but it passed away."

"Was it a girl?"

"No, a little boy."

"We had a little brother. He died too," says Katherine. "And mothers die as well."

"No they don't!" says Gertrude in fright.

"Yes they do. You don't know, you're still a baby."

These words make Gertrude huddle closer to me. "Mama isn't going to die, is she, Catrin?"

"Of course not," I say soothingly. Angelika's previous births went without complications, so I feel I can promise them that.

This time it ends up taking a bit longer. The midwife comes, Angelika's screams get weaker and weaker, it is light outside and there's still no baby. I curse my leg for keeping me so powerless and rooted to the spot, unable to support my friend. Finally, as the daylight streams into the house, I hear the shrill cry of a newborn. I watch the door tensely until Quentin appears.

"It's a little boy!"

"Congratulations! And Angelika? Is she all right?"

"Fine. Exhausted but very happy." And with that he's away again.

In the isolation of the box bed, I listen to the activity in the living room and am overcome with emotion. I'm glad when the girls come storming back in.

"We've got a little brother!"

"So I hear, how nice for you both."

"And he isn't dead," says Gertrude smugly. "And neither is Mama."

"What's his name?"

She has to think about it, her fine little brows knit together. "It's a difficult name . . ."

"He's called Allardusin," says Katherine.

"What a magnificent name."

"What was your baby called, Catrin?" asks Gertrude.

"He didn't have a name," I say. "He died before I'd thought of one."

They nod and run off to play outside.

Angelika is up and about surprisingly quickly. The very same day she comes shuffling her way through the house to sit with me. She has Truda bring her son and lay him in my arms. I look at his little face, the balled-up hands and tiny nails, smell that peculiar,

172

sweet baby smell and pass him back to Angelika with a smile. "He's beautiful."

"He is, isn't he? Quentin is so happy." Angelika beams down at her baby, full of pride and then looks at me. "You never told me what happened with your little boy. Was he still alive after the birth? Or would you rather not talk about it?"

"No, I'd rather not talk about it."

Angelika looks downcast. "I should never have brought it up, I'm sorry."

"It's fine."

But of course it isn't fine. Once she's left the kitchen with Allardusin and Truda has gone outside to hang the washing, I close the doors of the box bed and, for the first time in ages, I cry for my son.

After three more weeks, the day finally arrives for me to be allowed out of bed. With Angelika and her family around me, I've had enough company and distractions, but I long to be able to move around again. I wait impatiently for Evert, who's got hold of some crutches for me. My legs dangle over the edge of the bed. Smiling broadly, Evert comes in and hands me the wooden props. "These will have you back on your feet in no time. Well, foot anyway."

He lifts me up and the parts of my body he touches suddenly seem to glow. A few seconds later I'm standing on my good leg, leaning on the bed while Evert keeps hold of me. His breathing sounds laboured above my head, I hardly dare look up at him. Evert puts the crutches under my arms and takes a step back. "Give it a try."

As I take my first faltering steps, he stays close, one hand held out protectively. I soon get the hang of it and hobble up and down the hall.

"Finally," I say to Evert, who's watching with his arms folded. "I'm coming straight to the workshop with you."

"Are you sure?"

"Yes, of course I'm sure. I've been doing nothing for long enough. Painting won't do my leg any harm, so there's no reason not to get back to work."

"As long as you promise not to go gallivanting around the workshop for no reason. There's rubbish all over the floor."

"I'll stay at my bench like a good girl."

He nods at me approvingly. "Fine, I could certainly do with your help."

I say goodbye to Angelika in the living room. We hug and I give little Allard, as he's now known, a kiss.

"I'll miss you," Angelika says sadly. "It was nice having someone to talk to. You'll still be sleeping here for a while, won't you? You won't be able to go shopping or cook for yourself yet."

As much as I'd prefer to go back to my own house, and probably would manage with a bit of help, I must admit it's a relief to be freed from household tasks, so I agree.

"Then I'll see you tonight. Go and enjoy your painting. I think Evert is delighted to have you back," says my friend.

That sounds a bit ambiguous, but I decide to assume she means as an employee. Which seems plausible when I enter the workshop. By the look of it, production has doubled during my absence. The walls of the painters' studio, which had once been bare, are now lined with shelves groaning with unfired earthenware and both ovens are in use. There are crates of firewood, sacks of minerals and baskets of finished pieces ready for delivery. In one corner of the studio, a couple of lads are grinding pigment non-stop and every single seat at the workbench is occupied by a painter.

"We'll find a place for you," says Evert when he sees my face. "If the others squeeze together a little, you can sit at the corner. That'll be easier with your leg."

There's a racket coming from the courtyard and I shuffle over to the window on my crutches. The spot previously used by the cat for sunbathing is now rammed with handcarts, barrels and crates of clay and men are rushing to and fro.

"So busy," I remark to Evert, who comes to stand beside me.

"It's as much as I can do to keep up with the number of orders. They're coming in from all over the country, recently even from England."

"So it's a success."

"It's a huge success. And it was your idea, so you've definitely earned a raise. From now on you'll receive the same as I'd pay a man doing your job."

"In that case, I'm getting straight to work, before you think better of it." I've almost turned my back when someone else in the courtyard catches my eye. Jacob! At first I'm speechless, then I splutter, "What's *he* doing here?"

"He was looking for a job and I needed clay treaders," says Evert. "Why, is that a problem?"

At that moment, Jacob looks straight at me, as if he senses my presence. We're yards apart and there's a window between us, but I can feel the threat radiating from him. For a few seconds we maintain eye contact, and then he turns and continues on his way.

"No," I tell Evert, who's watching me expectantly. "It's no problem at all."

CHAPTER
TWENTY-EIGHT

Thankfully, Jacob keeps his distance. Even so, I still don't trust him and do my best to keep out of his way. And that's not so difficult, since our work keeps us in different parts of the workshop. After a while, my uneasiness about his presence ebbs away. Maybe he really was just looking for a job and I'm too suspicious.

My leg is healing well. Soon I'm able to leave my crutches aside and take a few tentative steps to grab something I need. I still need to lean on tables and cupboards, because I don't yet dare walk entirely unsupported.

The days grow shorter and with them our working hours. The demand for Dutch Porcelain, as we have come to call our new kind of earthenware, keeps on growing, so we're working harder than ever. We don't take any breaks, and even eat our lunch between tasks to make the best of the daylight.

Flowers, peacocks, dragons, ornamental trees and Chinese figures in long robes fill my days and nights. In the daytime I paint them, at night I dream about them. I decorate plates and vases and am getting better and better at it. I quickly come to see my work of two weeks earlier as completely amateurish and now trace my brush over the pot with a surer hand, more smoothly, in a single fluid motion without removing the tip once. Doing it this way means no blob of paint every time you put the brush to the surface, and gives you a much prettier end product. Frans and I experiment with different brushes and come to the conclusion that sable ones work best. We turn them into riggers, brushes with a long, fine tip, which we use to do the contours.

Even the firing process is refined. The raw product first goes into a trough of white tin glaze before being dried and painted with black cobalt oxide. The objects then get a layer of lead-based glaze to give them a high sheen.

After that, everything's baked again, and this phase is decisive for the final result. Stoking the fire is a painstaking task. If the fire's too hot, the colour will be ruined by the smoke and heat. It takes a while for us to determine precisely when the blue we're after develops.

Evert discovers that adding cooking salt to the tin glaze prevents the pot from being tinged yellow. He experiments with the firing temperature until he achieves the lustrous blue he has in mind. When pieces are set to be fired for the second time, he places them in fireclay containers called "saggers" so they're better protected from the heat. The pieces being fired for the first time are placed underneath, without protection. Triangular wedges, stays, prevent the objects from touching and sticking to each other.

Naturally, Dutch Porcelain has its imitators. Others around us have emulated our methods and enjoyed their own success. One pottery after another is established, but none of them manage to produce the same quality.

"How's your leg?"

I'm on my way home when Jacob appears next to me. It's the beginning of December and the street is slippery because of a layer of snow.

"Good," I say.

"Then why are you still on crutches?"

"Because it's slippery. I'm scared I'll fall."

"Let me help you. Take my arm."

"No, thank you." I soldier on resolutely.

"Catrin, I'm really not as much of a bastard as you seem to think. You misunderstood me that time in Amsterdam. You saw it as blackmail, I saw it as an act of mutual friendship and support. It's simply a matter of how you look at it."

I step out of the way of an old woman pulling a sleigh full of bundled kindling and ignore Jacob. He closes the distance in a couple of steps and grabs my arm.

"Truly, Catrin, I never wanted to scare you. I would never do anything to hurt you."

My crutches and his firm grip on my arm force me to stand still. "You threatened to report me and made off with half of my savings. What do you want to call it? I call it blackmail."

"I would never have turned you in."

"You say that now. What do I care? My money's gone, and yours probably is too. I was wondering when you'd be back for the rest."

"You can keep your money. That's not what I'm after."

"Oh no? So what do you want from me? You can't tell me this was the only place you could find a job, here in Delft with Evert."

Jacob grabs my shoulder and forces me to look at him. "What I want is your friendship. We've all got a dark side and sometimes it comes to the fore. You're no better."

I can hardly deny it.

"I want to make up for it, Catrin. I brought you that salve, didn't I? You could have died if I hadn't."

"Yes, and then you wouldn't have been able to get anything else out of me. That would have been a shame."

He releases me unexpectedly, with a sad expression. "I understand, I deserve that. I'll leave you alone, maybe that way you'll believe me."

He is about to leave, but I stick out a crutch and stop him. "What have you told them back home in De Rijp?"

"Nothing."

"Not to anyone?"

"No. I've only been back once, as it happens."

"And?"

"People think it's odd that you left so suddenly. They're talking."

"And what are they saying?"

Jacob shrugs. "The usual gossip. You know how it goes."

"Do they think that I . . ."

"Put it this way: no one would be surprised. But suspicion isn't enough."

It's starting to snow again. I watch the falling flakes and wonder whether it's snowing at home as well. "I can never go back," I murmur. "Mart doesn't trust me. He won't wait for a judge."

I see something like sympathy in Jacob's eyes. "If you ask me, you're better off staying here. Just as long as you know they won't be hearing anything from me."

I nod, hitch up my crutches and hobble home.

I know without looking outside that it has snowed during the night. It's early morning and there's a strange glow in the living room. Last night I left the shutters open, so now the light is streaming in. I climb out of bed, grab my crutches and go over to the window. The yard is covered with a thick layer of snow. I stand gazing out until I get too cold. I won't be able to get back to sleep, so I may as well get dressed. I'm worried about how I will get to work through all this snow.

The answer appears an hour or so later, once I've eaten and the hustle and bustle on the street outside shows that the working day has started. There's a knock at the door and I'm not surprised to find Evert standing on my doorstep.

"I thought the snow might be difficult on your crutches, so I've come to fetch you."

I smile and let him in. "How kind of you."

"Kind? I wouldn't dream of letting my best painter wind up back in bed with another broken leg." Evert winks. "It's high time you tried walking without those things. I talked to Bohm the surgeon yesterday and he said you can put weight on your leg again."

"I'm too scared to."

"How long has it been? Almost eight weeks? The break should have healed by now."

"My leg feels so strange. So limp."

"Your muscles are weak, you need to get them moving again. Just try it. Come on, I'll help you." Ignoring my protests, he takes my crutches away and grabs my hands. "Walk, Catrin. If anything goes wrong, I'll catch you."

I take one uncertain step.

"Now try your bad leg," says Evert.

I take another step, only to fall straight into Evert's arms. "I can't, I'm not strong enough."

"Don't give up yet. It didn't hurt, did it?"

He's right, and I really do want to get off my crutches, so I give it another try. This time it goes a little better.

"I don't know whether I dare try it without you helping me."

"You don't need to. I won't let go of you. I'm never letting go of you again."

I look up in surprise and find myself face to face with him. "What did you say?"

"You heard me. I'm asking you to marry me. Maybe it's a strange time to ask, but I have to know what you think of the idea. If you could ever love me. If you say you can, even a tiny bit, then that's enough for me. Sleep on it for a few days and tell me then."

"I don't need to think about it."

"No?" He looks at me uncertainly and I see a glimmer of satisfaction in his eyes.

I throw my arms around him and kiss him hard and deeply.

CHAPTER
TWENTY-NINE

Maybe it's my abiding sense of loneliness or maybe it's me adjusting my dreams to match reality. It takes so much effort to go through life alone. Maybe I'm accepting this proposal because it's the best thing for me under the circumstances. Maybe I do love Evert somewhere deep in my heart. Otherwise, I would have asked for time to think it over.

I don't really know. The only thing I know for sure is that I want someone in my life who's there for me.

We're in no rush to get to work. Evert is too much of a gentleman to try to go all the way so soon but we spend some time getting to know each other. Lying together in bed, he says, "If you start asking yourself later today or tomorrow what in God's name you've done, I'll understand."

I stare at him in shock. "Do you think I said yes because of a moment of madness or something?"

"Perhaps. I know I took you by surprise."

"The proposal was a surprise and I didn't stop and think about it, but that's a good sign. If you have to spend days thinking about it, you've probably got your answer."

"That's true. But still, if you have any second thoughts . . ."

I don't have any second thoughts and we set the date for 28 December. It gives us only three weeks, just enough time to prepare for the ceremony.

For a few days after his proposal, Evert is cautious, almost nervous with me, as if he's waiting for me to tell him it was all a huge mistake. With every day that passes, I'm more sure of my decision. I'm coming to see that there are different kinds of love: my fleeting infatuation with Govert, the overwhelming desire that bound me and Matthias, and the meeting of the minds I feel with Evert. No burning desire, no physical attraction confounding my decision-making but rather a feeling of familiarity and affection. That's good enough for me, I can't ask for more. And I don't deserve more.

Our friends are delighted about our engagement. All and sundry come to wish us well.

"This is exactly what I've been hoping for," says Angelika happily.

Even the workers at the pottery congratulate me, some more enthusiastically than others. Frans gives me a curt nod, Jacob leans back and looks at me in wonder. "So you're marrying the boss," he says. "Nicely done."

I ignore both of them.

My first wedding was one big party that went on for days. In accordance with country tradition, I was first kidnapped by Govert, then taken back by my brothers, after which I had to formally declare my acceptance of Govert. After that the preparations for the wedding could begin, a party the whole village was invited to. We used the farmyard and the threshing floor for the celebration and there still wasn't enough room. The cows were scared by the wild dancing, when everyone tried to make as big a racket as possible by banging and clattering whatever came to hand. At the end of the evening, Govert and I tried to sneak off but they were all keeping a close eye on us and we ended up being carried upstairs to our marriage bed on their shoulders to cheers and hoots. The biggest challenge was getting the revellers to leave, and it was only thanks to Govert's height and broad shoulders that they didn't give us a helping hand taking off our wedding clothes.

The day Evert and I say our vows, on a cold, sunny afternoon, is a quieter affair. People go all out for a first marriage; with second weddings they try to be a bit more discreet. I don't mind, I don't feel much like celebrating without my family there. I sent them an invitation but received the response that Delft was too far away and they couldn't leave their duties for that long.

Evert is also struggling with the fact that only our friends are here. Even though he's nothing but smiles all day, you can see the sadness in his eyes about what's missing. Adriaan and Brigitta send their best wishes but don't come.

"It'll take them a while to get used to the fact that you're marrying their former housekeeper," I say in the coach on the way to the church.

"That's their problem." Evert kisses my hand. "For the first time in five years I'm happy again, and I'm not letting anyone take that away from me."

The coach stops at the market, where friends and distant relatives of Evert's are waiting by the entrance to the church. A big cheer goes up as I step down in my cornflower blue, lace-edged gown and for a moment I feel a little less alone. I walk into the church on Evert's arm under a shower of petals. I had known he was well-liked in Delft, but only now do I see how well. Half the town seems to have come out, and those who haven't been invited are standing in the market square to watch.

Once we've exchanged our wedding vows and the time comes to put a ring on each other's finger, all the onlookers, inside and outside, applaud loudly.

A small number of guests are invited to join us for the wedding breakfast at the Mechelen Inn. There are speeches, toasts, jokes and anecdotes, followed by even more toasts.

My wedding night is as I expected, tender and restrained. Evert's lovemaking doesn't awaken the same wild lust in me as his brother's. The next morning, I wake up early and spend a long time gazing at my husband's face. He seems older now, sleeping on his back, with a double chin and bags under his eyes from many sleepless nights. His mouth is slightly open and he's snoring gently.

I try to go back to sleep for a while. I don't manage more than a brief doze. I can hear Anna clattering around in the kitchen, lighting the fire. She's a quiet

187

but hardworking woman whose husband died a year ago. She has two grown-up children who she doesn't want to burden by giving up her job, which is why at sixty she's doing all of Evert's backbreaking household chores. Mine too. It wasn't too long ago that I was a housekeeper, now I've got one of my own.

My thoughts immediately turn to Amsterdam, the house on Keizersgracht and then, involuntarily, to Matthias. I see his face before me, hear his voice as if I'd only just spoken to him. This stirs up a bittersweet pain. How is he going to react when he comes back and finds me married to his brother? Maybe he won't care, maybe he doesn't even think about me any more.

"So," says Jacob one morning when I come into the workshop and there's only the two of us there. "You're Mistress Van Nulandt now. How does it feel?"

"No different from when I was Barentsdochter."

"I don't believe that. It must be a strange feeling, having your employers as your in-laws," he says, sniggering.

He's right. Evert being my husband doesn't feel strange in the least, but that I can now call Adriaan my brother-in-law and Brigitta my sister-in-law definitely does. Let alone Matthias.

"Good work, Catrin," whispers Jacob in my ear. "I knew we were cut from the same cloth."

Jacob isn't the only one who has to get used to the situation. I'm the boss's wife now and am treated according to this new position. Jokes of the type employees always make about their boss suddenly cease and no one dares complain when the work rate is too high or Evert tells someone off.

It's only once they notice I never tell him about anything that goes on behind his back that the atmosphere returns to normal. We close down for Christmas and don't work over New Year either. In keeping with tradition, the New Year is greeted with parties in the inns, bonfires and a great deal of noise intended to drive out evil spirits.

Children run all over town with rattles, drums and the lids of pots and pans, while teenagers and adults get out their rifles and shoot into the air with carbide charges and gunpowder, making for big bangs.

Rather than spending my New Year's Eve with cups and plates, I spend it with Anna up to our ears in candied fruit, beer, fat and flour, making lardy cakes all day. They aren't only meant for our friends but for the wassailers who go door to door on the first of January. Just like in De Rijp, it's traditional for people to sing a New Year's song or recite a proverb wishing good luck in exchange for something tasty or a few coppers.

I'd been expecting Angelika to drop in with the children, but they don't come. I've hardly seen her since the wedding, even though we were speaking almost every day at first. It's niggling me. I know something's going on, I'm certain of it.

With my mind made up, I wrap a couple of the finished cakes in a cloth and go to see her. Angelika jumps when she finds me at the door.

"I've brought you a treat," I say.

Katherine and Gertrude come hollering to greet me. Their mother quiets them, sounding flustered. I wink and give the girls a cake. An uneasy silence falls.

"I hope 1655 will be a more peaceful year," I say.

"I hope it will be for you as well." Angelika eyes me uncomfortably.

"Is something wrong?" I ask.

"No, not at all. I had a bad night, that's all. The girls couldn't sleep because of all the noise and just as they were going off, Allard woke for his feed."

"I understand," I say. "You get some rest."

She nods, smiles and shuts the door.

The whole town is up all night; no one is even thinking about going to bed. That includes me and Evert, we're going to the Mechelen Inn. Johannes comes over as soon as he sees me. He kisses my hand. "Catrin! It's been far too long. How's your leg? You're walking again."

"Yes, but it took some time. It started to seem like it was made of jelly," I say. "And how are you?" I know he's depressed after losing Carel.

"I'm fine. I have my work and life goes on. Although I have realised a few things."

"Like what?"

"That life is too short and you mustn't waste your time on earth. Painting is my passion, I trained for years and qualified as a master craftsman, and look how I spend my days." He gestures at the bar. "Keeping an inn is a good job, but you can't do anything else on the

190

side. It's one or the other and I'm longing to feel a brush in my hand again."

"You're going back to painting!"

"Yes. We've found someone to run the inn, and I've hired a workshop to turn into my studio. I can't wait to get started."

"Good." I smile at him.

"Your painting lessons came to an abrupt end," Johannes goes on. "If you're looking for a new teacher . . ."

"That's kind of you, but you don't have the time. And I'm busy too. It feels strange *not* having a brush in my hand. Like I'm missing a finger."

Johannes laughs. "Well, just remember: if you change your mind, you're always welcome."

"Wouldn't Catherina object?"

"For the past few months, Catherina has been the happiest woman in the world." His voice brims with pride and happiness.

I look over at his wife, who's standing across the room. Her growing belly is clearly visible under her yellow smock.

"Congratulations!" I blurt out, surprised. "You're going to be a father, how wonderful. When is the baby due?"

"Only three months to go now. We've lost a couple before, so we kept the pregnancy a secret for a long time."

"Catherina is glowing."

"Yes, she's so happy. Miscarriages are hard, especially late in the pregnancy. It was a boy both times." A shadow of grief passes over his face.

"I know all about that," I say, but my words are lost as we're buffeted by a line , of dancers who form a ring around Johannes, putting an end to our conversation.

Angelika and Quentin have stayed at home with the children. They drop in on New Year's Day to wish us the best. They don't stay long.

"Are you and Quentin not getting along?" I ask Evert.

"No, but he has been very distant." Evert takes a thoughtful sip of wine. "So you've noticed it too."

"I barely see Angelika any more. Could it have something to do with us getting married?"

"I can't imagine that it would. They were more enthusiastic than anyone about it."

"Then it's something else, something we don't know about. Should I ask Angelika?"

Evert shakes his head. "It isn't necessarily anything to do with us. Perhaps they're having problems themselves."

"If they are, then I want to know that, too. They're our friends!"

"Friendship means trusting that everything's all right," says Evert. "Leave them be. If they need us, they'll come to us."

CHAPTER
THIRTY

Evert turns out to be right. The new year isn't even a week old when Quentin comes by on Sunday afternoon to have a word. He doesn't ask me to leave, so I stay in the parlour as well. Anna pours us each a glass of beer and puts cheese and olives on the table.

"Spit it out," Evert says once she's gone. "What's on your mind, lad?"

Quentin isn't a man to beat around the bush. "I'm setting up on my own."

These words are followed by a stony silence. I hold my breath and look from one man to the other. To my surprise, Evert seems to be taking the news relatively well. He fills his pipe and lights it from a spill he sticks into the fire.

"I thought it was something like that."

"Did you?"

"You're about to present your work to the guild and become a master. Why would you stay on after that?"

Quentin eyes him warily. "So you don't mind? We'll be competitors, Evert."

"I'm sad to see you go, of course, but the market is big enough for the both of us."

"I know your secret firing method."

"Yes, and you're going to use it. There's nothing to be done about that. I assume you've got enough sense not to go spreading it about."

"No, of course I won't. If we cooperate and send each other jobs now and again, we can maintain a monopoly." Quentin grabs his beer and takes a hearty gulp. "I'm so relieved you're reacting like this. I've been worried sick."

"How are you going to go about it? Have you got enough capital?"

"I'm going into business with Wouter van Eenhoorn. He told me David van der Piet's pottery on East End Canal is going on the market. Wouter's got the cash and I've got the know-how, so he suggested setting up a company together."

"Why are they selling?" I ask.

Quentin takes another sip of his beer and looks at me. "David bought the premises for his son Jan, he had kilns installed and got everything ready to begin production. But sonny boy had other plans and now the old man's stuck with the business. He wants someone to take it off his hands and asked whether Wouter knew anyone. That's where the idea got started. We're planning to buy the house next door so we can turn it into a shop."

"Cornelia's house, next-door to Bohm, the surgeon," says Evert.

"The very same. That's up for sale as well."

"Sounds good. When's all this going to happen?"

"It'll be a while yet," says Quentin. "I've still got to finish my official masterpiece."

194

"So you're staying for now. That's good, that gives me time to find a new assistant." Evert takes a puff of his pipe and blows the smoke into the room.

The equanimity with which he receives Quentin's news just keeps on amazing me.

"What am I supposed to do?" he says, once his friend has left. "I always knew Quentin wouldn't remain an assistant forever, he's far too enterprising for that. And I meant what I said: there's enough business for us both."

"He knows how to make Dutch Porcelain, which minerals you need and how to fire the pots. He can do it just as well as you. Aren't you worried about that?"

Evert shakes his head. "I learned it all through trial and error, others may do the same. There are already potters taking steps in the right direction. The only thing they still don't understand is how to stop the white pottery from yellowing. They're convinced it requires some mysterious ingredient from abroad." He chuckles. "They haven't got a clue that all you need is good old cooking salt and potash. No one knows that, just us."

"And Quentin."

"Yes, but he's got enough sense to keep it to himself."

"He'll have to tell Wouter van Eenhoorn. Before you know it, all of Delft will be in on the secret."

Evert stands up and kisses me on the neck. "Don't be so gloomy, darling. You never manage to keep anything successful all to yourself for long. And we'll be able to make plenty of pots before it comes to that."

Angelika is just as relieved as Quentin that we know about their plans and that Evert has taken the news so well.

"Of course it's not *illegal* to set up a rival company," she says, "but in this case the whole thing was a bit delicate."

"Because we're such good friends," I say.

She nods. "And because of those secret techniques. Which Quentin will share with as few people as possible, naturally. He's planning to have every employee sign a secrecy contract."

"That's a good idea."

"Isn't it? You could do the same, then we know it'll be kept between us."

Later that evening, I bring it up with Evert, who nods in agreement. "I've spoken to Quentin about it and I'm going to have a contract drawn up too. By the notary, completely official. Oh, and we need a name for the company, Catrin."

"A name? It's a pottery, not a tavern."

"I think it's a good move, now that competition is growing. We could put a little symbol on our pieces as a kind of hallmark. Then it'll be clear what company it comes from."

The next day, I mull it over as I'm painting. I'm absorbed, working on a picture of an exquisite, fragile flower the Chinese call the "lotus" and that stands for purity of spirit and internal growth. It sprouts under

196

water, in the mud, only growing towards the light and reaching the surface when the time is right. Maybe that's why I like painting it so much. I scrutinise my work. Then, in a flash, I turn over the piece I'm working on and paint a tiny lotus on the bottom with a few flicks of my brush. Evert thinks The Lotus Flower is a brilliant name for the company, which is lucky because by the time I suggest it to him the plate is already in the kiln. From that moment on, everything we make gets a flower and the letter L on the bottom.

On 26 February, Quentin and Van Eenhoorn buy David Anthonisz van der Piet's house on the west end of East End Canal, followed by the house next door to it a week later. Quentin moves into the annex behind it with his family. A nanny is taken on to look after the children, since Angelika will be working in the shop. They're not ready to open yet because Quentin will only present his work to the guild in May and until he does, and is accepted, he's not allowed to trade.

Spring is in the air as I set out one morning to do my shopping. Anna usually does it, but now and then I feel like going to the market myself. I'm on my way to the fish stalls when Jacob pops up next to me. Aside from the daily exchange of pleasantries, we've had almost no contact for months and I still feel uneasy in his company.

"Morning, Catrin. Are you off to buy fish?"

I presume this is merely an opening gambit and wait for the rest to follow.

"I am too. It's tasty and cheaper than meat," he says as he joins a queue behind me.

"That's true."

We wait for our turn in awkward silence. To give myself something else to focus on, I watch the two storks with clipped wings that are gobbling up the guts and off-cuts left on the ground. They work for the city and are wearing black and white collars.

"They've got those in Alkmaar too," says Jacob.

"What?"

"Storks around the fish stalls on Verdronkenoord."

"They have."

"Do you ever think about home?"

"All the time."

"I don't. I'm glad I got away from there."

It dawns on me that I hardly know anything about Jacob. "Why? You've got family in De Rijp, haven't you?"

"Yes, a religious fanatic mother and a father with loose fists and a quick temper. I'm the youngest of eleven, I barely know my brothers and sisters."

"That's a shame."

He shrugs. "Well, the ties that bind can strangle you too. Otherwise I'd probably still be there, milking cows."

I nod, not knowing what else to say. But Jacob goes on.

"I can understand it because of how my dad was. What you did, I mean. So you can count on me as far as that goes."

This puts me right back on alert. "Great."

"People from the same village should help each other out, don't you think?"

I look at him suspiciously.

"Don't be so mistrustful, I didn't mean anything by it. I only thought . . ." He stops and scratches his head.

"What do you want, Jacob?"

"Well, I've been working as a treader for a while now and preparing clay is starting to bore me. It's heavy, dirty work. And with Quentin going, Evert's going to need to train someone else up. It'll probably be Klaas. Which means someone needs to replace him emptying the kilns and cleaning out the scraps from the firing."

"You want to train as a potter?"

"It's a good skill to have. And with so many new companies getting involved, the boom looks set to continue. So, yes, I reckon it would be a good move for me."

"Why are you telling *me* this? You should be talking to Evert."

"True. But everyone knows you've got a lot of influence over what goes on at the company. Your opinion counts. Evert listens to you. So if you suggest that he trains me, he'll do it."

I struggle to hold in a gasp. I knew that he'd need me again for something one day. Jacob in the workshop? It doesn't bear thinking about. At the moment he spends his whole working day in one of the outbuildings and I don't have to see him, but the kilns are right next to the studio.

"It's such a small favour, Catrin. You'll do it for me, won't you?" Jacob's voice sounds friendly, almost taken aback that I'm hesitating. There's a smile on his face and I feel my resistance crumble. Perhaps I was wrong about him, perhaps he never meant me any harm and his request is exactly what it seems: him asking me to put in a good word. He hasn't bothered me at all over the last few months, but this isn't the only consideration that swings it for me. Some people are better kept on side.

"Very well," I say. "I'll do my best."

CHAPTER
THIRTY-ONE

"You miss your family," Evert says during dinner. After I told him about Jacob's request, he sat for a while without saying anything. I wait, watching his thoughtful face and wondering which answer I'm hoping for.

"Would it help you if I trained Jacob?" he asks finally.

"It won't make me miss my family any less, of course, but Jacob is the only person I can talk about them with."

"I understand. It's fine with me. Jacob is a hard worker, he'll be good at it. If it makes you happy, I'll train him up."

"Does that mean you're going to teach him all the firing techniques? I wouldn't do that if I were you."

Evert looks startled. "I thought you wanted me to train him?"

"Yes, but he doesn't need to know everything. The fewer people who know about the technique, the better."

"Don't worry, I don't teach everything to every apprentice. I wasn't born yesterday."

From then on, I see Jacob much more often. Now that he works inside, he's near me all day. His duties consist of collecting the painted earthenware to be baked and filling and emptying the kilns. After that, he joins the other workshop boys packing the ceramics for shipping.

As Evert said, Jacob is a hard worker and he takes his training seriously. He thanks me with a wink, which I answer with a weak laugh. I ask myself what he would have done if Evert had said no.

The first two months of the new year pass quickly. The first anniversary of Govert's death finds me in church, the only place where my mind can be quieted. From the minute I woke up I've been tortured by my thoughts. Evert understood when I asked for the afternoon off, of course. If there's anyone who knows what it feels like to be haunted by ghosts from the past, it's him.

As I sit there on the pew, I feel the bruises on my skin all over again, the split lip, the ringing in my ears from Govert's last blow before he collapsed into bed and succumbed to his drunken stupor. I'd had to endure his violent outbursts from the day we were married, but it got even worse around the anniversary of our son's death. I saw in his eyes that something was wrong, knew that he remembered as much as I did how our baby had been lost. He'd come back that Sunday from the pub after much too much to drink and wanted to kiss me. I shrank from his boozy breath and an instant later he was knocking me to the ground.

After a couple more kicks to my belly and legs, he stumbled to the bed and threw himself down on it. It was only when I knew he wasn't getting back up that I

202

picked myself up off the floor and crept outside to bathe my bleeding lip at the pump in the farmyard. Jacob and Jannet had the day off, so at least I was spared the humiliation of their sympathy.

I went back inside and stood in the doorway to the living room. No sound was coming from the bed. Many men snore when they've been drinking, but Govert only made the occasional sound, deep in his throat, followed by long pauses when it seemed like he'd stopped breathing. When we were first married I was frightened by it and shook his shoulder. He shoved me off with an irritable, "Give over, stupid cow." Whenever it happened after that, I knew better and counted the seconds when the breathing stopped only to be disappointed every time I heard him start again.

I don't know what it was that drove me to it that day rather than any other. The beating he'd doled out that day was no different from the time before, a variation on a theme that would probably last my whole life. I'd long realised he'd never change and that I'd always be having to hide an injury somewhere on my body. My children too, if I ever had any. That day I saw with fresh clarity the woman I was becoming: subdued, skittish, introverted, unable to laugh or love. I knew that kind of woman, there were enough of them in the village. I'd always pitied them, even though they made me angry too.

On a sudden impulse, I ran to the bed and grabbed a pillow. My hands weren't shaking and I didn't hesitate for a second.

I bent over Govert. His mouth was slightly open, far enough to reveal the gaps where his molars had once been. He moved his head and for a moment it seemed he was going to open his eyes, but before he could I slammed the pillow down on his face, hard. He woke up, struggled and fought. The drink had taken a good portion of his reflexes and strength. He was no match for me. Months of pent-up anger and humiliation welled inside me, making me stronger than I will ever be again.

It was over faster than I thought it would be. Before long I could feel the fight going out of him, and then the lack of air made him sag under my hands. I kept on pressing the pillow to his face for a while, just to be certain. I only took it away once I was sure he was dead. And then I looked at him, not daring to breathe.

It would be to my credit if I'd been struck with remorse, if I'd at least been shocked, but the only thing I felt at the time was relief.

He was dead. Finally.

"Can I be of any service?"

I jump at the deep, warm voice and see the minister standing in the aisle. He looks concerned.

"I've been watching you for a while and was touched by the intensity of your prayers. If I can be of any help to you . . ." He recognises me then: "You're Evert van Nulandt's wife."

"Yes, I'm Catrin. You married us a couple of months ago."

He nods and sits down next to me.

204

"I've been wondering something," I say hesitantly.

"Yes?"

"Are our mistakes always forgiven, Reverend?"

He gives me a sidelong glance. "That depends. In principle, yes. No one makes it through life without making mistakes, we're all sinners. But everyone can seek God's forgiveness."

"How?"

"By asking for it and showing proper remorse, by living a better life. There are different ways."

"And if you don't feel remorse?"

His expression clouds over with concern. "That makes it harder."

I look at my hands, lying clasped in my lap. "Do you think there's such a thing as sins you have no choice but to commit?"

"We always have a choice, Catrin. The only thing God asks of us is to turn away from bad choices. Of course, I can imagine it's difficult to do that sometimes."

"Have you ever been in a situation where you made the wrong choice?"

"Yes, of course, when I was young. Back then I turned away from God and didn't serve him. Thankfully that time is far behind me now."

"Because you felt remorse and decided to live a better life."

"Exactly."

I fall quiet.

His eyes search my face. "Is your problem really so big, Catrin? Why are you afraid of God's judgement?"

"Like I said . . . because I feel no remorse."

"Do you regret breaking God's laws?"

"Yes, I regret that."

"Because you're afraid of being punished, or because you recognise that you did wrong?"

"The first one. But I'm not a bad person, Reverend. My whole life I've tried to do the right thing. I'm obedient to my parents and husband. When I pass a beggar I always give him something. Doesn't that count for something in His judgement?" I don't mention that I've twice slept with a man outside of marriage, you can't really compare that to the reason I'm here.

"You can't make up for your transgressions like that, Catrin. God doesn't make bargains. Every sin is punished."

I shudder. "Am I going to hell?"

"You don't go there just like that. You know that Jesus came to earth and died for our sins. A sin damages your relationship with God and will be punished, but not with the loss of eternal life. God's love is so great that in some cases He can forgive our inability to feel remorse."

"How do you know if you've been forgiven?"

The minister smiles and puts his hand on his heart. "You feel it."

CHAPTER
THIRTY-TWO

I leave the church feeling slightly reassured. My talk with the minister has done me good. Somehow the sunlight seems friendlier, less glaring, and the crush in the marketplace seems less claustrophobic. I stand still and enjoy the lovely weather and the feeling of the lively press of people around me. But suddenly my thoughts turn to my family and an intense longing puts a lump in my throat.

"Penny for them . . ."

I turn to find Adelaide's smiling face close to mine. She's with her daughter, who bobs a curtsy.

"I was just wondering whether to go to work or keep on playing truant a little longer and make the best of this beautiful weather," I say.

"You work hard enough. Evert will forgive you if you stay and have a chat with me."

"I'm sure you're right."

"I saw you come out of the church. What an unusual time to go." There's a note of discomfort in Adelaide's voice, as if she's loath to pry.

"It's the anniversary of Govert's death. My first husband."

"Oh yes, I knew you'd been married before. Evert told me. So today's the day you became a widow."

I nod.

"That must be hard for you." Adelaide strokes my arm sympathetically. "Do you feel like coming home with us? Then we can talk about it, if you want to."

That's the last thing I want to do, but before I can come up with an excuse she adds: "I want to have a word with you anyway."

Something in her expression makes refusing difficult, so I agree. We walk back to her house on Choir Street talking about this and that. It's a big house with an imposing, richly decorated gable. A house worthy of a bailiff and magistrate.

I cross the threshold reluctantly. In the hall hangs the painting I'd seen once before when I came to rent my house from them. This time, I take a closer look. I don't like it much, Isaac and Adelaide, sitting on a chair dressed in old-fashioned black, the children standing stiffly at either side. Janneke is standing next to her mother, Michael next to his father, little copies of their parents in their dark clothes.

"I don't think it's all that good a painting," says Adelaide. "We've commissioned Johannes to do another one, a bit less formal."

"He'll do a good job. Johannes really brings life into his work."

"Exactly. This is so stiff and old-fashioned." Adelaide leads the way to the sitting room at the back of the house. Janneke has gone out into the yard, where I see her rushing up and down with a ball. Adelaide and I sit on two high chairs by the window. The sun streams in through the polished glass. A maid comes in and asks whether she should make a pot of tea.

"Yes please, Aggie," says Adelaide, and asks me: "Have you heard of it: tea?"

I nod, I used to make it now and then for Brigitta. Once I tasted some secretly. I didn't think much of it. Too bitter for my taste. But it's an expensive drink so I accept the small stoneware beaker Aggie brings me with a grateful nod.

"Really you should have it in something else," says Adelaide. "Glass doesn't work, it gets too hot, and stoneware is so thick on the lips."

"Special little cups," I say.

"Yes, something pretty and fine. Tea is an expensive drink, you don't pour that into the same old cup you drink your milk out of."

I examine her cup; it's robust and heavy in my hand. "I'll talk to Evert about it. I'm sure we can come up with something a bit prettier. What do they drink their tea out of in the East?"

"Out of little bowls, I think. You don't see anything like them here."

I feel a sense of growing excitement, just as I do every time something new and creative occurs to me. I picture dozens, no, hundreds of drinking bowls set out in the kiln, delicately made and beautifully painted with an oriental scene. I'd dearly have liked to rush home then and there to work on a design, but I force my attention back to Adelaide's prattle. I only start paying proper attention when she asks about my stay in the infirmary.

"You were so dreadfully poorly," she says. "We were worried that you wouldn't make it once you got sick."

"The fever, yes. I felt terrible."

"You were delirious, talking gibberish. At least . . ." Adelaide stops and looks down at her black skirt.

"What?"

"I spent a long time telling myself that it had to be nonsense, that you were out of your mind. The alternative would be too awful."

My blood runs cold. "What do you mean? What on earth did I say?"

"You were talking about your husband. Govert, wasn't it?"

I nod mutely. Sometimes you know what's coming before it's said.

"You were saying his name, saying that it was your fault, that God was going to punish you. And something about suffocating."

It's as if my heart's fallen off its hook. Usually the heart beats faster when one has a fright, but not this time. Every few seconds I feel a dull thud, an ominous thump. I feel faint and take a sip of bitter tea to keep my wits about me.

"What did you mean by that, Catrin? Tell me." Adelaide's voice no longer sounds so friendly but rather commanding.

Saying that I have no idea isn't enough. I need to lay her suspicions to rest. "When he drank, his breathing became irregular. Sometimes he'd stop breathing for

210

what felt like minutes at a time. Then I'd get hold of him and shake him until he woke up." I look at the vase full of flowers on the table in an effort to escape Adelaide's penetrating gaze. "On the day he died, he came back from the tavern drunk. He stumbled into bed and fell asleep. Of course I should have stayed with him to keep an eye on him, but I was too busy. It was towards evening and there's still so much to be done on a farm at that time of day. So I went about my chores." I put the half-empty cup down on the table and venture a look at Adelaide, who's watching me sceptically. "When I came back in it was quiet, too quiet. I ran to the bed and Govert was lying there, with his mouth wide open." I look down and add in a whisper: "He wasn't breathing."

"What happened then?" Adelaide's voice sounds sympathetic, even though the suspicion isn't entirely gone from her eyes.

"I tried to wake him, shook him as hard as I could. It took a while for me to take in the fact that he was dead. I couldn't believe it."

"When you were sick you said that he'd suffocated."

"That's how he looked, with his mouth wide open. As if he was trying to take a breath but couldn't get any air."

Adelaide gives this some thought. "Was he on his back?"

"Yes."

"That's very dangerous. Your tongue can roll back and close off your throat. Normally, that wakes you up, but not if you're drunk. Was there vomit around his mouth?"

I shake my head, even though that would have been the ideal explanation. I would have mentioned it already if it was true.

Adelaide leans towards me and puts her hand on my arm. "You can't blame yourself, Catrin. It wasn't your fault."

"If only I'd stayed with him . . ."

"For hours? While, as you said, you had work to do? He shouldn't have been drunk."

"I suppose . . ." I sit quietly on my stool. "Who else knows about this?"

"About what you said when you were feverish? No one. If I'd told Isaac about it, he'd have had to get in touch with the sheriff in Alkmaar. I wanted to hear from you how it happened first."

"Did you think that I . . ."

"That's how it sounded, Catrin. I couldn't imagine it, but then again, how well do I really know you?"

"You're right. I would have been suspicious too."

"I'm glad you understand," Adelaide smiles. "I didn't know what to do. I haven't said a word to anyone, rumours would be going around before you know it. People are always inclined to think the worst."

"Absolutely. Thank you."

We sit together in awkward silence. At least, it's awkward for me. Adelaide seems to be lost in thought. "I was married before as well," she says suddenly. "Against my will. My parents chose for me and I had to go along with it. I was seventeen when I got married."

"So young."

"Much too young. My husband was a bit older and I didn't feel entirely attracted to him. Love didn't grow with the years either, as my parents had predicted. If there'd only been some sense of camaraderie between us, it would have been bearable, but my husband treated me like a servant. He belittled or ignored me. Every day I woke up with the bitter regret that I hadn't resisted the marriage. And then, after five years, I was freed from him. God sent an epidemic of scarlet fever and two weeks later I was a widow." She laces her fingers together and looks out the window at her daughter, who's still playing outside. "I nursed him during his illness — of course I did that — but I never prayed for his recovery. I sat next to him with my hands together and didn't know what to ask God for. In the end, I simply left it to Him and my husband died. I felt guilty about that for a long time. I thought if I'd begged harder for his life, my prayers might have been heard." She stares at her hands, tightly folded in her lap, and then up at me, "But we overestimate our own power in such things. Who knows if we're making choices or if those choices were made for us long ago? It seems it was God's will that he died."

Our eyes meet.

"Yes," I say. "I think it was."

CHAPTER
THIRTY-THREE

We're probably all tormented by feelings of guilt and fear. How well do you really know the people around you? Everyone has secrets, big and small, which, for better or worse, we build our lives around.

The fear that the truth will one day come to light had been dormant for a while. It never truly left me for a single second; at best it faded into the background, like a thief in a dark alley. Now that it has finally jumped out, it's taking some effort to shake it off.

Did Adelaide believe my story or was she only pretending to? I'm half-expecting the bailiff and his men to knock on my door, but a month later, when nothing has happened, I dare to believe that I'm safe.

Meanwhile, I'm working harder than ever. I sketch designs for bowls to drink out of with high, thin sides. I add pictures of roses and Chinamen drinking tea. When I show them to Evert, and he and Quentin start discussing how they're going to make them, I feel better for the first time in weeks. Work has a restorative effect on my spirits, it stops me from brooding, despite Jacob's continued presence. Even though he never approaches me, I still feel ill at ease with him there. He watches me. I can see him out of the corner of my eye as I'm painting. I feel his eyes on me when he doesn't think I'm looking. Sometimes I see him in the reflection of a window pane, sometimes I simply know.

As spring progresses, we bring the teacups, as Evert calls them, into production. They're a huge success from the start.

Meanwhile, Quentin and Angelika are preparing to open their business. On the first of June, Quentin registers with the guild as a master potter and he and Wouter van Eenhoorn open their own pottery, which they call The Porcelain Flask. Despite the competition, we can still hardly meet all our orders, so our friendship with Quentin doesn't come under any strain.

On Sundays, we often go out together, perhaps taking a boat trip beyond the city walls then going for a walk, always ending up at a tavern where we eat outside on wooden tables, enjoying the food, wine and each other's company. They're lovely trips, which always cheer me up.

"You're glowing, Catrin." Quentin studies me for a moment. "Do you see that, Evert? Your wife seems to be getting more beautiful every day."

"Well, it doesn't seem possible," says Evert, "but I have to admit that you're right."

He winks at me and I laugh. For a while it's been our delicious secret, but now, on this beautiful summer's day, we nod to each other and tell our friends the good news.

Their congratulations are loud and animated, and it's in this happy atmosphere that we recharge our glasses and toast to the future. For the first time in years, I'm completely happy.

But happiness is a slippery customer. Just as I let my guard down, lower my defences and dare to start believing that life can go smoothly, I hear something that makes the hairs on the back of my neck stand on end. I'm strolling through the market with Anna when someone says the word "plague".

I whip round to face the man announcing the news. He's forty or so, clad in a dark brown jerkin and breeches with a weathered face. There's a basket with carry straps at his feet.

"What was that?" I ask. "Plague?"

The pedlar nods solemnly. "I'm afraid so, mistress. It has come from France and it's on its way here."

"Where is it now?"

"Antwerp already. The plague travels fast."

I break out in a cold sweat and feel myself growing faint. More people gather around with frightened expressions.

"Which towns have the plague?" asks Anna.

"It would be quicker to list the ones that haven't. It's everywhere. More than half the inhabitants of Antwerp have died. There weren't enough coffins, so they've thrown all the victims into one big grave."

A wave of muttering travels through the crowd.

"Don't listen to that old fool! Half the town? How can he know that?" shouts the fishmonger from behind his stall.

"I'm from there, I've seen it with my own eyes," says the pedlar.

"Is that right? Why haven't you got the plague then? Maybe you *have*. What are you doing here, man? People like you will bring the sickness inside the walls!"

Noises of assent are heard from the crowd, many faces turn angrily on the pedlar.

"I haven't fallen ill because I was smart enough to avoid the towns," says the man loudly. "And because I've got medicine to ward off the plague. Here!" He rummages in his basket and pulls out a vial. "This elixir kept me safe. If someone's already got the plague, it does no good. The medicine works preventively. Two sips, three times a day and the sickness passes you by."

"What's in that stuff?" sniffs a doughty woman, her arms folded across her chest.

"It's a secret recipe that's been in my family for years. No, I won't say what's in it, I'm a businessman, mistress. I have to make a living. The elixir is for sale, but I don't have many vials left. I saved many lives on my way here. Don't you believe me? I'm standing here, aren't I? How else could I have travelled unharmed through a plague area?" He pulls out another couple of vials and holds them aloft. "For those who act fast! You'll see soon enough whether I'm telling the truth, when the foul vapours of the plague reach the city."

Uncertain, I look at the vials. "How much do they cost?"

"Ten stivers per vial, mistress. That's not a lot for something that could save your life."

"Let's buy one," says Anna, sounding scared.

"Who says that the plague's even going round? I haven't heard anything about it." The fishmonger, with a cod in one hand and a filleting knife in the other, snorts, cuts the head off the fish and throws it to the ground.

A well-dressed man joins us. "It's true," he says. "I trade with people in Antwerp and the sickness is raging there at the moment. In Breda and Den Bosch too, so it might well come further north."

In the meantime, a large crowd has gathered, pressing in around the pedlar, and the merchant's words are passed from person to person. A young woman with a child on her arm forces her way to the front and sticks out her hand. "I'll take one of them bottles," she says.

The other people hesitate for a second but then one after another they open their purses and go up to the pedlar. I check to see if I've got ten stivers, Anna does the same. As I'm counting, I feel a hand on my shoulder.

"Don't be fooled, Catrin. No one has a cure for the plague, least of all this man." Johannes takes my arm and leads me away.

"You don't know that. He hasn't been infected," I say, looking back at the press of people around the pedlar.

"He's probably been nowhere near Antwerp and only heard about the plague by word of mouth. If the best doctors haven't been able to find a remedy, why would he have one? You can't believe that."

I drop the coins back into my purse with a sigh. "You're right. Anna, put your money away."

"You're frightened, everyone gets frightened by reports like that. And crooks like him know how to turn it to their advantage."

"Do you think the plague really is headed this way?" I ask.

"I don't know. Maybe it is raging around the South, but that doesn't necessarily mean it's coming here. An epidemic that breaks out like that can disappear just as quickly."

He leads me to a corner of the market square. "My new studio is near here. Do you want to see it?"

"Yes, please," I say, glad of the distraction.

We walk along Voldersgracht and stop by a house with a stepped gable and a little arched gateway to one side. Johannes pushes open the door and leads us into the alley. Halfway up there's a low door through which we enter. Anna stays standing shyly on the threshold, I go right in. The studio is a square room with high windows that let in a beautiful, muted light. In the centre of the room, there are two easels surrounded by tables covered in paint pots, brushes, scrapers and rags. Blank canvases line three walls, while the fourth is almost entirely taken up by a fireplace.

"I can work here in winter too," says Johannes, nodding towards the hearth. "And the studio faces north, so hardly any sun gets in. It's perfect."

"You're right. What a wonderful space!" I go over to the canvas on the easel. "You're hard at work, I see."

"Yes. I'm going to call this canvas *Christ in the House of Martha and Mary*. It's almost finished. What do you think?"

I take a step back. I don't much care for religious subjects but this tableau of Jesus talking to two women has something homely and familiar. Only the vague aureola surrounding Jesus' head betrays his divinity. The lively colours, the lifelike faces of the three people and their natural relationship with each other, which looks completely un-posed, gives the painting a power that leaves me holding my breath, transfixed.

"It's magnificent, Johannes. Truly magnificent."

"So you like it then?" He nods with satisfaction, then studies me from head to toe. "There's something different about you . . . Something to do with the way you're holding yourself."

I laugh, a little embarrassed. "You might well be right. I'm expecting. More than four months gone now."

"Really? That's fantastic. Congratulations!" He looks me over with a broad smile, then something in his expression changes. His smile vanishes and his eyes shine. "The way you're standing there right now, in that pale light, with that yellow jacket, that's how I'd like to paint you."

I don't know what to do with myself. Johannes scrutinises me intensely, as if he's trying to ingrain something in his memory.

"If only you could pose for me," he says, more to himself than to me.

I have no idea what to say, so I say nothing, transfixed in his gaze.

220

Then Johannes seems to come round with a jerk, as if from a daydream. "I've got it," he says, his eyes still on me. "I'll remember."

CHAPTER
THIRTY-FOUR

On the way home, Anna and I are unusually subdued. The plague dominates my thoughts. How is it possible that life is going on as normal, people are talking and laughing together, children are shrieking with pleasure as they chase after a cat, and the stallholders in the market are standing around cracking jokes as usual. You'd expect the plague to be the only topic of conversation.

Maybe it's me who's worrying too much, maybe because my pregnancy is making me more sensitive. Antwerp is far away, after all.

But I can't help feeling nervous. As soon as I'm home, I go in search of Evert. He's standing in the yard giving instructions about unloading a delivery of firewood. Once he's paid the delivery man and the apprentices are carrying the wood inside, I tell him what I heard in the market.

"The plague? Where?" asks Evert.

"In Antwerp, Breda and Den Bosch."

"I haven't heard anything about that." Evert gestures to Klaas, who comes over to ask something, then turns back to me. "Don't worry too much, darling. Even if that is the case, it doesn't mean it'll come to Delft."

"But it could." I put my hand on my belly, feeling like I could cry.

Evert looks at me, concerned, and walks off with a "Wait one moment." I see him talking to the wood merchant, who's giving his horse a drink out of a bucket, before waving me over.

"Tell my wife how things are in the South," he says as I approach.

The wood merchant nods reassuringly. "Nothing's happening, mistress. This morning I spoke to someone from Den Bosch and I didn't hear anything about the plague. I think that fellow on the market just wanted to make some money. You've only got to mention the word 'plague' and the exchanges get flooded with so-called miracle cures."

"Someone else vouched for the truth of his story," I say, still not reassured. "A man in fine clothes said the plague had spread to Breda and Den Bosch."

"An accomplice," Evert says with a dark voice. "Characters like that never work alone. I'd lay money that they're sitting in a tavern as we speak, counting their ill-gotten gains — wouldn't you?"

With a nod of assent, the wood merchant climbs onto his cart and takes the reins. "And if it is true, we can't do anything about it anyway," he says. "We'd be in God's hands."

Those words echo in my mind for the rest of the evening. The simple truth of them doesn't make me feel any better. The plague is always raging somewhere; five years ago it was in Alkmaar, but De Rijp has been spared for a long time. So long that I've never been confronted with it. Which isn't to say I have no concept of what it must be like to be hit by that dreadful disease. My grandparents and parents witnessed terrible epidemics. Everyone knows someone who died. The plague must be a terror. You can't do anything for those who come down with the pneumonic plague, the plague in their lungs. High temperature combined with stabbing chest pains and worsening shortness of breath swiftly give way to unconsciousness, followed by death. The bubonic plague offers a slightly better chance of survival but puts you through hell for days. The first sign you've got the black death is a temperature, followed by fever, after which lumps come up in various places on your body. They grow into dark sores and then hard, pus-filled swellings called buboes. The illness can last ten days. Only a small number of people survive this period. After that, the plague either disappears or attacks anew, with new buboes and heavy internal bleeding. No one survives the second stage.

For now, there doesn't seem to be any immediate danger. Because of our business, we speak to delivery men, ship's captains and travelling sales people every day, and we always ask them about the plague. Reports from the South are contradictory. One says the number of deaths in Breda and Den Bosch is high, another says nothing's going on. A third tells us there have been a few deaths but the plague hasn't taken hold. It now seems that Antwerp is the last affected town and the disease is fading away.

"You see, it's dying out," says Evert, once the salesman who was visiting our shop has left. He puts an arm around my waist and kisses my neck. "Everything's going to be fine."

In mid-July the blow comes. I hear the news buzzing around the poultry market between Choir Street and the Poel Bridge as I approach. The plague has hit Dordrecht and Gorinchem, and hard. Everyone is talking about it, there isn't anyone who isn't concerned. The town crier does the rounds, announcing that the city authorities are taking measures to prevent the plague from being brought to Delft.

I see Angelika standing holding hands with her daughters and go up to them. She turns to me with a white face. "Catrin, have you heard?"

"Yes, but they're taking measures. They'll bar the gates."

"They say the plague is spread by poisonous fumes. How do they intend to stop them?"

"I don't know." I catch sight of Katherine and Gertrude, who are gazing up at us, terrified.

"What is it, the plague?" asks Gertrude timidly.

"It's a sickness," I say, "but it's far off."

"How far?"

"All the way over in Dordrecht."

"Then why is everyone so scared?" Katherine looks around with interest.

"We're going," says Angelika. "I just need to drop by the apothecary's. I'm sure they'll have some kind of protective powder to take. You should get something too, before they run out."

I nod and watch them go, the trusting girls holding their mother's hand. Since my little conversation with Johannes, I no longer believe in those cures. What he said sounded logical: if they did help, the plague wouldn't exist any more. Whether you die or not is in God's hands.

My hand goes to my belly and I bite my lip.

No one knows how the plague spreads, but they do know it's catching. Putting a stop to all the trade with the surrounding area and other towns is impossible — people need food. But there are stringent checks on those who seek to enter the city. There's a suspicion that the plague vapours stick to skin, hair and clothing, and so itinerant pedlars, theatre companies, cart-drivers and ship's captains are no longer welcome. Other travellers are subjected to close questioning and anyone who is coming from an area hit by the plague is told to turn right around.

Trade goes on as usual with the areas where there's no plague, though this is risky too. Many merchants from the affected areas attempt to get in by taking a detour. The gatekeepers keep a close eye on how people look, but they can't guarantee they won't admit someone who's been infected. Often the people themselves don't know they're ill.

In neighbouring cities, the checks are just as strict. Despite this, the plague has spread to Gouda and

Rotterdam. The disease can't get much closer to Delft than that.

"Are you afraid?" asks Jacob when we're in the shop together.

I'm busy dusting the display pieces for the sake of the odd customer we still see. Jacob puts a crate of straw on the table and carefully places a large vase inside it, destined for a rich merchant in Amsterdam.

"Yes, aren't you? Everyone is afraid," I say. "This will be the last thing we can send. There's a good chance it won't even be allowed into Amsterdam."

"Nothing's been sent back so far. There's no plague here."

"No, not yet. But apparently it's bad in Rotterdam, and that's not far away."

"Schiedam is only a stone's throw from Rotterdam and there's nothing happening there. So you can't say much based on that." He gives me a sidelong glance. "You've finally got everything on an even keel and the plague breaks out." We carry on working in silence. "You know, Catrin, I admire you," he says after a while. "I never thought you had it in you to take care of yourself so well. We're really quite alike, you and I."

I frown. "You think so?"

"Absolutely. We both want a better life and are prepared to do what's necessary to get it. To start with, all you had was a good job; now you're married to the boss and carrying his child. I take my hat off to you!"

"Just to be absolutely clear, I married Evert because I love him," I say coldly.

He snickers. "Undoubtedly. But the fact that he has a successful business didn't hurt. And it did me good too. I hope the plague doesn't ruin it all for us."

CHAPTER
THIRTY-FIVE

That night I press myself to Evert's side. It's warm and we're lying under sheets with the doors of the box bed open. Sleep escapes us.

"I want you to leave here," he says out of the blue.

In the half-darkness I look up at him. "To run away, you mean?"

"Yes. It's getting too dangerous for my taste."

"The plague could pass Delft by. With all the measures the city authorities have taken, it definitely might."

"Every city takes measures, the same ones. It's no guarantee. You could go to your family."

I roll onto my back and stare at the planks above my head. Go home . . . Yes, I could do that. The plague is spreading much less rapidly in the countryside. And I would see my parents again and my brothers. The villagers too, but with the plague approaching they'll have more on their minds than my return. Then I realise Evert is only talking about me.

"And what about you? You'll come too, won't you?"

"No, I've got a business to run. The number of orders has gone down since the plague came to the country. The commissions I do have are far too important to neglect."

"You can't think I'd go alone? We'll be safe in De Rijp and it would be a good opportunity for you to get to know my family. I'm not going without you."

"You have to," says Evert firmly. "Before it starts here too. I don't want you or the little one to take any chances."

"I don't want you to take any chances!"

He strokes my cheek. "It can't be any other way, my love. In a couple of days, I'm sending a load of dishes to Den Helder by boat. Wout Kock is the skipper, you know him. You can travel with him as far as Alkmaar and go to De Rijp from there."

I'm quiet for a second. "You've thought all this through already."

"Yes, and there's nothing to discuss, Catrin. I really want you to go. I lost my wife and children once before, I can't let it happen again."

People who flee from the plague are not popular. They disrupt trade and public life, crippling the city before the sickness has even arrived. The city authorities put up signs trying to persuade the people of Delft they're in no danger and that fleeing isn't necessary.

So far, the people have listened, but the morning after my conversation with Evert, a rumour goes round about the first victims of the plague in Delft.

Panic breaks out immediately. Those who can afford to go head to houses outside the walls or to relatives in other cities. Most people stay.

230

"There's no sense in running," says Adelaide when we bump into each other. "God has long decided who will get sick and who won't. Those who flee take their sins with them."

"If it's already decided, why are the city authorities shutting the gates and passing all kinds of new laws? God has no pity for the foolish, He wants us to use the sense he gave us."

"He made the plague catching, and He decides who gets it and who doesn't. And whether you survive it. So we're going to stay here. And you should too."

I don't answer, merely put a hand on my belly. Maybe I will take my sins with me and dying a miserable death is my just deserts, but my baby has got nothing to do with that. As soon as I get home, I rush straight upstairs to pack.

That afternoon and evening, I say goodbye to my friends. We give each other long hugs.

"I hope the plague spreads no further north and you're safe there," says Johannes.

"You and your family should leave too."

"Maybe we will." We look at each other and smile, but without a hint of merriment.

During my last night at home, Evert and I make love for hours. With every caress and each kiss, I'm conscious of the fact that this could be the last time. Eventually we fall asleep and as the morning light enters through the shutters, I weep.

"Don't cry, my love. It'll be all right." Evert tenderly wipes the tears from my face and kisses me.

"Promise me you'll leave at once if it gets bad here. Important orders Or not."

"I promise. I do. I want to see you again and get to know my child."

We get up and get dressed. Evert takes my bundle and we walk along the canal, where streaks of morning mist hang over the water. Wout is already there, he's helping Klaas get the cargo on board.

I haven't said goodbye to Jacob, but now suddenly find myself face to face with him. He doesn't say anything but looks me right in the eye for a couple of seconds. "Watch out for Mart," he says finally, before turning and walking back into the shop.

"Now then, you two should get going. It's a long journey." Evert hands my things to Wout and pulls me into his arms.

A final kiss, a long embrace and I climb aboard. The boat is big, with a deck house that offers protection from the elements. I sit myself down on the bench and wave to Evert as Wout unmoors the boat and pushes off from the quay.

He blows me a kiss and stands watching as we pass under the Chapel Bridge.

It's cold this early in the morning. Luckily I foresaw this and put on extra layers. As we make our way up the River Schie, I'm overcome by a crushing weariness. The past few months have been busy at work, I'm now five months pregnant, susceptible to back pain and not sleeping so well any more. In any case, I've spent more time lying fretting than sleeping over the past few weeks. I stretch out on the bench, pull a blanket over me and drift off.

I sleep for a good deal of the morning, so we're a fair distance further on by the time I open my eyes again. I sit up stiffly. The sun is beaming into the deck house, I'm sweating. I take off a layer of clothing and go outside. Straightaway a fresh breeze caresses my face. I look out at the peaceful polder landscape that surrounds us. The meadows are filled with summer flowers, bulrushes rustle along the river bank, sunlight shimmers on the water.

I take a deep breath and join Wout, who's standing at the wheel. Two strong young men who've come to assist along the way and guard the cargo nod to me.

"Whereabouts are we?" I ask.

Wout glances at me. "More than halfway already. You've been asleep for a good while."

We chat about the weather and our expected arrival time in Leiden. Neither of us says a word about what we've left behind.

We travel on without making any stops and arrive in Leiden in the early evening. It takes no little effort to get inside the city, Wout's manifest is scrutinised closely. No one here knows the plague has hit Delft and eventually we're allowed in. After a brief night's sleep in an inn — when we get up it's not even fully light — we leave again. Once again, I get some sleep on board the boat. It's set to be a long day; the distance we've got to cover is a bit more than yesterday. By the time we're finally in Haarlem that evening, I'm exhausted. Luckily,

Alkmaar isn't all that far now. This means we set off a little later the next morning.

When the city walls come into view at the end of the afternoon, my heart starts beating faster. I leave the deck house and go to stand by the rail, my shawl wrapped around me against the stiff breeze. There is Alkmaar. It is over a year ago I set out from there, uncertain about the future that lay ahead. And now look, I have a job I like, I'm married and I'm expecting a baby. Who'd have thought it?

Smiling, I take in the familiar skyline of the city, the windmills along the River Zeglis, the lofty towers of the city gates and the cathedral, and a wave of emotion floods over me. I'm home.

CHAPTER
THIRTY-SIX

In Alkmaar, life is going on as usual. Barges are coming and going, cargo is being loaded and unloaded and people are trading at the cheese market. Here and there, I hear people talking about the plague but it isn't the talk of the town here. I soon realise people believe the sickness has remained confined to the South. I don't intend to draw attention to myself by telling anyone the truth.

I said goodbye to Wout and the lads at Tree Gate before going from tavern to tavern along Brewer's Quay. The cheese market has just finished. Usually my father and brothers sit drinking or finishing off bits of business in the pub for a while. Not for too long, they've always got the journey home ahead of them. It seems they've left in good time today, too, because I can't find them.

I keep looking for a while in the inns near the cheese market and when that brings me no joy either, I walk further into the city to the Thirteen Beams. It's been more than a year since I last saw Emil and Bertha. I quicken my step, almost breaking into a run for the last stretch. A little out of breath, I push open the door.

Our reunion is even more enthusiastic than I expect. Bertha screams and drops a tankard, Emil comes towards me with open arms and pulls me into a tight hug.

"Catrin! How is it possible! I never thought I'd see you again," says Bertha tearfully.

To my surprise, she starts crying, and I put my arm around her. "Of course you would, why did you think that?"

She pulls me into the back, to their living room. "Where have you been? You've got to tell me everything."

I don't intend to do that, and begin a vague story that Bertha quickly interrupts.

"You were in Amsterdam but you didn't stay there," she says. "You left without letting us know where you were going. Why, Catrin?"

"I sent word, but it obviously didn't get through." It's hard to lie to her face and Bertha isn't fooled.

"That's not true. You did a moonlit flit and sent no word. I think I know why."

Our eyes meet. I'm the first to look away.

"You ran," Bertha says gently. "The bailiff has been here looking for you. He wanted to talk to you."

I look at her again and see my fear reflected in Bertha's eyes. "Did he say what about?"

"About Govert."

A silence falls, which I break with a deep sigh. "Tell me everything, Bertha."

"No, you tell me everything. Is it true what they're saying?"

"What are they saying?"

"That you killed your husband."

236

If you want to keep something secret, you can't trust anyone, even your best friends. I can't lie to Bertha but I can't confess my crime either, so I keep quiet.

"Oh God," says Bertha. "Don't say anything, I understand. I think I knew as soon as it happened. But after everything that bastard did to you, I can hardly blame you."

"Govert was stone drunk. He fell into bed and stopped breathing."

"I believe you, lovely, and I'd stick to that story. Don't tell anyone any different, not even me, then they have nothing to use against you." She takes my hand and continues. "Emil knows Van Venn, the bailiff. Govert's brother went to him because he didn't believe what happened."

"Mart. He can't stand the fact that the whole inheritance went to me after one year of marriage."

"Yes, Emil said the brother had his own reasons for blackening your name. So put it down to that."

"What did the bailiff say, exactly?"

"That he wanted to ask you some questions. He hung around, Emil gave him a few beers and then he told us the doctor who examined Govert said that he had lots of red dots oh his eyeballs. That points to him having suffocated."

"So he wants to talk to me." It's impossible to hide my alarm from Bertha. My heart is hammering painfully in my chest and I can feel the colour draining from my face.

"I wouldn't stick around, if I were you. You'd have been better off not coming back at all."

"Bertha's right." We turn to Emil, who's standing in the doorway. "One minute they just want to talk to you and the next they're putting you to the question," he says.

I struggle to swallow. I've heard enough stories about their methods to have a vivid picture of what that would involve. Visions of thumbscrews and pulleys for wrenching joints apart appear before my eyes. It's not hard to get a confession that way. If your guilt is in doubt; they resort to those methods assuming God will help you to endure the torture if you're innocent.

"You need to get out of here, Catrin," says Bertha. "I don't know where you've been all this time, but you'd be better off going back there."

"I can't," I whisper. "Not right now anyway."

"Why not?"

For a second, I question whether I should tell her, then I decide to be honest. "There's plague where I've come from."

This news comes as more of a shock than my silent admission of guilt. Bertha slaps her hand over her mouth, Emil stiffens.

"*What* did you say?" he chokes.

"There were two or three cases when I left the city, and that was in an area where I never go. So I can't be carrying it," I say hastily. "But you see now that I can't go back."

Bertha and Emil exchange glances. "Which city are you talking about?" Bertha asks in a high-pitched voice, full of fear. "Is it near Alkmaar?"

"No, I travelled for three days to get here. You don't need to be afraid."

But they are, of course.

"Breda is much further than three days away. They said the plague had hit Breda, but it must be much closer." Bertha looks at me, her eyes huge.

"They say all kinds of things. And who says the plague will spread north? It could just as easily spread east, or die down."

It makes no difference what I say, they're suddenly looking at me differently. Bertha shuffles back, wiping her hands on her apron.

"You can't stay here," she says apologetically. "There's no room."

"Oh," I say.

"It's the truth. I'm sorry."

"It doesn't matter, there are plenty of inns in Alkmaar. I'll go and find one right away."

We stand looking at each other a little awkwardly, then Emil gestures to the door. "You should be able to find something at the Morien's Head."

I nod, look back one last time at Bertha, who stands rooted to the spot with her arms folded. When she continues to say nothing, I leave.

CHAPTER
THIRTY-SEVEN

I'd like to leave Alkmaar but I'm better off staying. As long as I don't know what the mood in my village is like, I'd rather not be seen there. Travelling to De Rijp in secret is impossible. Everyone who travels that route knows each other and if I go on foot I'll be spotted sooner or later. If I want to see my family, I'm better off waiting until they come back to the cheese market.

I find dingy lodgings on Houttil Square with Stien, an old woman who rents out all the rooms in her house and lives in a little shed in the yard. It's right by where the market is held. That works out well because I want to stay out of sight as far as I can. I get my fresh air in the yard and only venture out into the street to fetch something to eat.

It's a shame, I would have liked to speak to old acquaintances and walk around the city a little. Instead, I help Stien with her vegetable patch. Naturally, she's curious and wonders why I'm hiding myself away. To keep her from becoming suspicious, I've prepared my story. I'm unmarried, pregnant and running away from my angry family. I'm waiting for the baby's father, who's at sea and doesn't know yet.

Stien accepts my story at face value, she's probably heard stranger things. She takes on the role of protector, does my shopping and cooks for me, so I don't have to go out at all any more. Her warmth and generosity make me feel terribly guilty for lying like that, but I push the feelings aside. I'm not doing her any harm, after all.

After a couple of days, she comes home with news about the approaching plague, which has been raging for a while in The Hague, Rotterdam and Delft and has reportedly spread to Leiden and Amsterdam.

"It's on its way," she says sombrely. "Not long now and it'll be our turn."

"How bad is it in Delft?" I ask, but she doesn't know. Rumours are going around that there are a hundred victims a day in Leiden and Amsterdam.

"There's nothing in Haarlem yet, so maybe we'll be spared as well," says Stien.

The situation in Haarlem is monitored with great concern. Every day, crowds rush to Tree Gate to hear what the men from the boats have to say.

In Leiden bodies are being left on the street to be collected, in Amsterdam, ringing the bells for the dead has been banned because it causes so much fear. My thoughts regularly turn to Adriaan and Brigitta.

Despite all these sombre reports, life in Alkmaar goes on as usual. There are a few restrictions, since strangers are no longer allowed within the walls. Only farmers from the surrounding areas are admitted to the city to supply the market. The weekly cheese market is going ahead on Friday as well. This week's may be the last, so they're expecting crowds. On Thursday evening, the first farmers begin coming into the city with carts and wagons via the dyke, and on barges up the River Zeglis.

They don't just bring cheese but also vegetables and fruit, bread and rusks, chickens and other poultry, fish and meat. Alkmaar doesn't have a big central square for holding a market so little stalls spring up along every bridge and canal path. Only the stretch of quayside by the weighing house is reserved for the cheese market. Houses were demolished last year to make more space and create something resembling a small square.

I venture out into the streets in the hope of seeing my family. My father will want to make the most of this opportunity to get rid of as many of his cheeses as possible before the plague comes to put a stop to his business, my mother will already have pulled up the beetroots, leeks and cabbages from the vegetable patch. But no matter how hard I look, I don't find them. Disappointed, I am about to turn and head back to my room when Bertha comes round the corner. There's no point pretending we haven't seen each other, we practically bumped into one another. She stops, visibly uncomfortable with the situation.

I hold open my arms. "I don't have the plague, Bertha."

"I never said you did. We just didn't have any room."

"If I was infected, I'd be sick by now. Half the town would have caught it."

"I know. Oh, Catrin, I'm sorry. We were scared to death when you started talking about the plague. But we were telling the truth, we didn't have any space. Although you would have been able to stay in our private quarters, of course."

"It's fine. I understand."

"You're my friend. At least, I hope you still are. I should have helped you instead of sending you away."

We embrace and Bertha asks where I'm staying. I say that it's better she doesn't know in case the bailiff comes back to make more enquiries.

"I'd never tell him. And he has other things on his plate, now that the plague is on its way. It seems people can't talk about anything else."

"When it comes to it, you both need to go away, to your family in Schagen."

"And what about the inn? We can't leave it unattended. You know what would happen."

I do know. Even though it's understandable that people flee, it doesn't make them popular with those who stay behind. Not everyone has the means to up and leave, and all too often the houses of those who run from the plague end up looted or vandalised.

"You have to go anyway," I insist. "Better to lose your inn than your life."

Bertha shakes her head despondently. "I know for a fact that Emil won't hear of it. He says God ordains who will get the plague, so there's no point running away. And I agree with him."

"I don't," I say. "God has no sympathy for the foolhardy. He gave us minds to think and feet to run, and if the plague comes, I intend to use them."

The next day our hopes that Alkmaar will be spared are dashed. The news blows through the city like a gale: nine sick!

The victims are admitted to the plague house on Paternoster Row straightaway. Not only to treat them but also to isolate them and prevent it from spreading, since in the meantime, the city has filled up with traders and farmers from the surrounding area.

I'm up early. The first cheeses are being piled up by the weighing house, every layer neatly covered with grass to protect the cheese from the sun. From seven o'clock onwards, goods can be laid out, the market begins at ten. Long before then I'm standing in front of the weighing house. From there I have a good view of the goods being delivered via the canals and the activity inside the building itself. This is where all the sold cheeses are weighed to establish how much tax is to be handed over to the city. Inside are two giant scales flanked by weighing masters who supervise the process.

Outside on the quayside, the cheeses are piled up in neat rows. It's a good deal less busy than I'd been expecting. The word "plague" is dropped constantly and from snatches of conversation I learn that many farmers turned back at the gate. My parents must have done the same, otherwise I would have seen them. Despite the growing conviction that they aren't coming, I carry on looking out for them.

To my right is the White Rose apothecary's shop, which is doing a roaring trade. There's a queue all the way to the bridge.

"Garlic and cloves," says one person. "If you chew on them all day, you're protected from the plague fumes."

An old man informs everyone that you have to spread a paste made of sourdough, pigeon droppings, onions, figs, lily bulbs and scorpion oil onto the swellings. The last ingredient is the only one that is hard to come by; he hopes the apothecary has it.

Everyone knows of a medicine. The more exotic the ingredients, the more faith people have in it. I remember that Dr Geelvinck, who treated Brigitta, recommended something too. What was it again? We were talking about the medicinal properties of laudanum. He told me there was an oriental medicine in it, opium, a wonder drug that was even said to ward off the plague.

In a rush of hope, I join the queue. Laudanum is expensive; when I picked it up for Brigitta I'd been shocked, but I have enough money with me. If it works, no price is too high.

It takes a while until I can get inside the shop. It's dingy after the glaring sunlight. My eyes slowly become accustomed to the change and an amazing display of exotic items emerges from the gloom. In cupboards that reach to the ceiling are pots and jars with mysterious labels, the shelves are covered with stones of every imaginable colour, dried salamanders, whale bone and little skeletons and tubs of peppercorns, cloves and mustard seed.

Apothecary Moeriaans peers at me enquiringly from behind the counter. I've been here many times, but not so often that he knows me. I ask for laudanum and he raises his eyebrows.

"Laudanum? For the plague?"

"Yes. It works preventively."

"Who told you that?"

"A doctor in Amsterdam."

Boudewijn Moeriaans sniffs. "Where they're dying in the streets?"

I shrug, there's no point getting into a discussion with the man. "Have you got it or not?"

"Of course we have, how much do you want?"

"How much have you got?"

It has grown quiet in the shop. The other customers are following the exchange with interest, and when Moeriaans puts one little crockery jug after another on the counter, they start muttering. After the tenth jug, I hold up my hand, I can't afford any more. This is costing me a fortune. Externally unruffled, I count out the coins. A commotion erupts behind me. I buy a bag and pack up the jugs. As I leave the apothecary's, the other customers surge forward to buy up the rest of the supply.

I'm walking back through the cheese market with the bag in my arms when I see my father. He's talking to the market master about where he can set up his cheeses, a conversation accompanied by a lot of arm-waving. The market master points to the right and when my father turns round, he sees me. His mouth falls open. He pushes his way through the crowd towards me.

246

I set off in his direction too, and at the midpoint of the square we fall into each other's arms.

"Catrin, dear God, Catrin!" he stammers.

My father has never been particularly sentimental, but now his hug almost crushes me.

"What brings you here all of a sudden? You look well!" He takes a closer look and his eyes pause on my belly. His eyes meet mine and I nod, laughing. A broad smile spreads across his face. "Where are your mother and the boys? Won't they be pleased!"

That's putting it mildly. When my mother and my brothers come strolling up, there is a joyful reunion and I'm pulled from one person to another and hugged much too tightly. They all talk at once and ask different questions at the same time, until my father puts an end to it.

"Quieten down, you lot. Catrin can't get a word in like this. We've not got time to chat anyway. We need to get this stuff sold and head home."

"There's plague in the city, Pa," I say.

"That's why we need to be quick. We heard on the way here that it had reached Alkmaar, but we were almost here by then. So we'll sell this lot, turn tail and run."

At precisely ten o'clock, the bell is rung to signal that the market is open. Despite my fear of being discovered by the sheriff, I help my mother at her stall selling fruit and vegetables. In the meantime, the boys and Pa are trading on the cheese market.

It's just the way it used to be. Now and again, I look over at my family members and a warm feeling floods

247

through me, like liquid happiness. My mother sees me looking and pinches my cheek.

"I'm so glad to see you again," she says. "And how wonderful that you're having a baby. How far along are you?"

"Five and a half months."

"Are you staying here until the birth? You're coming home with us, aren't you?"

I nod and we smile at each other.

Two hours later it's time to go. The remains of our last-sold cheeses are dribbling from the cheese carriers on the handcart as my father drops the profits into a leather wallet.

"We're off," he says.

CHAPTER
THIRTY-EIGHT

There's no time to say goodbye to Bertha and Emil. I rush back to Stien's house and gather my things. Stien isn't there, and I leave the rent I owe her on her bed. Then I grab my bundle of clothes and go out into the narrow street. Before I can close the door, I see Justice Van Veen rounding the corner, accompanied by four armed constables. One of them is walking ahead of the group carrying a long stick, the Rod of Justice, that has to be brought with them if they're carrying out an arrest.

I step back into the hall, slam the door and sprint for the yard. There, I throw my bag over the fence and climb after it with some difficulty.

I flee through gardens, courtyards and alleyways, glad that I know the city so well. After a considerable detour, I make it back to the cheese market, where my family is waiting for me in our boat.

"Gosh, don't you look hot," says Dirk as he's helping me aboard.

I say nothing, glancing over my shoulder to see if there's any danger as I sit down next to him. Dirk's gaze is watchful as he scans the quayside. He shuffles up so that his broad body obscures me from view. "Off we go, lads."

My pulse only returns to normal once we're gliding past Tree Gate, out of the city.

We've got a lot to talk about but, as always in my family, the most important things go undiscussed. The others give me a detailed description of the huge fire that consumed the village the year before and tell me about Dirk's marriage to Klara Simonsdochter. I know her, we played together as children. For my part, I tell them about my work as a housekeeper in Amsterdam and how I got the chance to work as a painter in a Delft pottery. I say nothing about Jacob. I say just as little about why I haven't been in touch, and no one asks me.

Everyone is delighted to hear that I'm having a baby.

"What a shame your husband didn't come too," my mother says. "I'd have loved to meet him."

Though we talk throughout the journey, after two hours, by which time the first farms of De Rijp are coming into view up ahead, Govert's name has still not been mentioned. But I do enquire casually about Mart.

"He's still trying to find out where you are," says my father. "But we haven't said anything."

With my face to the open water and my hair stuffed under my cap, I sit pressed up against Dirk so passers-by will mistake me for his wife. I'm relieved when we turn into the broad ditch that runs along our farm and moor up. For the first time ever, I'm glad my parents' house is so isolated.

Feeling emotional, I take in the familiar contours of the low building, the weathered thatch on the roof, the earth walls and ramshackle outbuildings.

Laurie jumps out onto the grass and gives me a hand climbing ashore.

A young woman comes running up to us, staring at me in astonishment. "Catrin!" she says, and gives me a hug. With her arm hooked through mine, she ushers me inside. "How wonderful to have you back. They've all missed you so much. How are you? Are you pregnant?"

I nod, smile at Klara and throw open the door. As soon as I'm in the kitchen, I'm overcome by a feeling of nostalgia. The pots and pans on the shelves on the wall, the long table my father made and where I ate as a little girl, the hearth with its decorative tiles of animals and people my mother used to make up stories about, the furniture I painted, it's all so familiar. I run my fingers over a flower motif on one of the cupboards and smile.

Rather than take unnecessary chances, I stay indoors as much as possible during the next few days. There's work enough to do around the farmhouse, there's no need for me to venture beyond the yard. And the plague is marching on. Alkmaar is being hit hard. From the farmyard, I can see the clouds of smoke coming from the barrels of pitch on the walls, burnt to ward off the poisonous vapours of the disease. My fearful thoughts keep turning in the same circle, from Evert to Bertha and Emil and back again.

Panic-stricken reports come to us from the boats carrying fellow villagers and people passing through along the back of the farm. It seems that in Alkmaar, several funerals are taking place at the cathedral every day. The open graves reportedly give off an appalling stench and an ever-growing number of front doors have a brass P nailed to them as a warning that there are sick people in the house.

Despite these measures, it's happening, the plague is being transmitted throughout the city. The authorities in Alkmaar aren't taking any chances: furs, skins, wool and second-hand clothes are all banned, pawnshops and clothing merchants have to cease trading. In reality, everyone is giving them a wide berth as it is, so the new by-law isn't necessary. The same applies to salesmen from elsewhere selling furs, stockings and caps; they're summarily ordered to leave town.

The farmers have to do business outside the city walls. Grain isn't banned, but the sale of vegetables and fruit is restricted. Certain products are thought to aid the spread of the disease and trade as a whole dies off as people become more cautious. Plums especially are no longer in demand because of their striking resemblance to plague buboes.

Only ten and a half miles separate De Rijp from the city and we live in constant fear that the plague will reach us. My father chases off any stranger who comes near the farmyard and forbids us all from going into the village. We become self-sufficient.

I give each of my family members a tiny jug of laudanum, which is received with the usual scepticism. There are so many cures going around that no one knows what to believe any more, but when I add that a patrician's doctor in Amsterdam recommended it, they are convinced.

One week after my return I feel my baby move for the first time on the very same day the plague arrives in De Rijp.

A village has no gates you can bar, no walls to keep out unwanted outsiders. It lies defenceless in the middle of the fields. Once, when I was a child, I longed to live in the heart of the village, right by the school and near other children so I would have someone to play with. Now I'm grateful our farm is on the outermost edge, one of the last houses before the polder landscape stretches out uninterrupted for miles.

We go about our work in tense silence, glancing up when the heavy funeral bells ring out over the fields.

August begins, swelteringly hot, with a shower of tepid rain now and again. My father and the boys are busy making hay and spend every hour of daylight out in the fields. One day I'm standing churning butter in the barn when a figure appears in the doorway, blocking the light. I look up without stopping, in the assumption that it's my father or one of my brothers. But it's Govert's brother, and his expression promises nothing good.

I drop the handle of the plunger in fright.

"Catrin," he says. "You know, I thought it was you."

It takes me a while to recover my ability to speak. "Mart . . . can I help you?"

He laughs unpleasantly. "I would say so, yes. I've been waiting a long time to see you again. A long time. I was beginning to wonder whether Jacob would ever manage to find you."

"Jacob? What do you mean?"

"He was supposed to track you down for me, but he couldn't. And now you're back all of a sudden."

"What are you talking about? Jacob found me almost straightaway, in Amsterdam. Eighteen months ago at least."

"Is that so? Then that sack of shit has been having me on. But it doesn't matter, you're here now. It's high time we had a little chat."

Govert was a big guy and his brother is no less imposing. It's unnerving, seeing him standing there with his red face, sweat patches under his arms, glowering down at me. I find myself looking around, as if I don't already know the door he's blocking is my only escape route.

"What . . . what do you want to talk about?" I ask weakly.

"About Gove. About his death. According to the bailiff, there's no proof — but you and me both know how it is. Everyone knows. You're not going to admit it, though, are you? No, you're never going to admit it."

He moves slowly in my direction, weaving slightly as if he's drunk. My hands grip the lid of the churn.

"He suffocated," says Mart. "You could see it in his eyes. The doctor said he could have choked on his own vomit. Did you see any vomit, Catrin? I didn't. A bit of spit, but not enough to choke on. According to that

254

quack, it could have been the cause. By the time I'd arranged for another doctor from Alkmaar to come and look at Govert, he was already in the ground. You were in a rush, of course, I can understand that."

I stare at him, unable to speak. There's something strange about his eyes, and his voice sounds odd. As if his tongue is swollen in his mouth. A feeling of foreboding creeps over me.

"Stay where you are," I warn.

"I only want to say hello. Let me give you a hug, Catrin."

"Stay away from me, Mart."

He pays no heed and slowly comes closer. I prepare to defend myself and then to my surprise he pulls down his trousers.

Terrified, I recoil, but he's not planning what I think. He pulls up his tunic to reveal his parts. And his groin, where a disgusting purplish-red lump stands out vividly against his white skin.

There's a ringing in my ears. I suck in my breath with a sharp sound.

"This is my parting gift to you." Mart pulls up his trousers. "I can't die without hugging my beloved sister-in-law one last time, can I? After that, everything will be forgiven and forgotten, then it's in God's hands. What is it, Catrin? You look so pale all of a sudden. Have you so little trust in His judgement?"

My knuckles are white from gripping the butter churn. There's no escape from the corner I'm standing in. I lift the lid off the churn and pull out the plunger.

"Not another step. I'll use it!" I hold up the oak handle with its heavy round end threateningly.

Mart lunges at me. He grabs the handle and tries to yank it from my grip. I hold on with all my strength and wrench the plunger out of his hands. I have no hesitation in striking out with it. The blow catches him on the shoulder. His face contorts with such a grimace of pain that I suspect there's another swelling in his armpit. There's no space for sympathy now. I lift the plunger above my head, ready to deliver another blow, but Mart throws himself forward. He trips over the butter churn and lands half on top of me. I scream and scream, with my eyes closed and his heavy, boil-covered body on top of me. Then I hear my mother's voice in the distance and stop screaming. I realise Mart is no longer moving.

Crying, my breath coming in fits and starts, I work my way out from under his body and crawl away. Leaning on the wall, I watch my mother bend over Mart with a length of wood. Klara is standing behind her, her hand over her mouth.

I stand up and look at the motionless body, filled with revulsion. "He's got the plague. Oh God, he collapsed on top of me!"

"Take off your clothes, then I'll burn them," my mother says. "Scrub yourself down under the pump. Now, Catrin, don't just stand there."

I take one more look at Mart, then turn and run out of the barn.

CHAPTER
THIRTY-NINE

I've never taken my clothes off so fast. Right there in the farmyard, in full view of anyone who might happen by.

So this is how God has decided to settle the score: through Govert's brother. How appropriate. But I don't give in that easily. I wash my body with water from the pump and dash inside to put fresh clothes on. By the time I come back outside, all that remains of my clothes is a pile of burnt remnants, which my mother is sweeping up and throwing on the rubbish heap.

Just then my father comes into the farmyard with Laurie and Dirk.

"I saw smoke," he says, looking in confusion at the blackened patch on the ground.

My mother waves him over and opens the barn door, which she'd locked. "He attacked Catrin." She nods towards Mart's body. "He's got the plague."

My father, who had been about to go in, freezes at the word. "The plague?"

"What was he doing here?" Dirk asks.

"He came for Catrin."

We all stare down at Mart. My father doesn't say a word, neither do the boys. Mart is slowly coming round and groans.

257

"What do we do with him?" asks Laurie.

"Nothing," my father says, turning away abruptly. "Leave him to fend for himself. Don't go near him."

At the end of the day, I slip into the barn, despite the ban. From a safe distance, I look at Mart, who's lying on his back staring at the ceiling. He slowly turns his head in my direction and opens his mouth, revealing a swollen, blackened tongue. I take a step back, trembling.

"Don't leave," he says. The words are almost unintelligible. "Please."

I turn, ignoring his strangled cries, and grab a wooden cup from the shelf. I fill it at the pump and go back. I don't dare get too close; I set it on the ground and nudge it over to Mart using a broom. He puts his lips to the edge and drinks.

I watch him as he does. It's a fearful sight: there's blood coming from his nose and mouth, his eyes are bright with fever. Where his tunic is hitched up, I can see purple and black blotches underneath his skin. And swellings, even more than there were this morning.

Next to his head is an empty mug, so someone else has been in here and whoever it was gave him water too. We can do no more.

"Catrin," he says hoarsely as I'm turning to leave.

I look down at him, waiting.

"Govert . . . did you do it or not?"

For a second I'm fighting an internal battle, then I murmur, "Does it even matter any more?"

He slowly shakes his head and looks up, as if he can already glimpse where he's going.

When my father goes to check on him the next morning, Mart is dead. Pa and Laurie wind the body in a sheet and drag it to the edge of the road. It will be collected tomorrow by a cart, along with all the other victims of the plague.

My mother and I clean the barn with buckets of hot water, then burn all our clothes. After that, the barn door is bolted and we go back to our daily chores.

For days we keep a close eye on each other and ourselves. Every little cough, the tiniest rise in body temperature or slight headache is cause for concern. My condition is monitored especially closely. When I wake up, the first thing I do is check my armpits and inner thighs. I run my hands over my body again and again, looking and feeling. I prod with my fingers and each time I don't find anything under my skin I feel a surge of relief. The rest of the day I stay alert, because the plague can appear at any time. Along with the others, I take laudanum three times a day. It makes me calmer, a bit listless. Whether because of the laudanum or because I still have some kind of credit left with God, I don't know, but I don't get sick and neither does my family. After a week, I dare to believe we've escaped the plague.

The sickness has blown through the village like a gale, leaving many victims in its wake. We also hear second- and third-hand news of the situation in Alkmaar. When I see a pedlar going past one day, I run to the edge of the farmyard and ask him whether he knows anything about the inn, the Thirteen Beams.

"The one near Goblin Gate, miss? Yes, that one's closed. There's a big P nailed to the door."

I stare at the man in shock. "They can't both be . . ."

"If one gets the plague it's usually not long before the other does. But who knows, miss. There are people who survive. Don't give up hope."

I try not to, but it isn't easy.

The next day someone comes along who confirms the Thirteen Beams is shut and the innkeeper and his wife have both died. That night, I cry myself to sleep.

By mid-August, the number of new cases of the plague in Alkmaar is going down and I start to think about returning to Delft.

My mother would rather keep me home until the birth, but it's too long a wait for me. My belly is already getting in the way and if I wait any longer, travelling will be too difficult. Travelling *after* the birth doesn't seem like a good idea. Besides which, I want to go back. I miss Evert and I worry. Not just about him but about my friends. There are so many contradictory reports about the situation in different cities that I have no idea what to expect.

On a cloudy, windy day, I leave. Saying goodbye is especially hard when we don't know how long it will be before we see each other again. My father gives up a day of work to take me some of the way on his cart.

As we're trundling along towards Zaanstreek, my father says, "I'm not happy about you travelling on your own like this. And in your condition, too. How are you going to get all the way to Delft?"

"I want to take the horse-boat from Haarlem."

"If they find out where you're from, they'll never take you. Everyone from the North is under suspicion."

"I know. If I have to, I'll walk." I watch the landscape go by for a while, lost in thought. "Don't you think it strange, Pa, that there's been no plague in Haarlem and other towns?"

"The people in the towns that were hit probably sinned more. It gets to the point where God's had enough."

"He seems to have more patience with some people than others."

My father glances sidelong at my face. "I don't know why either, love. You never get a good answer to questions like that, not even from the Church. We've all got to try and lead good lives as best we can."

"And is that enough?"

"I think so. We're alive, we're healthy, the plague passed us by. So we must have been doing something right."

We pass the hamlet of Spykerboor and take the road to Knollendam. From there I'll carry on alone. I stare straight ahead, vacillating about what I'm about to confess.

"Pa, there's something I need to tell you."

He lets the reins drop onto the horse's back and shakes his head. "No, child," he says, "you don't need to tell me anything."

We say goodbye on the path along the dyke bordering the Zaan River. A hug, a kiss and my father turns the cart around. He waves and begins his journey home. The reeds rustle in the wind as I watch him leave. It's not until he disappears behind a stand of trees that I turn away and pick up my bundle.

If I get a move on, I can reach Haarlem before nightfall.

CHAPTER
FORTY

It's a long but not unpleasant walk. The dyke takes me from Knollendam to Assendelft alongside the gently babbling water and past dozens of wood mills. I can rely on them for a drink of water, sometimes even a mug of milk. There are taverns where I can rest and have something to eat, and they have bandages to bind my painful feet.

A farmer sees my swollen belly and offers me a lift on his cart all the way to Westzaan. The plague bypassed this area and feels far away. I enjoy the meadow landscape, the buzzards and hen harriers circling high above my head and the quiet villages we pass through.

In Westzaan, I bid farewell to the farmer and wander around the harbour a little. It's crammed with windmills and sawmills as well as boats from near and far. It doesn't take much to find a cheap spot on one of the barges which stand ready to leave, brown sails clattering and snapping in the wind. The captain tells me I can forget about Haarlem, no one is being let in. The plague is raging through Leiden, so he can't go there either.

"I'm dropping my cargo off in Spaarnwoude, from there the Haarlemmers can fetch what they need themselves. And then I'm going back to Zaandam, it's safe there," he says.

"Do you know anyone who could take me further?"

He nods. "It should be fine. Where are you headed? Delft? That's a long way from Spaarnwoude."

"Is the plague still going around in Delft?"

"Not according to the latest reports."

"How bad was it there?"

"Not so bad as in Leiden or Amsterdam, but the funeral bells were ringing out a fair bit there too."

With a mind consumed by fearful thoughts, I settle down amidst the cargo and don't say another word for the whole journey.

I stay the night in Spaarnwoude. The horse-drawn barges are no longer running, but the captain who dropped me off arranges for me to transfer to a different boat the next day. Now that the regular connection has been severed, there's an enormous traffic of other barges, dinghies and rafts on the canals and waterways. Anything that can float is being pressed into service.

Outside the city walls, business is still going on, even around Leiden, the city the scariest stories have been told about. Our skipper keeps sailing right on past. He sets me down in Leiderdorp and heads in the other direction. I stop at an inn for the night and get back on the road early the next day.

Sadly, I don't manage to find anyone willing to take me. No one's willing to risk having a stranger to the area on board. No one's willing to take me overland in the back of their cart either.

"You say you're not from Leiden, but I've no way of checking," says a farmer with a cart full of beetroot. "I don't think anybody will take the risk, miss."

There's nothing for it but to walk the last stretch. I can't go very fast, but even at my slow pace I can get home today.

I follow the towpath along the Vliet River, which leads in a straight line to Delft. I'm tormented by blisters, even through the bandages. When it gets so bad I can't take another step, I rest, but never for too long. This close to home, every moment of delay is one too many. For a long time, I've managed to keep the torturous uncertainty about Evert's fate at the back of my mind, but now there's no avoiding it. I need to know how he is, whether he's ill, whether he's still alive.

I keep on walking, blindly putting one foot in front of the other, ignoring my exhaustion. No one offers me a lift and I don't ask for one. Almost every house I pass tells the same story, with a bundle of straw or the letter P on its door. In the hamlets I pass through, there's a heavy stench that sticks in my chest. I'd prefer to bypass all the villages, but it would be too much of a detour. So I go through them, passing along silent streets that seem to have had the life leeched out of them. Many of the shops and houses have been boarded shut, the marketplaces are empty. Even with my feet hurting so terribly, I find myself speeding up. Each time I leave a ghost village like that behind, I heave a sigh of relief.

Halfway through the day, I get hungry. The walls of Delft seem close but I'm not home and dry yet. Certainly not with an empty stomach. I turn onto a path leading to a farm and walk into the yard. A dog on a chain is barking madly. No one comes. My gaze goes to the front door and I don't see a P.

I'd prefer not to go into the farmhouse without permission but there doesn't seem to be anyone here so I have no choice. I stand on the threshold to the kitchen and call out a couple of times. No one appears. There's bread, fruit and cheese on the low table. I eye them greedily but keep moving.

I carefully push the door open. A dark hallway stretches out before me. I hear a noise from somewhere inside and freeze. I listen, alert. The sound doesn't come again, but suddenly there's a foul smell in the air around me. I turn, about to leave, but then I hear the sound again. Something thumping on wood.

Even though there's a voice in my head screaming at me to run, I don't. I open the nearest door which, as I had expected, leads into the living room. I'm hit by a terrible stench, a smell I've come to know all too well.

Someone is lying in the box bed. The thumps are coming from the hands and feet lashing out inside, accompanied by strangled cries and now and then a wailing gurgle. My heart's in my throat from fear and horror. From a distance I can see it's not a grown-up lying there but a child.

I slowly walk over to the bed, every step a victory over my own instincts. It's a little girl, seven at most.

Damp, blonde hair sticks to her face, which is flushed bright red from the fever. Her chest is heaving but she still doesn't seem to be getting enough air. A thin sheet half covers her, heavy with sweat and pus. Her fragile little body has at least six dark blue swellings and various other bruises, her whole body is tinged an unnatural colour.

"Oh my God," I whisper.

You don't have to be a doctor to see this girl is a lost cause. I know a little about medicinal herbs for minor ailments like a sore throat or problems during your monthlies, but what can you give someone who's dying of the plague? The little bit of laudanum I still have won't save her. At most, it will offer some relief.

I go to get my bag, which I've left standing by the kitchen door. As soon as I come into the kitchen, I know something has changed. There's less light coming inside. In the same instant I see why: the doorway is blocked by a man, and he's glaring at me.

CHAPTER
FORTY-ONE

For a few beats everything is quiet, then I say, "I'm sorry, I heard someone calling out."

He says nothing but continues to glare at me. Now that I look more closely, I see he's still a boy. No older than fifteen, I reckon, very tall and with a split in his top lip that goes all the way to his nose.

"I just wanted to get my things. There's something to drink in there that can help that little girl." I gesture to my bundle.

After a long look, he grabs my bag and hands it to me.

Relieved, I put it on the table and rifle through it. The boy comes to stand beside me.

"That girl in the bed, she must be your sister," I say.

He nods.

"What's her name?"

"Wilhelmina. She's sick."

"Yes, I saw."

"She's dying."

Something in his behaviour and the way he talks is odd, and it's not because of his harelip. I study him for a moment before continuing.

"I can't make her better," I say gently. "But I can make sure she's in less pain. Do you think that's a good idea?"

He nods and I pull out my last little jug of laudanum. As we're walking back to the living room he says, "First they get sick and then they die. All of them."

"Apart from you. Why is that?"

He shrugs.

"What's your name?" I ask.

"Lucas."

"I'm Catrin. Are there any other people in the house, Lucas?"

"They're all dead. Are you going to die too?"

"I'm not planning on it." That reminds me, I still need to take my laudanum. I remember seeing mugs in the cupboard when I was in here before. I grab three of them and pour a slug of laudanum into each one. I give one to Lucas and drain another myself.

Lucas eyes the yellowish liquid suspiciously. "What is it?"

"Drink up, then you won't get ill."

While Lucas is pulling a face and draining his mug, I see to Wilhelmina. I don't really want to touch her but there's no other way. She needs to sit up to be able to drink. I stuff an extra pillow under her head so she's more upright and I can let the laudanum trickle in between her cracked lips. She drinks greedily, as if she's past being able to tell how bitter it is.

"Mama," she mumbles, and grabs my hand.

I stiffen, but I can't bring myself to pull it away.

"Hush now," I say gently as she begins to cry. "I'm here." I brush the damp hair off her face and feel my heart overflow with pity. To quiet her, I sing an old lullaby while the laudanum begins to do its work. The taut expression on her pinched little face begins to fade and it's not long before she falls asleep. I carefully withdraw my hand.

"Is she dead?" asks Lucas, who's been standing behind me the whole time.

"No, she's sleeping."

"Ma went to sleep too, but she didn't wake up."

I come away from the bedside and ask, "Where is your mother now?"

Lucas beckons and leads me back through the kitchen and outside. I notice then what I failed to see when I came in. In the yard, next to the outbuildings are six freshly dug graves.

That night I sleep alongside Wilhelmina on the floor with the windows wide open to get rid of the smell. I daren't use the bedding belonging to her deceased family members so I'm lying on my bundle.

I'm no longer afraid of the plague, or maybe I'm simply too worn down to keep on resisting the inevitable. If my time's up, it's up. I'm no longer willing to be driven on, nor am I prepared to abandon a dying child. If you do get what you deserve, then let God take note of that.

It's a restless night, during which I frequently stumble, half-asleep, over to the bed to give Wilhelmina something to drink or comfort her. By the time dawn comes, there's blood trickling from her nose and mouth. I stay by her side until she dies, her hand in mine.

In the morning, Lucas reappears. I have no idea where he spent the night but wherever it was, it wasn't on the farm. Maybe he prefers the open air, which isn't hard to understand. He has two dead hares dangling in one hand. I'd been finding little pelts all over the house and now it's clear who the poacher in the family is. It wouldn't surprise me if Lucas spent most of his time wandering around the neighbourhood, even when his family was ill. That's probably why he's still alive.

I give him his dose of laudanum, take my own dose and gently prepare him for the news that his sister has died. He barely reacts. In a few steps he's at the bedside, looking down at the emaciated little body. He turns on his heel and stalks out of the room.

I find him in the yard, digging the seventh grave.

"Wouldn't you rather give your sister a Christian burial?" I ask. "We can have her picked up."

Lucas shakes his head and carries on digging. I watch for a while and reflect that he probably prefers to keep his family together than see them in a mass grave. They will be reburied later.

Once the hole is deep enough, we go back into the farmhouse together, wrap Wilhelmina in a sheet, carry her out to the grave and lay her down in it. Lucas fills it, I pick some of the yellow roses that grow next to the house with an exuberant beauty that is jarring. I adorn each grave with a couple of roses. We stand gazing at them for a while in silence.

"Is there anyone you can go to?" I ask finally. "Have you got family in the area?"

"Uncle Jan and Aunty Barbara in Delft."

"Then you must go to them."

He shakes his head. "I want to stay here."

This is unthinkable, of course. He's too young to live alone on a farm. It's probably a tenant farm, since I've seen no valuables to suggest any level of prosperity. The animals might be theirs, but I doubt it. The landowner will soon lease the farm to someone else and they'd have to find somewhere for Lucas to go. It's clear he isn't normal and can't be treated like your average fifteen-year-old. This, combined with his harelip, leaves him few options. I can picture him leading a life of vagrancy, being exploited by employers or put on display at the fair. People can be very harsh when it comes to someone who's different.

"We can go together. I need to go to Delft too." I look at him and wait, half expecting him to shake his head again. To my surprise, he nods and walks back into the house. When I go after him to see what he's doing, I find him packing his things.

Whether we're allowed to or not, we are taking the horse and cart. I search the house for valuable items and pack them into a sack. Lucas probably doesn't attach much importance to them, but this could change one day. I take something from each member of his family: Wilhelmina's doll, the decorative clips his mother used to fasten her lace cap, his father's pipe, a

272

hairbrush belonging to an older sister, his little brothers' catapults and caps. I never get to know their names: Lucas refuses to talk about them.

While he's hitching up the horse, I milk the cows, which are lowing piteously. It's a familiar task and I'm done in a jiffy. We take the milk with us in small cans with lids. Even the remaining food, like cheese and dried sausages, is loaded up, and I pick all the fruit from the trees for good measure. Even the plums, despite their bad reputation. I can't imagine, after all I've been through, that I'm going to catch the plague by eating a plum. Finally, I untie the dog, which runs off immediately.

After that, I climb onto the cart and Lucas comes and sits next to me. As we drive out of the farmyard, I take one last glance over my shoulder at the little row of graves.

Lucas stares straight ahead.

CHAPTER
FORTY-TWO

We reach Delft shortly after midday. We drive under the imposing archway of The Hague Gate and trundle into town. Throughout the journey, I've been in such a state of fearful tension that the reins are sticking to my damp palms. I continuously scan the streets for signs of how bad the plague has been here. I'm pleased. I see fewer Ps nailed to the doors along Old Delft Street than I had expected.

Following Lucas's directions, I drive to Molen Street where his family lives. They have a bakery and Uncle Jan has just come out to blow his horn, signalling that there's fresh bread. At least, I assume it's Uncle Jan because Lucas is waving to him.

The man lets go of the horn and approaches us slowly. He stops at a distance. "Lucas," he says.

I jump down from the driving seat and introduce myself. In a few short sentences I tell him how I came to know his nephew and that the rest of the family is dead.

"They're dead? All of them?" A look of defeat appears on Jan's face, and at the same time he takes a step backwards. "And now you're bringing him here? Do you want us to get the plague too?"

"Lucas isn't sick. If he'd been infected, we'd be seeing it by now. You're his uncle, can you take him in?"

Jan doesn't answer straightaway. A thin woman with a pinched face appears behind him, looking us up and down. "Who are they, Jan? Oh God in heaven, is that Lucas?" For a second she's astounded, then she realises why her nephew's on her doorstep.

"Cornelis and Maria are dead," she whispers.

"Are they Lucas's parents?" I ask.

"Yes. Maria's my sister. And the other children? Are they all . . ."

I nod.

Tears appear in Barbara's eyes but she makes no moves to welcome her nephew. Lucas stays sitting in the wagon and stares down at his aunt and uncle expressionlessly.

"He hasn't got the plague," I say.

"No, it doesn't look like it." Barbara hesitates for a second before walking over to the cart. "Come down, lad, then we'll go inside. Are these your things?"

"It's all his, apart from this." I grab my pack out of the back. "If you've got any more questions, I live on The Gheer. The Lotus Flower pottery."

"We know it," says Jan.

"Do you know if . . ." Afraid to hear the answer, I stop talking halfway through my question.

They both shake their heads. "We never go to that part of town," says Jan.

"I understand. I'll just have to go and see. All the best, Lucas."

"Bye," he says.

I nod, turn and walk away.

I rush back through town to my house. On the market square I glance anxiously at the Mechelen Inn, which thankfully has no P on the door. I stride over the square and go up Corn Market, which leads onto The Gheer. As I go, I count the Ps and bundles of straw on the doors and feel a cautious optimism begin to grow. When The Lotus Flower comes into view I break into a run over the last stretch.

The shock of the huge white P on the door is like a blow to the chest. All the air is knocked out of me, I can feel myself growing faint. I stand frozen in front of the door to the pottery. It can't be true.

The shop has been boarded shut, the fold-down hatches from the windows are floating uselessly in the canal, all life has been extinguished. I go to the window and peer inside through a gap between two planks. The goods are in the shop as usual. There's no one to be seen.

"Catrin?"

I turn quickly. Jacob is standing behind me with his cap in his hands.

"You're back," he says.

I look at him without saying anything, trying to put off the inevitable question. But I don't even need to ask, the answer is written all over Jacob's face.

"Evert?" I whisper.

"It was quick. He got a boil and it was all over. Some people fight for days, but it wasn't like that." He keeps

276

turning his cap over and over in his hands and sighs. "The employees all fled. Anna had already gone. Suddenly there was no one left. That's why I just nailed the whole thing shut."

The sadness that wells up in me is so raw I'm gasping for breath. I wobble and Jacob grabs my arm.

"Come with me," he says.

He takes me to Angelika and Quentin, who receive me with open arms. They take me to the living room and give me red wine to bring a little colour back to my cheeks.

I listen numbly to their story of Evert's last days and his concern for me. They say he made them promise to look after me. They confirm that he didn't suffer for long and died quicker than they'd all expected. And then the conversation turns to the other victims we know, like Adelaide and her twins. Isaac is the only one left, spared because he was away on business in Haarlem. By the time he came back to Delft, his wife and children had already been buried.

Anna died too. A couple of days after I left, she fled to a niece in Leiden to escape the plague. She found herself in the very city where the plague wrought the most havoc. Her children, who stayed in Delft and remain in good health, brought the sad tidings.

The terrible news strikes me dumb. There's no next step with grief, you only have as many tears as your body can produce. At a certain point, you can't even cry any more, you just go very quiet.

I slowly get up.

"What are you going to do?" asks Angelika.

"I'm going home," I say. "Quentin, Jacob, could you take those planks off the windows please? I want to go inside."

There's an uncanny silence in the workshop. The vats of tin glaze, the potter's wheels and the crates of finished pottery are standing there as if it's a normal Sunday and the work's going to go on as usual tomorrow. Only the dried-out paint in the pots and the cold ovens reveal there's nothing more going on. Now that the planks have been removed from the windows, sunlight is streaming in again, revealing the layer of dust covering the trays of earthenware and the tables.

"If there's anything I can do for you . . ." says Quentin.

Without turning around I say, "I'd just like to be alone for a while."

Their footsteps retreat, the door closes. I take a deep breath, shut my eyes and let the pain come.

"Evert," I whisper.

Over the past few weeks I've imagined our reunion so often it's hard to believe I'm never going to see him again, that he has vanished from my life without my being able to care for him in his final hours, without my being able to say a proper goodbye. What did he feel when he discovered the swelling? Did he think of me when the fever wracked his body and internal bleeding made him weak? And where was he buried? In the church or in a mass grave, as often happens during an epidemic? I hope with all my heart it was the church.

278

I wander aimlessly through the empty workshops, through the shop, and go upstairs. There's a musty air in the living quarters, the smell of rooms where windows have not been opened for a long time. Otherwise it's as though Evert could return at any moment. A plate of beans and fish untouched on the table, a jug of stale beer next to it. An accounts book open on the table, which he was probably leafing through when the plague overcame him.

The sheets and the straw mattress have been taken off the bed. The regulations dictate that whenever anyone dies of the plague, their bedding has to be burnt to prevent infection.

I stare down at the empty bed for a couple of seconds, then I throw open the windows.

Evert has been laid to rest in the New Church. Accompanied by Quentin, Angelika, Johannes and Digna, I visit his grave. I stand for a long time staring down at the flagstones with the inscription and trying to imagine him lying under them. Still in a state of disbelief, I squat down and trace the letters of his name.

Matthias should be here, and Adriaan. I sent word to Amsterdam and got a letter back saying Adriaan was recuperating from the plague and too weak to travel. Brigitta was fine. And Matthias is sailing in some far-flung corner of the globe with no inkling of what's been going on here.

Maybe he'll never come back, he'll stay away in that unknown world. Maybe he's dead too.

"You made Evert very happy, Catrin," says Johannes. "And he hadn't been a happy man for a long time. I'm glad he had a few wonderful months."

I simply nod and walk over to Adelaide's grave. We pray, then stand talking for a while before slowly leaving the church.

"Maybe it's a little early to be asking, but do you know what you're going to do now?" Angelika asks once we're home. She has come back with me and we're having a drink in a sunny corner of the abandoned yard.

I take a sip of beer and shake my head. "No idea."

"You could sell the company. It's going well, it'll bring in a pile of money. And it's yours now."

That's true. I don't need to go looking for a job, I don't need to keep house for anyone or mop a kitchen, I've got a business. A business I don't know the first thing about.

"There's interest in The Lotus Flower. A couple of people have already enquired about whether it's going on the market."

"I don't know," I say. "It doesn't feel right."

"I understand, lovey, I really do. You played a big part in its success, it will be hard to see it passing into other hands. But what are you supposed to do, with Evert gone? As his widow, you've got the right to continue his business, but as a woman, you're not entitled to sign contracts. You have to leave the business side of things to a man."

"I can take on a foreman."

280

"Or you can sell the company to Quentin and me, and come to work for us. We could do with a good painter."

"Do you mean that?"

"Of course. We'll pay you a good wage."

I turn my gaze to where Quentin and Jacob are filling in the nail-holes in the window frames with a mixture of sawdust and wood glue.

Kicking in my belly distracts me and I look down. What would Evert have wanted? For me to be able to provide for myself and our child, for starters. Undoubtedly, he'd have liked to pass his company on to his child, be it a boy or a girl. What I want has nothing to do with it, I owe it to him to try and keep The Lotus Flower going.

CHAPTER
FORTY-THREE

It turns out to be no trouble finding new workers. As soon as I let it be known I'm going to reopen The Lotus Flower, they stream in from all over. Highly skilled craftspeople, some of them from far away to the south, who fled when the plague was raging in Flanders. I take on a new housekeeper, Hilly, a young woman in her early twenties who knows how to work.

And in all fairness, Jacob is a great help too. Who would have thought I'd ever value him like this? Together we judge the suitability of the potters, painters, treaders, bailers and stokers who come asking for work. I'm the one who makes the final decision, but Jacob asks such good questions and has such reasonable arguments that I can't ignore his opinion.

I rehire Klaas and Lambert, who both took refuge from the plague with their families nearby and are glad to be able to get back to work. Jacob doesn't see them as an asset and tries to change my mind, but I dig my heels in. Evert never complained about these lads, and he'd definitely have kept them on.

"It's your funeral," says Jacob, shrugging. "The problem isn't that they're young, it's that they're slow, too. Lazy. But for the time being, we need people. We can always get rid of them later."

He's using the word "we" a lot, I notice, but I don't say anything about it. It's probably an expression of his investment. As long as it's clear who's in charge, I don't much care.

One week after my return, I find Frans on my doorstep. "I heard you were back," he says. "And that Evert's dead."

"Yes."

"I'm sorry. My condolences."

I nod.

"Is it true The Lotus Flower is opening again?"

"Yes, in a few days."

"Are *you* going to run the company?"

"Yes. I'd like you to come back, Frans. I need you."

Frans observes me in silence for a few seconds. "How are you going to go about it?"

"As a widow, I'm entitled to continue my husband's business. I just need a master potter, and someone who can deal with the business side of things for me."

"And have you got anyone?"

"Not yet. Jacob is helping me, but he doesn't know anything of those matters."

Frowning, Frans's eyes wander up along the gable of the shop. "I do. Evert always included me in his deals."

"Excellent, then you can deal with the administration, the contracts, the deliveries, that sort of thing, and I'll run the studio. We'll hire someone to take care of the kilns."

"I want a raise."

"You'll get one," I say, and hold the door open a little wider.

Hard work is an excellent remedy for grief. It doesn't fill the emptiness in your soul but it does ensure you've got no time to dwell on it for long. I miss Evert, I miss his sturdy, warm body, his deep voice and the loving way he looked at me. Will anyone else ever look at me like that again? Fine, Jacob, but that's different. His eyes seem to burn through my clothing, no matter how many layers I've got on.

Whenever we need to discuss business matters, I make sure I'm not alone with him. And there's plenty to discuss. Quentin helps me find a master potter, Christiaan Zegers, who has only been living with his family in Delft for a short time. Once he's in the picture, everything falls into place in no time. The Lotus Flower comes back to life. Carts full of clay roll into the yard and dump their loads into brick troughs, so the air bubbles can be stamped out of them. In the workshops, potters are sitting behind their wheels, the vats are filled with tin glaze and the ovens are brought up to temperature. White-and-blue pottery is being produced again and business is booming. That I, a woman, am running the company doesn't seem to bother anyone, as long as they get a good-quality product. And they do. It has a perfectly glazed surface and the cobalt blue decorations are skilful and precise.

We get so many orders that the drying tables are full of clay plates, bowls and platters waiting until they're

284

dry enough to go in the kiln. I free up space in the attic of the living quarters so we can dry pieces there too.

One day I'm busy in the attic when someone comes clumping up the ladder. I glance over my shoulder and see Jacob's head appear out of the trapdoor. I straighten up immediately.

"I came to see whether you needed any help," says Jacob as he enters.

"No, I won't until later on this afternoon. The potters are still busy making everything. I'm getting some space ready."

"This is a lovely room. Nice and big."

I nod and turn my back, hoping he'll go away. And I hear footsteps, but they're coming closer. When I turn to face him, he's right behind me. I recoil but he immediately takes another step towards me. He says nothing, just looks at me and I know what's coming.

"Jacob, don't . . ." I say. He pulls me to him and presses his mouth to mine. I wrestle free from his grip and glare at him.

"What the hell are you thinking!"

"Come on, Catrin. You can't honestly say you don't feel something between us."

"I feel nothing. Oh, except annoyance about you coming up here to bother me. Go downstairs and leave me alone."

He looks at me, stunned, then chuckles lightly. "Always so stubborn. A man has to make an effort to get you, eh? You like that. Well, I think that's all well and good, but we've been playing that game for long enough. I want things to be clear."

"Game? What are you talking about? I think I've made myself abundantly clear."

For a second, my reaction seems to wrong-foot him but he soon recovers. He puts his hands in his pockets to show he won't touch me again. "I love you."

Now it's my turn to be surprised. "What did you say?"

"You heard me. I love you. I want you. I was already in love with you back when you were married to Govert."

I can hardly believe my ears. "Then you've got a funny way of showing it."

"Why? I've never done you any harm, have I? I protected you."

"You threatened me, blackmailed me and demanded half my savings."

Jacob heaves a sigh. "Are we back on that again? I did you a huge favour by keeping my mouth shut and in exchange for that you gave me a helping hand when I was broke. Wasn't that a fair exchange? Catrin, listen, giving you up was the last thing I would have done. Mart hired me to track you down, but I never told him where you were. Why? Because I've always known we're meant for each other. Don't you see how alike we are? We're two of a kind. We know what we want and won't let anyone stop us from getting it."

In the silence that follows, I can't think of anything to say except that he's got the whole thing wrong, but that doesn't seem a sensible thing to say while I'm alone with him here in the attic. We stare at each other until Jacob pipes up again.

"I've overwhelmed you," he says. "It's too soon after Evert's death, even if we both know why you married him. Not that I blame you, I understand completely. Just let me know when you're ready for a new relationship. I'll wait for you."

And with those words, he turns and goes downstairs.

CHAPTER
FORTY-FOUR

Sometimes, when you think you understand life with all its highs and lows, when you think it can no longer throw you with all its terrible surprises, it takes a turn you hadn't foreseen. I have no idea how to handle this situation, or what Jacob will do if I refuse him. At the same time, I ask myself whether I haven't judged him wrongly. It doesn't matter, I'm not attracted to him. I don't need him either, there are enough suitors who will appreciate the charms of a widow with a successful business. Remarrying is the best option for most women when they find themselves on their own, but for now I have no desire whatsoever to find another husband.

One Saturday morning, after I've handed out the wages, Klaas stays behind. He waits until everyone else has left the office. "I'd like to say something," he says. I wait expectantly.

"I just wanted to say I'm glad you carried on the company. The boss would've liked that."

"I think so, too." I smile warmly.

"And I haven't said so before, but I think it's a real shame he's gone."

"Yes," I say softly.

"I don't understand it either. I was afraid I'd get sick, too. The boss said it was only a cold and he didn't have the plague, so I didn't need to go. Then he showed me he didn't have any swellings, so I stayed. The next day he didn't appear, and when Frans went to look, he was dead."

"Sit down, Klaas. Tell me, how long was my husband ill? When did it start?"

"He had a bad cold for a couple of days. He said it wasn't the plague and it didn't seem like it either. No one knew exactly how the plague looks when it starts, so we were worried. A couple of lads left then, not wanting to take the chance. Because the boss was so sure it wasn't anything serious, and because he didn't have any boils, I stayed on. He really needed me once half of the lads had gone."

"That was very loyal of you. And then? Did he get a fever, was he in any pain?"

"He was tired. Mistress Angelika van Cleynhoven came by and I heard the boss telling her he was going to go to bed early."

"Was Mistress van Cleynhoven worried?"

"At first she was. She asked him a few questions about what was ailing him, and then she said he should have a long sleep and it would get better."

It could be that the plague struck him down in a single evening. I've heard stories of that happening. And Evert *had* been under the weather for a few days before that. But I still don't see how it could have carried him off so fast. "Who was the last person to see my husband, Klaas?"

"Jacob," says the boy. "He made some medicine and went upstairs with a little cup to give the boss."

I try to picture the room as I saw it when I came home. There was no cup. "What kind of medicine was it?"

Klaas shrugs. "It was a funny colour. Once I'd cleaned the workshop I came upstairs too. I knew I wasn't supposed to, I had no business going into the boss's house, but Jacob had been gone for so long and I wanted to see if I could help. I was halfway up the stairs when he came down. He sent me away and said the boss was sleeping."

"How did Jacob seem when you saw him? Did he jump?"

"A bit. Not much, he just waved me away and told me to go back downstairs."

"Did you happen to go back and have another look later on?"

Klaas shakes his head. "I believed him, I thought the boss was sleeping."

Something in his tone grabs my attention. "You believed him then, but not later?"

"The next day, when I heard the boss was dead, I kept thinking about that medicine. Jacob came downstairs with the empty cup and held it a bit behind him. Something dribbled out of it and when I went to look the next day I saw something on the ladder. Only a tiny bit, but it had dried into the wood completely. I keep on wondering what sort of medicine it could be."

Our eyes meet. The silence between us is pregnant with unspoken thoughts.

290

"Thank you, Klaas," I say. "Let's agree to keep this between us."

As soon as Klaas has left, I jump up to go and examine the ladder in my house.

That same evening, I'm sitting in the living room at Angelika and Quentin's. They were about to have their dinner when I came in, so I was invited to join them. During the meal, surrounded by the children, I don't raise the topic I wish to discuss, but as soon as they've gone to bed, I bring up Evert's final days.

Angelika and Quentin exchange worried glances. They were naturally under the impression that I was doing better than this and have no desire to distress me again. But apparently I seem calm enough because Angelika tells me what I want to hear.

"I did go and see him in the late afternoon. He wasn't feeling well — he had a sore throat and he was very tired — but he wasn't too worried about it, or he was pretending not to be; I'm not sure which. I advised him to go to bed early and he said he would. That's the last time I saw him."

"And the next day, when you heard that he'd died?"

"That's when I went to your house," says Quentin. "Frans had found Evert dead and came to tell me. He was lying there, quite peacefully, as if he'd died in his sleep. The plague must have done its work quickly. That's often the way."

"How do you know he had the plague? Did you see swellings?"

"No, he was covered in sheets up to his chest. I didn't look underneath them because I saw a blue-black tinge around his neck. To be honest, I didn't dare go near him."

"And Frans?"

"Frans didn't touch him. He was right behind me when I left the room."

"And then the body collectors came and picked him up?" I say.

Quentin nods. "I'm sorry, Catrin," he says, without saying exactly what he's sorry about; probably that he stayed away from his best friend while he was sick, and that after his death he made it no further than the doorway.

I thank my friends for the meal and walk back to The Gheer. The days are getting shorter again, the mist is creeping onto the canal earlier each day. Lights are burning in the workshop from candles and ovens that never go out. Frans is on the evening and night shift and is just arriving with a basket of wood as I come in. We've never spoken in any detail about the circumstances surrounding Evert's death. I ask about them, but I don't learn much from his story. He confirms what Quentin told me. Evert was lying peacefully in his bed. The only things that showed him to have been a victim of the plague were the bruises around his chest and throat.

"There must have been a swelling somewhere too," I say.

"There probably was, but I didn't see it." Frans gives an apologetic shrug. "And I didn't look for one either, Catrin. I didn't dare touch him."

292

"I understand," I say.

And I do understand, all too well. Not only what Frans said but everything. I suspected it this afternoon when I examined the mark on the ladder, and I know for sure once I go upstairs and search the box bed. Since my homecoming I've not slept in there. Even though the infected bedding and the straw mattress are gone, I still don't dare lie in it. There's another box bed in the kitchen and I'm using that now. Otherwise I would have seen the conspicuous smear on the wood inside our own bedframe much sooner.

CHAPTER
FORTY-FIVE

That night I don't sleep a wink. Hour after hour, thoughts churn in my mind and I don't drift off until shortly before dawn. Not for long. When I wake up, it feels like I've only just closed my eyes. I don't know what's woken me. It's Sunday and outside on the usually bustling street, a serene peace reigns.

Sitting at the window, with a view of the empty yard, I think through my plans one more time. The conversation I'm about to have will be the start of enormous problems, but could also put an end to the disquiet in my mind.

I dress smartly, put on my prettiest lace cap and, after a light breakfast, walk over to the New Church. Evert and I always took this walk together; now there's a painful absence next to me. But that doesn't last for long. On my way, I encounter so many acquaintances that we end up arriving at the church in a big group. As I take my seat, my eyes travel to Isaac, sitting in his pew with a bowed head and without his wife and children. There are many Delft families in mourning, but no one has been hit as hard as him.

After the service, I make sure I end up next to him as we're walking back up the aisle.

"Catrin." He smiles weakly.

"How are you?"

"Hmm . . . I think you can probably imagine."

I nod.

"And you? Are you managing?"

"I am."

"It must be hard to find yourself a widow for the second time in eighteen months."

"It's not easy, but I'm getting through it."

Side by side, we walk out of the church into the September sun.

"Adelaide and the children were wearing little bags of stone shavings around their necks," says Isaac. "She was convinced it would protect them. A lot of people in Delft were wearing chips of stone when the plague hit; in some places there are grooves chipped out of the walls. I said it couldn't be God's will to damage the church."

"I'm gradually coming to the conclusion that I've no idea what God's will is any more," I say, and Isaac nods in agreement.

"Life isn't easy," he sighs, "but we can't blame Him for that. Man is full of sin."

"As bailiff, you know all about that."

"Right. It's infuriating how rarely people abide by the laws and commandments. Old, young, men, women . . . In most cases it's only minor transgressions, but still."

"Is that so? Are there so few serious cases? Murders, for example?"

"There are many crimes committed that end in death. Premeditated murder is less common. A couple of months ago, I was asked to assist at the trial in Leiden of a woman who'd poisoned her husband because she'd fallen in love with someone else. Afterwards she'd fled to Delft."

"And was she convicted?"

"Yes, of course. She went to the gallows."

We stop in the middle of the market square.

"But how do you prove something like that?" I ask.

"That she had poisoned her husband? Simple: they found rat poison in her cesspit. She'd thrown away what was left. And according to the doctor, the symptoms her husband displayed had been a match for those found in cases of poisoning."

"Someone else could have given it him."

"There was no one else with a motive. When we got hold of her lover, he admitted the woman had been planning something of the sort for a while. He was against it himself, but she'd gone ahead anyway. We couldn't pin anything on him, there was no evidence to implicate him. But there was against her. In the end, she admitted she was guilty."

"After being put to the question."

"No, you can only resort to that if the criminal is caught in the act. And even then, only if we need a confession to carry out the verdict. If there's doubt, then we don't put people to the question, but we do carry out a forceful interrogation. A couple of days' solitary confinement in the dungeon tends to help too.

296

The rack is not something we resort to if we can help it; after all, this is the seventeenth century."

"So if someone keeps on denying it, they can't be convicted?"

"That's about the size of it. Unless they're caught in the act by multiple people."

"By multiple people?"

"Yes. One witness is not enough. If that were the case, somebody could be convicted merely because someone else wants to get him or her in trouble. That's why we require supporting evidence."

It's as if the sun is suddenly shining more brightly, getting warmer, as if the sounds and colours around me are becoming more vivid and cheerful.

"Is it like that in every city?" I ask.

"Of course. The law applies to the whole country. But where are these questions coming from, Catrin? You haven't got anything on your conscience, I hope." He laughs as he says this, but his eyes search my face.

I hurriedly come up with a reason for my interest. "I've got an employee I suspect of stealing. I was wondering how to deal with it."

"If you need help, I'd gladly bring him in."

"It's only a suspicion. The things might have just been misplaced. I'll keep an eye on it. Thank you, Isaac" I smile and move to turn as if I'm going home.

"You're welcome. You can always come to me."

With a nod and another smile, I bid him farewell and walk away. As I'm leaving the market and turning into a side street, I risk a glance over my shoulder and see that Isaac is watching me go.

CHAPTER
FORTY-SIX

The second conversation I need to have is one I'd rather put off until Monday, when there will be people around, but when I get home, the door to the workshop is open. I go inside and see Jacob standing by the ovens.

"What are you doing here?" I ask.

"Keeping an eye on the fire," says Jacob, his gaze fixed on one of the kilns.

"Didn't you go to church?"

"No, I haven't been going there for a long time." He turns to face me. "And I wanted to speak to you. It's been long enough, Catrin. I want an answer."

"Tomorrow."

"No, today. You already know what you're going to say to me tomorrow."

"Fine then. I'm not going to marry you, Jacob. I don't love you and I don't see any advantage in marrying you from a business point of view either." There, I've said it. Calmly and collectedly.

Jacob's face transforms, as if it's made of liquid. A cold glint appears in his eyes and his smile vanishes. "No advantage from a business point of view? You're clearly not thinking straight, Catrin. I can bring down this whole company, and you."

"I think not." My quiet self-assurance makes him uncertain; I can see it in his slight frown. "By the way, you're fired. I almost forgot to say."

He approaches me slowly. "You can't do that. You can't fire me."

"Yes, I can. I just did. I want you to pack your things and leave Delft. If you're still here tomorrow morning, then I'm going to the bailiff and having you investigated for murder."

His face is a picture. "*You're* going to inform on *me?*"

"For murdering Evert. I don't know what you gave him, but it certainly didn't make him better. What was in it? I reckon it was digitalis, foxglove, so that his heart stopped immediately. You know enough about herbs to make some kind of concoction. Handy, a plague epidemic like that. An excellent opportunity to get someone out of the way without arousing suspicion. I think you mixed larger and larger amounts into his food until he died. That explains why he was lying there so peacefully. He had a heart attack."

Jacob laughs. It sounds like a warning and he doesn't seem shocked. "He had the plague, Catrin. Several people saw that."

"What did they see? The blue stains you put on his neck? Last night, I stood mixing paint until I had midnight blue. The exact colour that would suggest a bruise. Unfortunately, you spilt some. On the ladder and on the edge of the bed."

Jacob comes closer, still smiling. "But of course, you're not going to tell anyone that. Because you're not

299

so innocent yourself, my dear little Catrin. You never told me how it feels, pressing a pillow down on someone's face until he suffocates. Did Govert wake up? Did he fight? Did he know what was coming? At least Evert didn't know what was happening; you can't say the same about what you did. So excuse me, but you're no better."

"Govert abused me! He murdered my baby, he made my life a living hell. He would have murdered *me* one day, if I hadn't got there first."

"It's still murder. I don't see the difference."

"The difference is that Evert never did anything to you. In fact, he showed you nothing but kindness. You murdered him so you could marry me and take over the company. As if I'd ever have gone along with that! You make me sick!" I spit the words in his face.

Jacob grabs my arm. "And yet that is what's going to happen. You're going to be my beautiful, obedient wife and together we're going to make this a successful business. I'll be a father to your child and we'll have children together, too. I'm already looking forward to getting started." He grins broadly.

"Keep dreaming, because that's never going to happen," I say, wrenching myself free. "You can't threaten or blackmail me any longer. I spoke to Isaac, the sheriff, and he told me that one witness isn't enough to get someone convicted. There needs to be supporting evidence, and there isn't. Sadly, the same applies to you, otherwise you'd be in prison now. But I trust that God will punish you."

300

A leaden silence falls, in which we each wait for the other to break their gaze.

"Fine," says Jacob finally. "If that's how things are . . . You can have your way, Catrin. I'm offering you protection and a comfortable life, but if you don't want them, I'm not going to force you. I'll be damned if I'll let you take my job away from me, though. Look!" He shows me his arms, which are covered in burns. "I've put my heart and soul into this business, I've got a right to my fair share. You can buy me out."

"What are you on about? I'm not giving you a thing! Get out of here, and be quick about it."

He laughs. "Fiery as always. It's a shame, we're such a good match. But on second thought, I'd prefer a well-behaved wife. What to do with you, though? You're actually crazy enough to go to the bailiff." He looks about himself, frowning, then goes over to the oven. "I know. You opened the kiln for some reason or other, your sleeve caught and there was a fire. There was no one around to help you . . . How tragic. They'll find your charred body among the rubble and all your new friends will mourn at your funeral. But by then I'll be far away."

He pulls open the door of the kiln and sticks a long piece of wood inside. Then he holds the burning end of the wood against the basket of kindling until it catches fire.

"Stop it!" I fly at him, push him to one side and kick over the basket so I can stamp out the flames.

Laughing, he sets fire to more things, flames spring up next to the supply of paint and oil and next to the packing straw for the delivery crates. After a slow start, everything is now ablaze.

I look around wildly. There's no water on hand to put it out, my business is doomed!

I run towards the open door but Jacob blocks the way, a piece of burning wood held in his hand like a sword. His face is twisted in the most evil expression, a grimace that renders him barely recognisable.

"Jacob, please!"

He shows no sign of emotion whatsoever as he drives me into a corner, blocking my attempts to escape with the flaming stick in his hand. The workshop is filling with smoke by this time and I hold my arm up to cover my mouth.

"You said you loved me! Let's talk, I —"

"Shut it!" he says. "We've talked enough. I gave you every chance, now it's done." He holds out the flaming torch to my billowing skirt. The lace ribbons catch and crackle, the fire spreads upwards in a straight line. I throw the thick fabric of my skirt over them to put them out, but Jacob is pressing the burning wood to my clothes in so many places that I haven't got enough hands. I start to scream.

"Stop that! Be quiet!" He lifts the piece of wood.

With my hands over my head, I ready myself to catch the blow and scream as I see the burning end rushing down at me.

As I'm waiting for the blow to come, Jacob collapses. He falls to the ground like a ragdoll, the torch still in his hands. Klaas is standing behind him with an axe.

Blood is spreading across the floor, along with something else that's coming from Jacob's head.

Speechless, I look to Klaas, who stares back at me, his face contorted in horror.

People appear in the doorway. Lit up by the flames, they form an indistinguishable mass. They shout for water and try to smother the flames with hastily removed articles of clothing. Two women slap at the smouldering flames on my jerkin and skirt and get me outside, where a crowd is forming. Windows and doors are thrown open, there's shouting coming from all around. A fire that gets out of hand can destroy the whole town, so within minutes everyone is on the streets. Several chains form between the pottery and the canal, where buckets of water are drawn and passed from person to person along the line.

I lend a hand. I'm not in any pain, the flames didn't get through the thick layers of clothing. I sweat to save my business and don't stop even once to look inside, where Jacob's body is burning to ash.

CHAPTER
FORTY-SEVEN

Klaas is locked in a dungeon and subjected to interrogation, but thankfully he doesn't stay locked up for long. After two days, he's released. The magistrates show clemency because, when all is said and done, he did prevent Delft from being razed to the ground. And there were enough witnesses to attest to the fact that I was being threatened. Isaac's testimony, that I had suspected an employee of stealing, but had no proof, coupled with my repeated assertions that this employee was Jacob put the matter to rest, although I suspect the saving of the city carried more weight in the end.

Even The Lotus Flower came out of the whole thing well. There was a great deal of damage, but the workshop was saved by the quick action of my neighbours. After the restoration work, which costs me a lot of money, we got back to work as quickly as possible.

Now I have an excellent master potter in Christiaan, and Klaas has replaced Jacob.

The stain Jacob's blood left on the floor fades over the weeks that follow. The way he died makes me shudder, but I don't dwell on it. Every time I see the mark, it hits me afresh that he's gone from my life, that there's no longer anyone who knows my secret. I'm free. It seems I've built up some credit with God after all.

September and October rush by and we're stuck inside for days as the rain beats against the window panes. On one of those wet, windy days, painting apprentice, Hendrik, is sitting doodling on one of the misfires. I walk past him with a medicine jar that needs painting, glance over his shoulder and stop walking. Next to the vague lines testing the thickness of the paint is a row of little windmills with their sails in various positions.

"That's lovely," I say. "Give me that pot for a second."

Hendrik hands me his work, surprised at my interest. I walk over to Christiaan with it. He's busy in the workshop with the vats of tin glaze and is giving instructions to a new employee. I wait until he's finished and hold up the pot.

"Windmills?" He raises his eyebrows.

"It looks good, doesn't it?"

"I don't know. People want oriental designs."

"And we're going to keep making them. But perhaps the customers would like these too. Windmills and other Dutch images. City panoramas, for example."

Christiaan scrutinises the pot. "I suppose we could do the walls and gate towers of different cities. Each city could have its own pottery."

I give him a big smile and go back to the studio to talk the idea over with Frans.

"I don't know." His face clouds with doubt. "We're so busy as it is. Where's the demand for this?"

"If we don't try, we'll never know. Make a couple of drawings of the gates of Amsterdam, then I'll do a couple of the Delft ones."

He shrugs. "You're the boss."

Frans is right, we are too busy to be setting up a new line of earthenware. But 1 don't see why we should let that stop us. I believe that it can be a success, with just as much certainty as when I suggested to Evert that we make oriental pottery ourselves.

As the autumn goes on, I'm working harder than ever. With my fat belly, I can barely do much more than sit, so I make the best use of my time. Frans and I sketch various designs and, once we're satisfied, we produce stencils and move on to painting real pieces. We start with windmills and ice-skaters, which immediately sell well. Then we bring out our city panoramas of Delft and Amsterdam. The demand for them exceeds even my expectations. Our Dutch Porcelain becomes so popular we broaden our range to include views of more cities, polder landscapes and ships.

Quentin and Angelika follow our example. We don't tread on each other's toes. The demand is such that our companies can barely meet it. We pass on commissions to each other and borrow workers as and when we need them.

Spurred on by our success, one pottery after another opens up, often in vacant breweries. Fifty years ago, Delft's beer industry was still flourishing, serving ocean-going ships, but when many cities began brewing their own ship's beer, most of the Delft companies shut down. Now the empty buildings, kitted out with work-shops and ovens, are turning out to be exceptionally well-suited for setting up potteries.

By the beginning of December, there are fifteen up and running, almost all of them on The Gheer. They are located next to each other in a neat row, the shops on the street side, the workshops behind. Thick clouds of smoke rise over the roofs and there's an all-pervading smell that never goes away. The city has found a new occupation.

On December the fifteenth, I give birth to a little girl and name her Eva. The birth is without complications. In the weeks that follow, the stream of visitors and presents, even from customers, doesn't stop. It's hard without Evert, even though Angelika and Quentin give me a lot of support.

Every time I look at Eva's face, at her fine, dark curls and those heavenly little hands and feet, I feel overwhelmed by an unprecedented feeling of happiness. Life hasn't always been easy for me, but finally even I've got a great deal to be grateful for.

One cold winter day, I'm walking across the poultry market with Angelika. I've left Eva with Hilly. As we're wandering among the stalls, I catch a fragment of conversation. The words "ship returning" and "Delfshaven" float over to me and I whip round with a start.

"What is it?" asks Angelika.

"Didn't you hear that?"

She shakes her head.

I walk back to the cluster of people standing chatting next to the butter stall. "Excuse me, but I couldn't help overhearing a little of your conversation. Has one of the VOC ships returned?"

The people stop talking and look at me. One of the men nods.

"From the East, with a hold full of spices. The cargo is piled in enormous bales on the quayside. But the crew didn't fare so well."

"Fewer than half of them are left," says the woman standing next to him. "Apparently, the voyage out was terrible, with storms, sickness and too little drinking water. They had to muster new men in the East to even get home."

"Which ship is it?" I look from one to another anxiously.

"The *Delft*," says the man.

From that moment on, I don't know a moment's peace. Fewer than half! Would Matthias still be alive? My feelings for him are locked up somewhere deep inside; it's as if we were never entirely separated. I'm sure I would have sensed it, if he had died. And so I wait, restless but hopeful.

Large, ocean-going vessels can't get all the way to Delft so they lay anchor at Delfshaven, where the cargo is transferred to smaller boats and brought into town. Even though it's freezing cold, I make sure I'm out on the streets and in the city harbour as much as possible to keep up with the news. The first crew members return to Delft and I ask after Matthias. To my relief, I hear that he has survived the journey. But no one knows where he went after he came ashore.

It's a sombre winter day, with heavy clouds that put an end to the working day earlier than usual. Everyone has gone home, apart from the stokers, and I'm tidying up in the office when someone arrives in the doorway. I know it's him before I've even turned around. I feel his presence.

I turn and there he is, almost unrecognisable with a tanned face, shoulder-length hair and a beard. Only his eyes are still the same: that unmistakable, bright blue gaze. And the way he looks at me with a kind of hunger makes the repressed desire in me flare up all over again.

We close the gap between us and I feel his arms around me. His grip is strong, a briny smell rises from his clothes.

"I've dreamed of this moment so often," he says quietly. "I was so afraid you'd be gone, disappeared without a trace, but you're here."

He strokes my hair, my back, and then he grabs me around the waist and holds me slightly away from him. His eyes take in every detail of my face. Next he bows his head to mine and a second later our lips meet. A wild wave of desire rushes over me. I clamp my arms around him and kiss him with abandon. I can hardly believe that he's back, that I can see him and touch him. We just keep kissing, touching, smiling and kissing again. Until I hear Eva crying. The sound is coming from close by and Hilly appears in my peripheral vision with Eva in her arms.

I gently push Matthias away. He looks round and then, bewildered, back at me.

Feeling a bit awkward, I walk over to Hilly and take my daughter from her.

"Matthias, this is Eva."

Slowly, what I'm trying to tell him seems to sink in.

"Eva," he repeats.

"My daughter." I pause for a second and then add, "And Evert's."

He stares at me, nonplussed. I have to swallow the lump in my throat before I can continue.

"We got married last year."

The change on Matthias's face is complete. Passion has given way to dismay and now a tinge of anger also appears in his eyes. "You were supposed to wait for me."

"I never promised anything. Eighteen months is a long time, Matthias."

"And all those months I thought only of you, I was sorry I'd left and prayed to God you wouldn't meet anyone else. And all the while you were busy getting married to my brother the second I was gone."

"That's not fair, that's not how it went."

"You married him, didn't you? So that's exactly how it went. You've even had his child." Then something seems to hit him. "Where is Evert, anyway?"

Another awkward silence falls. I avoid Matthias's eyes and take a deep breath.

"Sit down," I say.

CHAPTER
FORTY-EIGHT

I don't know which is worse: Matthias's anger that I married his brother, or his anguish about Evert's death. The shock hits him hard. He doesn't say anything, just stares into space with a hollow expression.

I reach out to comfort him. He shrinks away from my touch. He stalks out of the office and a moment later I see him walking away up The Gheer.

Devastated, I sink onto the edge of the desk. I expect him to come back, but it keeps getting later and later and there's no sign of him. I walk around with Eva, who can sense my disquiet and won't go to sleep. Once she's finally settled, I remain standing at the window for a long time.

Around midnight, I give up hope and go to bed. I lie on my side fretting. Where is he now? Will he come back tomorrow or will he leave Delft? Surely he has to understand I had no other choice, that life went on and I simply *couldn't* wait for him?

I get up early, feed Eva, open the doors of the workshop and let the men in. Once Frans has arrived and everyone is getting down to work, I give Hilly her instructions for the day, kiss Eva and walk over to the market square. I reach the Mechelen Inn and go inside.

"You're in early." Digna comes over with a look of concern.

"Has Matthias been in?"

"Yes, of course. He stayed here last night — but he's gone already."

"Did he say where he was going?"

"No. He might be with Johannes. He asked for the address of his studio." She looks at me sympathetically. "The news you gave him wasn't easy to hear. How did he take it?"

"Badly." I walk out the door again.

I rush over to Voldersgracht at a trot. I push open the door to Johannes's studio, full of hope. He's giving instructions to an apprentice when I come in.

"Catrin! Matthias just left." He comes over and leads me into the side room, out of the apprentices' earshot.

"How is he?"

"He's shocked and sad. Very sad."

"Was he angry?"

"With you? No, he understood. He said he was the one who went away, that it's only logical that you didn't sit around waiting. Well, actually *I* said that, and he admitted that I was right. He said he wasn't suited to committed relationships, he had nothing to offer you."

"Where did he go?"

"To the harbour."

I stare at Johannes and feel despair growing inside me. "After a year and a half, he's finally back and he's leaving again? Just like that?"

"I'm sorry." Johannes puts his arm around me. "I'm most sorry that he's come and thrown everything up in the air again, now that life is going a bit better for you. Let him go, Catrin. You deserve better."

I flash him a small smile and leave. I set off in the direction of the harbour, running as fast as I can. I keep an eye out on the way, but I don't spot Matthias anywhere. He's nowhere to be seen in the harbour either. My eyes dart between the many boats that are moored or just leaving. Am I too late?

I enquire with all the, sailors I encounter.

"Van Nulandt? Yes, he was looking for a boat to Amsterdam," one says. "There're enough of them headed there, so he must be on his way by now."

I stay standing on the quayside for a long time, gazing out over the water. Finally, I turn and trudge home, filled with an emptiness that robs me of all energy and lust for life.

When I get home, he's standing in the kitchen. Hilly is pouring him a glass of beer and he's looking at Eva, who's lying in her crib. One glance at my face is enough to send Hilly running from the room.

Flabbergasted, I lean against the doorpost. "I thought you'd gone."

"Without giving you the presents I brought you? Never." He gestures to the table, which is covered in strange things. I can hardly take them all in.

"Did you love him?" Matthias asks after a brief silence.

"Yes, and I miss him. I wasn't in love with Evert, but he was my best friend. I could count on him and he could count on me. Sometimes that's enough for a marriage." I tell him about all that's happened over the past eighteen months. The only part I leave out is Jacob; that has nothing to do with this. I relate everything as carefully as possible, the way Evert and I grew closer, our collaboration, my broken leg and how he supported me.

When I've finished, Matthias says, "I understand."

"Really?"

"Catrin, I've had a lot of time to think on my travels. I realised I should have been more clear."

"About what?"

"About my feelings for you. Maybe I needed this voyage to know what I wanted."

"And that is?"

I wait for the words I never thought I'd hear again, and at the same time ask myself whether I'll believe them. Whether I'll ever dare to rely on him.

Rather than saying those words, he gestures to all the objects on the table. He tells me what they all are: coral, amber, fossils, starfish and precious stones. They come from the Cape Verde Islands, the Southern Cape of Africa, Madagascar, Mozambique and Ceylon. Names that mean nothing to me, but that evoke mysterious worlds. Worlds where he was thinking of me, from whence he brought back little pieces. For me.

I listen to his stories, watch the life return to his eyes as he relives his journey.

"It sounds amazing," I say at last. "It must have been a great adventure."

"A dangerous adventure, but it was fantastic"

"You love travelling, you need it."

314

He hears the subtle change in my voice, stands up and walks over to me. "I need you as well. While I was out there, I thought about you constantly, but now that I'm back . . ."

"You want to go again."

"Not immediately. But one day . . . yes."

"Then you have to go. You'll be unhappy if you stay on dry land."

"I'll be unhappy without you, too." His eyes seek mine and hold my gaze.

A silence falls.

"One thing doesn't rule out the other," I say softly. "This time I would wait for you."

Moved, he watches my face. "Really?" He comes to stand in front of me and strokes my lip with his thumb.

"I need to go away now," he murmurs. "Not for long, a couple of days. And then we'll talk."

I nod and he kisses me. Then he grabs his bag and leaves. I follow him out, wave after him as he goes up the road, and smile to myself because even though I know that he'll often leave me, I also know that he'll always come back.

Glossary

Baller A worker in a pottery who rolls chunks of clay into balls ready for the potter to use on the wheel.

Batavia Capital of the Dutch East Indies on the island of Java. The city is now known as Jakarta, the capital of modern-day Indonesia.

Bontekoe Journaal A diary account of the voyage of the *Nieuw Hoorn*, an armed merchant ship, authored by the ship's captain, Willem Bontekoe. After setting off for Batavia in 1618, the *Nieuw Hoorn* was shipwrecked near Sumatra and the surviving crew endured a perilous journey in lifeboats to Batavia.

Hindeloopen A town in North Holland known for its colourful decorated furniture. Hindeloopen pieces often have floral motifs similar to what you might expect to see on an old-fashioned gypsy caravan in the UK.

VOC The Dutch East India Company (Verenigde Oostindische Compagnie) was founded in 1603 to explore new territories in the Orient and establish trading routes for valuable commodities such as spices. The VOC was a company with shareholders and directors but also represented the Dutch government in negotiations and offered armed resistance to foreign powers.

Gracht A gracht is a narrow canal found in many old Dutch cities and will be familiar to those who have visited or seen pictures of Amsterdam. Used as alternatives to streets, grachts (grachten) were vital arteries for transporting produce and people in the past. Many warehouses and grand buildings in Dutch cities had doors leading directly onto them.

Weighing-house The weighing-house was an important public building in pre-modern Holland and Germany. Situated on or close to the market square, the weighing-house was where city officials would weigh produce sold at market on giant scales to establish how much tax was to be paid on it.

Afterword

Halfway through the seventeenth century, known to the Dutch as the Golden Age, Delft Blue stormed onto the market and became enormously popular within a very short time. Anyone who wanted to show he had both money and good taste bought some. The supply of original Chinese porcelain had been well-established in the period of 1620–47, thanks to the voyages of discovery and the VOC expeditions that followed, until a civil war in China put an end to it. From then on, a number of Dutch cities, including Delft, Haarlem and Amsterdam, tried making the beloved pottery themselves. They called it Dutch Porcelain; the name Delft Blue didn't come until much later.

Between 1654 and 1690, the number of potteries in Delft exploded; by around 1700 there were almost forty. The craze for decorative ceramics reached its peak between 1680 and 1730. Delft Blue found an important ambassador in Princess Mary II, the English wife of the Dutch Stadtholder Prince Willem II (William III of England). Her fascination with Delftware and enthusiasm for collecting it led to more orders from the nobility and royalty.

At the end of the eighteenth century, the earthenware industry collapsed due to competition from English porcelain. There was a revival in the mid-nineteenth century, but after the Second World War much of the once so beloved tableware was put away in the attic for good. Delft Blue was deemed fussy, old-fashioned tat. The only place its popularity remained undiminished was abroad, primarily in Japan and America.

The last few years have seen the white-and-blue pottery gradually being rediscovered in the Netherlands. KLM flies in Delft Blue aircraft and the loyalty scheme where you could collect little Delft Blue houses if you flew business class sparked a craze. Today there's no getting away from this centuries-old export. Everywhere, from the lifestyle section of the exclusive department store Bijenkorf to the shelves of bargain homeware chain Xenos, there is Delft Blue in the form of knick-knacks, oven gloves, duvet cushions, bike panniers and anything else you'd care to name.

The real Delft Blue is still an expensive porcelain that is much loved abroad. At The Porcelain Flask (De Porceleyne Fles) in Delft, the ceramics are still fired and painted by hand. It's worth the trip to take a look around the factory, along with the many foreign tourists, and see the painters at work.

The Porcelain Flask began on the Oosteinde (East End) but is now located on Rotterdamseweg, a little outside the old town in Delft. During the last century, another three companies were set up: The Delft Peacock (De Delftse Pauw), The Blue Tulip (De Blauwe

Tulp) and The Chandelier (De Candelaer). The four of them brought the name of Delft Blue to the attention of tourists and other enthusiasts.

The characters of Quentin (Quentin) and Angelika (Engeltje) van Cleynhoven are historical figures. In 1655, Quentin and Wouter van Eenhoorn took over a pottery they named The Porcelain Flask. In a trench on the grounds of number 171 Oosteinde, where the business began, a hundred and twenty objects from the early period of the ceramics factory were recently found, including a platter with the inscription "Engeltie Kleijnoven, 1673". This is probably a commemorative plate on the occasion of their twenty-fifth wedding anniversary. In the archive records, the name Cleynhoven is spelt with both a C and a K.

The Lotus Flower pottery never really existed. Nor did Catrin or Evert; they are figments of my imagination.

It goes without saying that Rembrandt, Nicolaes (Nicholas) Maes, Johannes Vermeer, his wife Catharina and his mother Digna are historical figures. Johannes' father, Reynier, was the owner of the Mechelen Inn on the market square. Following his death in 1652, Digna carried on with the business. Johannes and Catharina lived with her for a long time. Sadly, the inn is no longer standing; it was demolished in 1885 to widen Oude Manhuissteeg.

It isn't clear who Johannes' teacher was, but the name Carel Fabritius is often mentioned. He died at the age of thirty-two, during the explosion of the artillery depot.

Acknowledgements

I would like to thank Jessica van Erkel, product manager at The Porcelain Flask in Delft, for reading the manuscript of *Midnight Blue* and for her help with the research. Without her warm reception and the books she lent me, I would never have got hold of some important information. It was also truly wonderful of her to arrange a painting lesson for me with one of the painters at The Porcelain Flask, which means I now have a piece of Delft Blue at home made by yours truly.

I also want to thank my publisher, Wanda Gloude, for the idea of writing a novel about Delft Blue. Good ideas are always very welcome!

Suggested Further Reading

Russell Shorto, *Amsterdam* (London: Abacus, 2014)

Sources

Jos W.L. Hilkhuijsen (ed.), *Ach, lieve tijd. 740 jaar Delft en de Delftenaren* (Zwolle: Waanders, 1995–1997)

Wik Hoekstra-Klein, "De Porceleynne Fles: periode 1653–1850", in *Geschiedenis van de Delftse plateelbakkerijen*, deel 6. (Delft: Deltech, 2001)

Jonkvrouwe dr. C.H. de Jonge, *Delfts aardewerk* (Rotterdam: Nijgh & Van Ditmar, 1965)

J. Matusz, *Delfts aardewerk* (Amerongen: Gaade, 1977)

Annet Mooji, *De polsslag van de stad. 350 jaar academische geneeskunde in Amsterdam* (Amsterdam: De Arbeiderspers, 1999)

Leo Noordegraaf & Gerrit Valk, *De Gave Gods. De pest in Holland vanaf de late middeleeuwen* (Amsterdam: Bert Bakker, 1996)

Trudy van der Wees, *Door Delfts blauwe ogen* (Soest: Uitgeverij Boekscout.nl, 2012)

THE AWKWARD AGE

Francesca Segal

In a Victorian terraced house in north-west London, two families unite in imperfect harmony. After five years of widowhood, Julia is deeply, unexpectedly in love. If only her beloved daughter Gwen didn't hate James so much. At the very least, she could be civil to his son Nathan. Bringing together two households was never going to be easy; but Gwen's struggle for independence, and the teenagers' unexpected actions, will threaten Julia's fragile new happiness. This is a story about standing by the ones we love, even when they hurt us. We would do anything to make our children happy — wouldn't we?

DARKE

Rick Gekoski

Dr James Darke has expelled himself from the world. He writes compulsively in his "coming-of-old-age" journal; he eats little, and drinks and smokes a lot. Meditating on what he has lost — the loves of his life, both dead and alive — he tries to console himself with the wisdom of the great thinkers and poets, yet finds nothing but disappointment. But cracks of light appear in his carefully managed darkness, and he begins to emerge from his self-imposed exile, drawn by the tender, bruised filaments of love for his daughter and grandson . . .

COUSINS

Salley Vickers

1994: Young Will Tye has suffered an appalling accident. The terrible event ripples through three generations of the complex and eccentric Tye family and leads to the revelation of dark long-held secrets. Each family member holds some clue to the chain of events that may have led to the accident, and each holds themselves to blame. Most deeply affected is Will's cousin Cecelia, whose affinity with Will leaves her most vulnerable to his suffering, and whose own life is forever changed by how she will respond to it. Told through the eyes of three women close to Will — his sister, his grandmother and his aunt — and spanning from the outbreak of the Second World War to the present day, this is a story of selfishness, wrong choices, life, death, and ultimately love.

CURTAIN CALL

Anthony Quinn

On a sultry afternoon in 1936, a woman accidentally interrupts an attempted murder in a London hotel room. Nina Land, a West End actress, faces a dilemma: she's not supposed to be at the hotel in the first place, and certainly not with a married man. But once it becomes apparent that she may have seen the face of the man the newspapers have dubbed "the Tiepin Killer", she realises that another woman's life could be at stake . . . Tom, long-suffering secretary to an ageing theatre critic, has a secret of his own to protect. His chance encounter with a lost young woman who is haunted by premonitions of catastrophe closes the circle: it was she who narrowly escaped the killer's stranglehold that afternoon, and now walks the streets in terror of his finding her again . . .